The Colors We Desire

Belinda Benna

CW01496280

About the Author

Belinda Benna is an award-winning author whose moving romance novels are filled with emotion, allowing you to lose yourself between the lines and find yourself at the same time.
Experience stories that will make you cry, laugh, and fall in love-each with a message that will stay with you for a long time.

In her newsletter (www.belindabenna.com/newsletter), Belinda provides exclusive insights into unpublished manuscripts and her life as an author.

Keep in touch with Belinda:
Website: www.belindabenna.com
Instagram: @belinda_benna_author
Facebook: @Belinda Benna - Author
TikTok: @belinda_benna_author

the Colors we Desire

If you forget to enjoy life,
you forget yourself.

Prologue

Hanna

Eight years ago

Sometimes the rustling of the wind in the birch leaves sounds like music. And the daffodil heads sprouting among the first lush green shoots of the lawn next to me glow in a yellow hue that seems to outshine everything around them.

Just like today. Even though spring has begun to work wonders, I can already see off the road, as I am strolling along, how nature will change in the coming weeks.

I see the hepatica emerging, delicate buds forming on the branches of the apple trees. The scent of freshly mowed grass fills my nostrils, and the taste of sun-ripened strawberries lingers on my tongue.

In my imagination, I step onto a path. I immerse myself in a new world, wandering among vegetable patches and berry beds that appear out of nowhere in my mind's eye, passing by a sunlit terrace made of pinewood. It still looks lonely, but soon, the daisies will sprout new shoots. Their white and yellow blossoms will snuggle up to the wooden posts, and the lavender's scent will waft into the nose of anyone warming their soul in the spring sun on those rustic chairs.

All of this I can envision, and so much more. Back there, where the rose arch marks the entrance to a hidden trail, would be the perfect spot to create a pond with fish, water lilies, and reeds lining the shore, where even the most restless souls could find peace.

A place of power.

A place where everyone can be themselves.

"Hey," someone calls from a distance.

No, not yet. I want to stay in this dreamlike place for a moment longer.

"Watch out, you stupid cow!"

The loud roar of engines shatters the glass dome of my thoughts like a hammer blow. I tear myself away from the wreckage of my dream and blink rapidly to return to reality.

Searching for orientation, I look around. I find myself standing on the road, holding a cardboard box in my arms. The frayed ribbons of my apron and the worn corners of a photograph peek out.

Immediately in front of me, I spot three motorcycles with five girls and boys. Though their faces are hidden behind dark visors, their clothes indicate they must be around my age.

"Is she stupid or what?" Scornful laughter reaches my ears. "Why doesn't she get out of the way?"

Only now do I realize that I'm not just on the road but right in the middle of it. My pulse quickens instantly, and my palms become sweaty. Clutching the box tightly to my chest, I glance at the motorcycles.

"She's a beggar!" the girl with wild blond hair sticking out from under her helmet calls out. Her voice sounds familiar, but I can't place it. "She's blocking our path because she wants to beg from us."

No, I'm not…

"Exactly!" One of the boys laughs, the closed visor muffling his mocking tone. "No normal person would wear rags like those."

With pursed lips, I lower my gaze to my tattered sneakers, whose broken shoelaces I've replaced with garden twine.

In the corner of my eye, I see someone approaching me in brand-new leather ankle boots. "Wait a minute, I know her."

Feverishly, I try to identify the voice.

Is that Jakob?

Please, no.

I shake my head and march on before this gets even more uncomfortable than it already is.

Because you can never control yourself, Hanna. No wonder these things keep happening to you.

I don't know if it's my voice or my mother's now raging within me. I only know that she's speaking the truth.

By now, I've reached the edge of the road, but the motorcycles behind me remain eerily quiet.

Please, leave me alone, I silently beg. It's bad enough that less than an hour ago, I lost my apprenticeship, and I have no idea how I'm going to make it from here.

"I know her!" the male voice suddenly exclaims loudly. "That's Hanna Daydreamer!"

Damn.

I squeeze the corners of my cardboard box and quicken my pace.

The whole group follows with amused cheers. "Oh, so this is what she's become," sneers a woman, probably the blond one. "Suits her, don't you think?"

I desperately fight back the tears welling up inside me. Because now I know who these five are even though I still can't see their faces.

Jakob, Peter, Maria, Melanie, and Laura make up the coolest clique from my former school class. They not only witnessed me every day in class but were also in the audience during the project presentation.

Oh God, this just can't be happening.

"You've really made something of yourself, Hanna Daydreamer. Congratulations." Shortly after Jakob spits out the words, the engines finally rev up.

I dare to exhale. It will be over soon.

Keeping my gaze fixed ahead, I trudge along the road toward Semmtal.

The roar of the engines grows louder.

And even louder.

Soon, they will pass me. My heart thumps so hard against my chest that my whole body vibrates.

Shouting voices mingle with the motorcycles' rumble.

I hold my breath.

It's your own fault, Hanna. If you had just stopped daydreaming, they wouldn't have noticed you at all.

The motorcycles zoom past me so closely that I instinctively leap to the side. The cardboard box flies through the air, and I land on the outside of my foot, twisting my ankle.

A sharp pain shoots through me, and I collapse on the spot. I inhale sharply, the exhaust fumes from the bikes scratching at my lungs. Struggling, I prop myself up on my forearms and lift my head. That's when I see the blonde on the bike turn to me while the guy she's wrapped around from behind reduces speed.

"Freak!" she yells at the top of her lungs, flipping me off.

Then, at last, the five of them speed away, leaving me crouching by the roadside. Deep inside, I know the blond girl is right.

I am Hanna Daydreamer.

And Hanna Daydreamer is a freak.

On this planet, there is no place for me. So many times, my mother has tried to make me understand that, but I refused to believe it. The worlds in my head were too intoxicating, and the dreams in my imagination were too vast. I fought—and never once won.

I can't go on like this. Here and now, I must finally admit the truth, whether I like it or not. If I ever want to live a normal life, I have only one choice: I have to become someone else.

Chapter 1

Hanna

Today

The new guests will surely complain if I'm not finished in ten minutes.

With firm pressure, I wring out the mop. The hot water quickly turns my fingers fiery red, but I don't care. Nor do I mind the beads of sweat forming relentlessly on my forehead or the fact that my jeans are soaked from a little accident with the water bucket earlier. With determination, I push the mop across the floor, following the wood grain.

There's a rustling sound behind me, but I don't turn around. I need to prepare the cabin for the next vacationers, and my time is almost up. I'll probably have to skip cleaning under the red-and-white-checkered sofa, so at least I can scrub away the soot marks next to the Swedish stove.

"Wow, it's really busy in here," someone remarks.

Without interrupting my work, I glance around. In the rustic-furnished hallway, I see Elina. Her honey-blond hair shines in the incoming spring sunlight. "Hey," I say with a smile.

"Oh dear." She furrows her eyebrows in concern. "Do you have a headache again?"

How does she know that?

Quickly, I grab the water bucket. "I'm fine. What's new?" I ask, hoping she won't pry any further.

"I'm doing well. But you look tired." Suddenly, she's right next to me, giving me her penetrating doctor's gaze. "When was the last time you took a day off?"

A day off? How is that even possible? "I'm perfectly fit, and I enjoy my work." As if to prove it, I dip the mop cheerfully into the water.

From the corner of my eye, I see her tapping her chin with her index finger, giving me an intense look. She shouldn't. My life is what it is, and it could be much worse, so I won't complain.

"You're a great doctor, but sometimes you see things that don't exist," I add, winking at her.

Suddenly, she smiles at me. "And you're the best sister-in-law one could imagine. That's why I want you to be well."

Wait a second. Did she just say sister-in-law?

As if she can read my thoughts, she waves her hand in front of my face. I notice a delicate silver ring on her ring finger with three azure blue stones embedded in the metal.

"Wow," I whisper in awe and even pause in my work for a moment to pull her into a hug.

"That's amazing, isn't it? I want you to be one of my maids of honor. There'd be two of you. You remember my best friend Maya, right? She already said yes," she chatters away as I try to put on a carefree expression for her, kneeling to scrub away the soot marks.

Elina and my brother are the happiest couple I have ever seen. It's as if they see into each other's souls every day, finding beauty even in the darkest corners. Soon, they will start a family together. It's wonderful, and I should be happy for her. Yet all I feel is a painful longing.

With effort, I manage to lift the corners of my mouth. "It would be an honor for me."

I look around. After cleaning the living room, I need to tidy up the hallway, vacuum the doormat, and change the light bulb above the entrance door. I also have to prepare the floral welcome greeting for the new guests.

My God, how am I going to manage all this?

"It will be fantastic," Elina exclaims, jumping up with excitement, her eyes sparkling. "You won't believe what Noah came up with for the proposal. The entire observatory was lit up with candles. He waited for a night with many shooting stars. And then…"

She sighs blissfully, and my heart clenches. I swallow hard but keep my composure. Florian and I will get married someday too; I just need to be patient a little longer.

"Then he got down on one knee in front of me. He said his love for me was as vast as the sky above us. And that I am the star that will always shine for him." Elina lowers her eyelids bashfully. "It's quite cheesy, isn't it?" she adds softly.

With a determined headshake, I guide Elina toward the exit. Noah is ready to share his life with her. That's simply beautiful. "That's just how true love is," I say even though I've stopped believing in true love myself. It doesn't exist, at least not for me.

She steps back, allowing me to start mopping the hallway. Her cheeks turn rosy. "Absolutely."

"It will be the most fantastic day of your life," I say, then quickly finish my work, crouching down to grab the mop. I'll have to clean the narrow threshold manually, or it won't be properly clean.

"And it will be," she says with an enthusiastic expression, rolling up her sleeves. "I'll help you. The flowers are missing, right?"

Without waiting for my answer, she marches over to the cleaning trolley parked on the concrete slabs in front of the cabin and gathers a bunch of daisies.

I put the mop aside, swiftly vacuum the doormat, and finally look up at the light bulb.

How am I supposed to reach that? What if I use one of the patio chairs as a makeshift ladder?

You might end up getting hurt, and nobody wants that, my mother cautions me in my thoughts.

"Well, what do you think?" Elina proudly presents her handiwork.

"Beautiful," I say with gratitude, nodding as I accept the flowers from Elina and arrange them in a vase on the patio table.

She looks around, searching. "What else can I help you with?"

"We're done. I just need to—"

Florian's voice interrupts from a distance. "Hanna?"

"I'll be right there!" I immediately shout back, promising to return later with a ladder to change the light bulb. I turn to Elina. "Sorry, I have to go."

"No problem, my patients are waiting anyway." Her cheeks flush again. She finds more joy in her work than anyone else I know. Being a doctor is her dream, and she gets to live it every day.

How lucky is she?

With a quick hug, she bids me farewell and dances away through the garden while I hurry to join Florian.

15

I return the cleaning trolley to its shelter and climb the uneven stairs of our house adorned with rustic wooden beams. The third step creaks particularly loudly. We should replace it before an accident happens.

I open the door and step into the cozy, warm hallway. The scent of the bread I baked this morning lingers in the air, making my stomach growl. But Florian is my priority now. I slip off my shoes and, in the same moment, feel Florian embracing me from behind.

"The guests should be arriving any moment. Is the cabin ready for occupancy?" He nestles his cheek against mine, his beard tickling my skin.

I lean my head wearily against his shoulder. "Yes."

"Great." He quickly pulls away from me. "Come with me, I have news," he says suddenly in a tone I can't quite place. Serious, yet a little mysterious.

Curious, I follow him into the study and let him guide me to his desk, which occupies an entire side of the room. Disordered piles of papers coexist with full blue and red folders. Almost instinctively, I start picking up the scattered paper clips.

With a sigh, Florian drops into the imposing swivel chair and reaches for the computer mouse. Deep furrows appear on his forehead.

I slide the paper clips into their designated box. "What's wrong?"

"Well…" He clears his throat right away. "I didn't want to worry you, so I haven't said anything until now, but…"

"But?" Apprehension creeps up in me. His serious businesslike demeanor intensifies my feelings.

He strokes his blond hair with both hands and locks his fingers at the nape of his neck. "Our guesthouse is not doing as well as we hoped. And most of the income we get is used for repairs."

My apprehension turns into concern. In the past seven years, Florian has been handling the bookkeeping. Even though I don't have access to the finances, I can well imagine that it's true. There's always something broken, and our cabins are increasingly left empty. "The accommodations are showing their age."

"Exactly. And we don't have anything special to offer our guests. The late check-in and early checkout service hardly attracts anyone."

Does that mean I've cleaned the cabins in record time for the past few weeks for nothing?

He logs into his computer and opens the accounting software. "In the past three months, we have been in the red. And that's despite the fact that we don't even have to pay wages and have received the money from the grant I landed at the beginning of the year."

I lean against the desk, utterly bewildered. Is it really that bad? Why didn't he tell me earlier?

I could ask, but deep down, I already know the answer. He knows how much I fear ending up where I was before I met him. The thought of being on the streets with nothing but the clothes on my back and not knowing where the next meal will come from terrifies me.

Out of consideration for me, he didn't confront me with it; he wanted to solve the problem on his own. But now, it seems that the time has come when he can no longer keep it to himself.

"We need to take action," he adds unnecessarily, his expression serious.

Of course, we need to take action! This can't continue like this. "What if we add a conservatory?" I suggest, secretly imagining how we will design it.

With hanging chairs, a gently trickling waterfall, and plenty of large, lush green plants. Some orange trees with their fragrant blossoms to enchant the guests. We should also incorporate an aviary with parrots. Kids love the colorful feathered creatures, especially if they can talk. The image builds up in my mind, and I feel like I'm about to get lost in it.

That can't happen. My dreams have no place here. I quickly pinch my forearm. Then I glance at Florian, who is thankfully focused on the screen.

"Small changes won't help us. We need to think bigger," he says earnestly. "Much bigger."

"What do you suggest?" I reach for the loose stack of papers to straighten it up. "More funding?"

He immediately raises a calming hand. "Leave that to me. I already found a solution." His eyebrows rise, and the corners of his mouth twitch.

When he makes this expression, he looks like a little boy who has concocted something mischievous. Then he looks at me promisingly even though he already has my full attention.

"We're expanding."

Expanding? What does he mean by that?

"I found an estate in Tuscany for sale at the ridiculous price of only 400,000 euros. Five hectares of land with a main house and two outbuildings." His voice almost overflows with excitement. "I think we should buy it and turn it into a guesthouse."

My mind races with thoughts, flitting around so hectically that I can barely grasp them. Another bed-and-breakfast? In Italy? For such a huge sum?

Perplexed, I let the documents slide onto the desk. "But we can't afford that."

He spreads his arms wide, smiling gently. "Of course, we'll take out a loan."

Seeing the eager anticipation in his gaze, I know he expects an enthusiastic thank-you from me. I can't help but nod cautiously even though my fear has begun to consume me from within. The increasingly painful throbbing in my temples is tangible evidence of it.

As if sensing what's going on inside me despite my efforts, he stands from his chair and wraps his arms around me. "We have to invest if we want to achieve something. That's how it works in business." He softly strokes my back. "In a few years, everything will be different. We won't have to worry anymore and can take it easy."

"That would be amazing," I admit because the vision is simply too beautiful. Never again cleaning toilets, preparing breakfast boxes, or washing mountains of sheets and towels. Then I would have time to create a garden. I could…

"And it will be," he assures me because he knows how to make me happy. "You know I would never suggest anything that could harm our future." With a satisfied nod, Florian releases me from his embrace. Then he cups my cheeks with both hands, looking at me lovingly. "We'll make it together."

Of course, I know that. He would do anything to see me happy. "What do you want me to do?" I ask on impulse.

"It would be great if you traveled to Tuscany to visit the property. I need you and your knowledge of Italian on-site." Florian takes a seat on the chair again.

Yes, that makes sense. As a child, I spent a lot of time with my grandparents in South Tyrol. Even though I've only spoken Italian with guests lately, I should manage well in Italy. "Okay."

"The price is too good to be true. And the seller never shows up himself; he always sends a woman who claims to be his daughter. We need to make sure he's not trying to cheat us." He concentrates on the screen, opening three files at once. "You can also check possible excursions and take photos for the website and promotional brochure. We'll need a list of expected repairs and renovations to calculate the costs." The printer at the end of the desk hums and spits out several pages. "Don't worry, I've prepared checklists so you won't forget anything."

As I take the warm paper from the printer, I realize the list seems endless and probably contains every important detail. Florian has even provided fields for notes and listed questions with possible answers that I just have to check off. He knows me too well.

"I would love to accompany you, but time is ticking," he says as if trying to encourage me. He takes my hand and squeezes it tightly. "While you're there, I'll take care of the finances and talk to notaries and lawyers about contract clauses."

His cheeks are flushed, and his gestures become more animated.

He has planned everything without me. But it's one hundred percent for us.

I give him a grateful smile. If I were only half as

organized as he is, I would be able to contribute useful thoughts. But, of course, I can only think of one question. "Who will take care of the bed-and-breakfast while I'm away?" Since I moved here eight years ago, I've never been away for more than a few days.

"I have a solution for that too." He grins widely and hands me a sheet of paper with a photo and a résumé. "This is a student from the hotel management school in Innsbruck. She'll be doing her mandatory internship with us, which won't cost us much," he says proudly.

A seventeen-year-old is supposed to handle everything on her own? I'm not so sure about that.

"Natalie will have her first day the day after tomorrow, and you'll leave next Thursday. Until then, she'll have to learn everything, but I'm sure you'll be able to train her quickly." He reaches for a notepad and writes down a name and a phone number, then hands me the paper. "This is the supposed daughter of the seller and your contact person in Italy. She will show you around and help you with your tasks."

He really has thought of every detail. But that's just him. Florian has everything under control, and not for the first time, I feel how lost I would be without him. He hasn't just made a plan for a life of security. In addition, he has done all the preliminary work and even created a checklist to support me.

It's clear. Florian is the doer. I, on the other hand, am still just a daydreamer. Even though I've learned not to show it to anyone anymore, Hanna Daydreamer still lies dormant within me. Sometimes she threatens to awaken, but I won't let her. Because the world she dreams of simply doesn't exist.

I quickly reach for the piece of paper and attach it to

the other documents with a paper clip. When I look up again, I see him looking at me.

"Smart and structured action is now the most important thing," he says energetically. "It's early March. It will probably take a few weeks for both of us to complete our parts in the preparations. If construction work is necessary, it could be tight to open before summer."

He's right. I haven't thought about that yet. I meet his gaze and nod emphatically. "You can count on me," I say, determined not to make any mistakes. The plan is too significant, and our goal is too big.

Finally, we will have what is most important to me in life: security.

Chapter 2

Vico

My pounding heart matches the force of the waves crashing against the rocks. The blood rushes through my veins with anger and turmoil. Behind my closed eyelids, I see flickers of orange-red light, and I feel the hard stone ground beneath my feet. A hint of salt lingers on my tongue, and a cool breeze brushes against my forearms. With my head lowered, I open my eyes.

The first thing I see is my toes, gripping the rocky ground like a cat's claws. The edge of the cliff lies just ahead of me. Below, the water crashes violently against the cliffs, but it can't reach me. About twenty yards of pure emptiness exists between us.

Twenty yards of nothingness.

One more step forward, take a deep breath.

I'm about to do it.

I'm going to jump.

My heart races, and adrenaline floods my body. I can feel the energy coursing through my fingertips. The thrill fills me like nothing else in the world can. I am present, and I am ready. Everything else loses its significance.

With every muscle taut, I rise onto my tiptoes and lift my arms. This is my moment. Now or never.

In a single flowing movement, I bend my knees,

pick up momentum, and push myself powerfully off the rock.

I shoot upward.

But fractions of a second later, I fall into nothingness. I tuck my legs in, spinning around my axis.

The azure blue water is my guide. I keep it in sight, controlling my position in the air, letting my muscles work.

Another tucked somersault.

Now, extend all limbs. Even the tips of my toes.

The roar of the ocean grows louder. I can feel its energy, and the first cool drops touch my heated skin.

In a straight line, I race toward the water.

One last time, I check my position. It's perfect. Everything is perfect.

With a sense of bliss, I close my eyes. I want to savor the adrenaline rush as it surges through me.

With the force of a car crash, the water breaks my fall. If I let go now, my bones might break. So I give it my all. Every fiber of my being must work, as the sea engulfs me with its might.

Bam!

Just a moment ago, I was at the mercy of gravity, but now the water catches me. I let myself sink to the bottom and open my eyes. Above me, the sunlight breaks through the restless sea, painting flickering lines on the sandy floor. Seaweed sways blissfully in the current, and a crab hides under a rock beside me.

My heartbeat calms down, and a silence settles within me. It scares me, so I forcefully push off from the bottom and break the surface. I raise my arms high and let myself float in the water. The spectators on the cliffs above applaud, but I can't hear them over the deafening roar of the waves.

I swim energetically toward the waiting inflatable boat, pull myself up, and take a seat. Before I can brush my dripping, shoulder-length hair out of my face, the driver revs up the motor and steers toward the coast. Absorbing the harsh impact of the waves, I unzip my wetsuit and look around for the person I've put all my effort into this jump for: the talent scout.

Over there, on the low rock covered with coastal grass, he stands. His thinning hair flutters in the wind, and he's jotting something down on his notepad. Thanks to his oversized sunglasses, I can barely make out any movement in his facial expressions.

Please, let it be a good evaluation.

In my mind, I go through the jump again. Were my legs perfectly parallel during the stretched twist? Did I execute the flips cleanly? I know my body was in a flawless position upon entering the water. Anything else, I would feel clearly now because the sea does not forgive the slightest mistake. Still, that alone won't be enough to finally get a sponsorship deal. Not with the competition I've already seen jumping today.

A few minutes later, as I climb the steps carved into the cliff with bare feet and pass by the scout, he nods approvingly at me but doesn't approach me. Thankfully, I have no time to dwell on what that could mean as my buddies surround me.

Matteo holds out his fist. "Awesome," he says.

I can't help but crack a relieved grin. If my coach calls the jump *awesome*, then it was indeed awesome.

My chance is alive.

If I perform just as well in the next two rounds, I

might finally make my big dream come true—to make a living from cliff diving. I'll need the talent scout's recommendation to secure a sponsorship deal and move to the pro league. There's nothing I want more.

In the next hour, I do everything to deliver a flawless performance. With my final jump, I realize that fate is now in control. I can only hope it remembers that it owes me some redemption.

***

As I arrive at my VW bus in the gentle light of the evening sun after the show, I can't suppress a yawn. I'm exhausted. But also incredibly happy. Letting out a contented sigh, I sink onto the driver's seat and reach for a power bar from the half-empty pack. After barely taking the first bite, my phone rings.

It's a video call from Camilla. Chewing with pleasure, I answer the call. "Hey," I say, setting the phone down to grab my hoodie from the back seat.

Even though it's pleasantly warm here during the day, the approaching night still brings some colder temperatures.

"Vico? I can't see you." Her tone carries a sense of urgency. "What's wrong with this stupid thing again?"

"Just a moment." Quickly pulling the hoodie over my head, I reach for the phone and hold it up to my face. "I'm here." As soon as I utter the words, I pause. Even though Camilla's fringed short haircut hasn't changed in years and I already know her recently chubby cheeks, she seems foreign to me today.

My sister takes a deep breath and locks her gaze on me. "Where are you?" she asks.

"At the Amalfi Coast. Why?" I take another bite of my power bar and study her more closely. Her usually cheerful face is frozen in an expression of concern.

"I see," she replies without answering my question.

An uneasy feeling creeps up inside me. "Are you okay? You look a bit pale."

She remains silent, nervously fumbling with her ear. Her wedding ring glistens in gold. Something is not right with her. I can sense it.

I shouldn't let myself be affected by this restlessness. However, it happens anyway.

I put the half-eaten bar aside. "What's wrong?"

"Nothing," she whispers. "I'm just a little tired."

It may be true, but that can't be all. An uncomfortable silence settles between us. I could let it go, not ask any further. Yet I know I can't do that.

"Do you need me?" I ask. "Should I come back home?"

My God, what am I saying?

I can't go back there. The mere thought makes my stomach twist into knots. Cold sweat forms on my forehead. Besides, my next competition is this weekend.

Camilla shakes her head silently, but her eyes scream loudly, "Yes."

What now?

Should I pretend that everything is okay?

My throat feels constricted. The sky behind the windshield darkens rapidly. I wish I could freeze time, but that wouldn't help. No matter how many shivers run down my spine at the thought of returning to my hometown, I won't abandon my sister. Not after what she has done for me.

To relieve the tightness in my throat, I clear it loudly. "I'll leave early tomorrow morning."

My attempt to sound carefree has failed miserably. The forced croak probably gave me away. Hopefully, she won't notice that my smile is nothing but forced.

She nods, blinking noticeably often. Then she struggles to force her lips into a smile as well. "Thank you," she whispers and ends the call abruptly.

Whether I like it or not, in my imagination, the video continues, showing my little sister burying her face in her hands and sobbing loudly.

I bite my tongue until I taste the metallic tang of blood and start the engine. I have one evening and one night left—about fourteen hours when I'd better not dwell on what awaits me in the peaceful village where I grew up.

***

Despite all efforts to keep my thoughts anchored in the present, the night was restless. Fragments of memories crowded into my dreams. My father's face furrowed with worry. My mother's radiant smile as she tied my shoelaces. Camilla and I sitting silently in her bungalow's living room. Alessia's wide-eyed expression, and Aurora's incredulous stammering. The whole family gathered around the long wooden table in the living kitchen, drinking wine and laughing wholeheartedly.

All of it was there. And it felt all too real.

Consequently, I'm tired as I drive my camper along the country road. Hip-hop music blares so loudly from the radio that I can't hear the roar of the old engine anymore. I only feel the vibrations of the uneven road. I try to avoid the bumps caused by the powerful roots of pine trees that have torn through the asphalt over the years as I get closer and closer to my old home. The gently sloping hills let me know that I'm already quite near.

Too near. I'm not ready yet, unsure of how to deal with being back here.

Nevertheless, the first rooftops of Collina da Sogno appear in my view behind a row of cypresses. In less than ten minutes, I'll have to face whatever awaits me at home.

Tense, I signal and turn toward my hometown. I press the gas pedal of the sluggish van, and I see a cloud of soot rise behind me in the rearview mirror.

I shouldn't postpone the van's repairs any longer. Pietro could look at it, but that would mean staying at least one night. And that's not an option.

Just as I'm about to turn up the music even louder, I see a dark red compact car parked a few yards ahead. Its rear extends into the middle of the road, while the front points toward the ditch. The hazard lights are on, but I can't see anyone around. No warning triangle is set up either. Strange.

Now I'm close enough to see the license plate. The car is from Austria. Maybe someone just got lost. To make sure that nothing has happened, I slow down, pull over to the right side of the road, and peel myself out of the worn-out seat of my van.

"Hello? Are you okay?" I ask in Italian, repeating the words in German just to be safe even though I wouldn't understand the response unless it's *How are you?* or *What's your name?*

Nothing stirs. The car appears abandoned.

After failing to detect any signs of smoke or a flat tire, it appears that the Austrian driver didn't have any car trouble. Could she have just stopped her car in the middle of the road to take a leisurely stroll through the picturesque landscape?

Perhaps she ran out of gas.

I walk around the trunk and continue toward the front of the car. All the windows are rolled down, and a large travel bag sits on the back seat.

Finally, I spot the woman on the driver's seat.

She's sleeping.

Did she simply pull over to take a nap in the middle of the road?

I'm baffled as I crouch down to peek through the window, taking off my sunglasses. A familiar fragrance of freshly cut flowers, green leaves, and roses, like the ones you find in a flower shop fills the car.

The woman sleeps contentedly, her chest rising and falling beneath the seat belt that runs across her. She wears a simple white T-shirt and dark blue jeans. No jewelry, no makeup, no nail polish. Her nails are short, and her hands bear scratches. A thick scar runs under her chin.

As questionable as this sleeping woman might be, something about her is captivating. The occasional twitch of her lips and the movement of her closed eyelids make me smile. With her unstyled hair framing her delicate cheekbones, she looks as if she stepped out of a fairy tale, waiting for someone to wake her with a kiss. What if I were that someone?

Nonsense.

"Hey," I say softly so as not to startle her. "You can't

sleep here." She doesn't react. I repeat the words in English, but that doesn't get her attention either. I hesitantly touch her shoulder. "Hello." I gently shake her. "Wake up."

Still, there's no response from her, but my own emotions are stirred up. Fascination intertwines with concern.

What if she's not sleeping but is somehow sick? Maybe she had a heart attack or something.

How did first aid go again? Check for breathing and pulse? Yes, that can't be wrong. Then put her in the recovery position and call for help.

With a queasy feeling in my stomach, I open the car door and lean over her. Her breath grazes my neck. I reach for her wrist to feel for a pulse.

It's there, strong enough to almost unsettle mine.

So she doesn't need help. Yet I can't just walk away after closing the car door. I remain at a safe distance, observing her enchanting face. My heart races, and I can't stop wondering what color her eyes might be.

The deep chestnut brown of her hair? Or the vibrant azure blue of the sea along the southern Italian coast?

As I imagine what it would be like if she were to look at me, I feel that I can't leave until I know the answer. "Who are you?" I ask, surprised by my own thoughts.

The stranger's eyelids flutter. Her eyelashes rise and fall gently, like feathers in a barely perceptible breeze.

I'm captivated. I should say something.

Yes, that would be good. But what?

"Are you okay?" What a foolish question. Of course, she's okay. Besides, she might not even understand Italian. Why am I speaking such nonsense?

Suddenly, she opens her eyes and gazes directly at me.

My heart skips a beat.

The mystery of the stranger, which I was so eager to unravel, is solved.

And the answer is a breathtaking sea green.

Chapter 3

Hanna

Everything is glowing.

The blue eyes. The shoulder-length hair. The stubble.

I blink.

Where am I?

"Are you okay?" asks the rugged face on the other side of the car door. I think it's in Italian. Or was it English?

What's going on here?

Heat rises within me, an intense tingling creeping up from my wrist and spreading farther upward. I lower my gaze, but all I see is the tiny hairs on my forearms standing on end like they're magnetized.

I don't understand this. And that's not the only thing. With a nervous gesture, I touch my temples, trying to catch the fleeting thoughts that ghost through my mind.

"Sto bene," I stammer even though I don't really know if I'm fine.

The stranger smiles at me. I smile back and squint my eyes. The surreal glowing image of the man becomes clearer, and suddenly, I feel like I'm sinking into the blue of his eyes. They are like a mountain lake, refreshing and clear.

"I…" What was I going to say again?

Now he steps back. "This is not the best place for a nap," he explains.

What does he mean?

Was I trapped in a daydream? Did I let myself fall so deeply that I couldn't perceive anything anymore? Please, no.

I strain to dig into my memory. No. That's not what happened. My migraine attacked me!

The excitement about the upcoming departure kept me awake half the night. Add the long car ride, and I probably didn't drink enough either. I should have taken better care of myself. No wonder I had such a severe attack that I even saw double.

Of course, in my thoughts, my mother wags her finger in admonishment. *It could have been pretty damn dangerous.*

"Headache," I reply disoriented. "It was too uncertain to continue driving."

Although my Italian is usually good, I'm not sure if what I just mumbled was correct. He probably thinks I'm a bit crazy. Prepared for a dismissive expression, I look up at him.

"I understand," he says casually and shrugs.

Even though he acts as if it's not a big deal, I feel the urge to explain to him. "I stopped to take a pill." With my index finger, I point at my open handbag, from which the medication package is indeed sticking out. "It takes a little while to work." And while I was waiting, I must have fallen asleep.

Well done, Hanna.

"And how are you feeling now?" He looks at me attentively.

"I'm fine. I can continue driving," I reply, and that's

the truth. My pain has subsided, and only a heavy tiredness remains.

He buries his hands in the pockets of his frayed jeans. "Then have a safe journey."

"Thank you." I reach for the ignition key and turn it. "For everything," I add. After all, who knows what could have happened if he hadn't woken me up.

His mouth corners twitch upward, but there's also a strangely melancholic flicker in his eyes. He waves goodbye, and at the same time, I imagine his posture is pleading for me to stay.

Obviously, my mind is not working perfectly after the migraine attack.

I raise my hand in a greeting, too, and gently press the gas pedal. The car starts moving, and although I should concentrate on the road, my gaze keeps flicking to the rearview mirror. There, I see the stranger watching me for a while before he puts on a pair of aviator glasses and strolls back to his VW bus.

Chapter 4

Vico

The woman from earlier remains in my thoughts for the rest of the way. There was something about her that I can't grasp. Something I can't explain, yet I know it exists.

However, she can no longer distract me now that I'm forcing my camper into the driveway. My palms become instantly sweaty, and I grip the steering wheel tightly. I only have to cover a few hundred yards of gravel road lined with an avenue of cypress trees and knee-high grass, and then I'm here.

I'm back home.

Directly in front of me stands my family's mansion. Camilla's separately built carmine-red bungalow also appears next to the tall trees. Relieved that I don't have to enter the main house, I stop at the back of the bungalow. I turn off the engine, and the hip-hop music stops, leaving an eerie silence where I can hear my heart pounding.

I feel sick.

Nothing would please me more than turning back. But that's not an option. It's better to get it over with quickly, so I step out of the van and walk straight to the wooden front door. Before I can knock, it opens. However, Camilla's not standing in the tiled hallway. It's my youngest sister, Alessia.

With a sweeping gesture, she brushes her hip-length curls aside, her oversized neckline exposing her shoulder. "He's here!" she calls into the house before rushing into my arms.

I lift her and twirl her around, just like we used to do. And for a moment, it feels like the past.

Warm. Safe. Affectionate.

"Hey, little whirlwind." I can't help but smile.

"Finally." She sighs deeply, then breaks away from me, blinking rapidly. "Come inside," she says, turning on her heel and disappearing into the house.

The carefree moment is abruptly gone. I immediately feel like a storm is brewing inside me. It takes an effort to kick off my flip-flops and follow my sister into the modern, spacious kitchen. I spot Camilla sitting on a cream-colored armchair in front of the floor-to-ceiling window, holding her round belly with rosy cheeks.

Damn, that thing is huge. Are those twins? More like quadruplets.

"Don't worry, I'm staying away from the beach," she quips, playfully rolling her eyes at the ceiling fan, which is not usually needed in March but is lazily spinning today.

I give her a mischievous grin. "Good, then I don't have to call Greenpeace either." Camilla chuckles amusedly, and I walk toward her, giving her a cautious hug. She feels as warm as a radiator in the dead of winter. "How are you doing?" I ask. The pregnancy must be taking a toll on her.

Instead of answering, she nods against my shoulder. Then out of nowhere, she breaks into sobs.

First Alessia, and now Camilla. Every woman I

embrace today is either on the verge of tears or actually crying. For a split second, the sea-green eyes of the Austrian woman flash through my mind as if they could be my lifeline to avoid thinking about my sisters' behavior. But I have to address it.

Gently, I stroke Camilla's back. "What's wrong?" I try to keep my voice steady because I want to be there for her. "Is there something wrong with the babies?"

She waves it off and signals for me to sit on the blue-checkered corner sofa. Alessia hands me a tall grappa glass and places the bottle of clear marc brandy right next to it as if she's certain I'll be pouring myself a drink soon. I shake my head silently. No matter what they have to tell me, I can handle it without alcohol.

She doesn't look me in the eyes. Instead, she exchanges meaningful glances with Camilla and finally settles on the opposite side of the coffee table on the bright tiles of the floor. The fan rumbles on. The sofa creaks with every movement.

My God, can someone finally say something?

I look at Alessia, then at Camilla, urging them to speak. "Thank you for being here," she says with a fragile voice as if she's been practicing the lines. "We need your help." She pauses, swallows hard, and breathes shakily.

I slide closer and take her hand in mine. "Whatever it is, I'm here for you."

"There's something you need to know. Something… I've kept from you. And I'm sorry for not telling you earlier…" Camilla seeks help from Alessia, who seems to be the prompter trying to save her.

The uncertainty gnaws at my stomach and now my lungs as well. I feel like I can't get enough oxygen.

"Alessia, go ahead and tell her," Camilla finally says.

With a sudden burst of courage, Alessia blurts out, "Father is sick. And the business is bankrupt." As soon as she says the words, she jumps up, walks to the window, and turns her back to us.

I'm unable to gather my thoughts coherently, so I turn to Camilla, who has buried her face in her hands. Thick teardrops slowly trickle down the inside of her forearms, disappearing into the crooks of her elbows.

I want to ask her how this happened, how long she's known about it, and why she didn't reach out to me sooner. But at the same time, I'm so afraid of her answer that I can't bring myself to ask. More importantly, I suddenly realize what kind of help they want to ask me for.

They want me to return and help save the family legacy.

Their home.

Our home.

Accompanied by Alessia's soft sobs and Camilla's silent tears, I reach for the grappa, empty the glass in one gulp, and immediately refill it.

Fuck.

Abruptly, Alessia turns around, her curls swaying backward. "Father wants to speak to you." Her sober tone is unlike my little sister, whose voice usually carries a melodious lilt. "He's waiting in the library."

I clench my fingernails into my palms. "Fine," I say, though it's anything but fine.

No one responds, and I'm left speechless as well. Almost robotically, I rise to make my way there.

Suddenly, someone grabs my arm. "Wait."

I whirl around and meet Alessia's red-rimmed eyes.

I know that they see me as their rock in troubled waters. And that's what I want to be for them.

But right now, I truly can't handle any more bad news.

"Let's talk about it later," I say quickly, eager to get away.

Away from their tears, the sight of which brings me to my knees.

With my hands buried deep in the pockets of my jeans, I trudge along the beaten path to the back entrance of the main house. I avoid looking up, not wanting to see the venerable building or how it has changed in the almost four years of my absence. With my head down, I open the heavy wooden door with its intricately carved ornaments and step into the dimness of the hallway. Damp, cool air greets me. Only a few more steps along the uneven stone floor separate me from the library. There, I will come face-to-face with my father after all this time to explain to him why it is impossible for me to carry on his work.

My future lies on the highest cliffs in Europe. In the place that used to be my home, everything feels constricting.

I would perish if I were to stay here, where the same curtains still billow in the gentle breeze from the drafty windows. Just this hallway alone constricts my chest. For in my mind's eye, I see myself as a little boy, walking down the corridor with nothing but swimming trunks on my body and the taste of sugary grapes on my tongue. Laughing loudly because I could easily escape from my three sisters during our game of tag. Everything was good here for so long. But that time is irreversibly over. I don't belong here. From the

40

ruins of the past, I have painstakingly built a new life. A life that I love.

In the meantime, I have arrived at the library. The dark door with its metal fittings is only slightly ajar, but no sound can be heard from inside the room. The only thing that reaches my ears is the rushing of my own blood.

This is ridiculous. There's nothing to fear, so I pull myself together and step in confidently. The wooden floor creaks under my feet, and the air is so stale as if no one has ventilated this room for years. I even imagine still catching a whiff of the pungent smell of medical soap that hung in the air during my last stay in this room. My gaze sweeps over the floor-to-ceiling shelves covered in a thick layer of dust. None of the two thousand books seem to have been moved in years.

The room seems dead.

Just like my father, whom I now discover in an antique brown leather chair. He sits there motionless, staring out through the dirty window. His slippers, made of thin fabric, are frayed at the edges, and his jogging pants and faded shirt hang on him like on a coat hanger. His hands tremble in his lap. His fingernails are long, and his skin appears scaly and pallid.

My God, what has happened to him?

"Hello, Father," I say as I step closer to him.

He doesn't look up at me and doesn't utter a word. It's as if he doesn't even realize I'm here. But I'm acutely aware of his presence. I see every detail—the deeply furrowed forehead, the hair that is much too sparse for his nearly fifty-five years, the sunken cheeks, the grayish complexion. I don't understand. When I left Tuscany four years ago, he was stable. He had forgotten how to laugh joyfully and feel genuine happiness, but his muscles were strong, and behind his troubled expression was that iron will. Even though I couldn't see him, I felt he was there.

I was sure that everything would turn out fine. But the way he huddles on the armchair today, staring into the void behind me, speaks a clear language.

Father is not sick in the way I thought earlier. I turn around but don't see any medications or medical devices in this room. I don't even spot one of those health drinks. His body is healthy. But his soul is suffering, and there is only one possible explanation. The death of my mother has taken more than just the love of his life from him.

Gazing out the window over the gently sloping hills of Collina da Sogno, I clear my throat with effort.

"You wanted to talk to me?" I ask because I hesitate to inquire about his well-being. Not even a blind person could miss the aura of decline surrounding my father.

His armchair creaks softly, immediately capturing my attention. He nods sluggishly. "Thank you for coming," he murmurs wearily.

My stomach churns at the thought of what is about to happen.

He takes a deep breath as if preparing to dive underwater. "We're selling the estate."

What? This estate is his entire life. He inherited it from his father, and it was meant to be passed on to his children. Camilla agreed to take over the inheritance. All the details were settled.

I sink to my knees beside him in disbelief. "But then…"

"It will be over," Father completes my sentence. "It's done. Finally. Over."

Though he whispers his words, I sense the gravity behind them. He wants to sever all ties. Erase every memory.

The enthusiasm with which he fought for this patch of land his whole life no longer exists.

I don't know what to think about it, and even less can I comprehend what this information does to me. It's as if there's a void inside me, swallowing everything.

"A potential buyer has shown interest. He's coming today." Beads of sweat form on his forehead, indicating how strenuous this conversation is for him. "I don't want to burden your sister even more than she already is. Camilla is struggling enough to help me with the sale formalities. She clings to her homeland. But you…"

I don't. That's what he thinks. And he's probably right. Too many memories lurk here for me, too much nostalgia, and even more pain. The feeling of home died within me long ago. And that's for the best.

"Alessia prepared your old room for him. You must show him the estate and the grounds. I also promised that we would present him the sights of the surrounding area." He reaches for me. A cold nothingness brushes against my hand, as if a ghost were touching me. "He'll stay for three weeks to take a good look at everything. Then he must decide if he wants to buy, understand?"

The determination in his voice lacks the fragility that usually dominates it. He's serious. Whatever the reason this particular buyer is so eager, it seems to be the most important thing right now.

I don't want to ask because, in the end, it doesn't matter. I know that it's probably the best solution for everyone. We'll get it over with. Rip off the Band-Aid from our skin and endure the excruciating burning for a second, only to finally be free.

The fact that I have to stay for several weeks now doesn't sit well with me. But if it's necessary, I'll do it. I gently place my hand on his bony shoulder and nod. "I'll take care of it."

Chapter 5

Hanna

I pull up on the gravel forecourt of the grand estate. If I had realized earlier I was heading in the wrong direction, I would have arrived long ago. But my confusion after the embarrassing moment with the stranger by the roadside cost me at least forty minutes.

I can't let something like that happen again.

Florian is counting on me, and I can't disappoint him. As long as I'm here, I have to wear the mask of a serious investor. Determined, I swing open the car door, step out, and look around.

The stone facade of the main house rises with impressive calm against the pale blue sky. The square windows are hidden behind shutters whose white paint has mostly peeled off. The greenery obviously has been taking what they want in the courtyard for years. Ivy tugs at the rusty rain gutters, and bright purple heather proliferates on the wall ledges.

The more closely I look, the more dilapidated the estate appears. The metal chairs of the seating area in the sheltered corner are adorned with intricate ornaments, but they look so crooked as if they must withstand an eternal storm.

I stroll on and discover a pool sunken into the ground. Where deep blue water should invite for a splash, there's a green soup swirling, its surface covered with pine needle nests. A brown-spotted frog clings to a small branch, eyeing me skeptically.

There is probably still a lot to explore here. Up ahead, for example, where the stone staircase seems to lead to a higher terrace. Lined with herb beds that are hardly recognizable anymore, the steps wind around a bay window. As I approach, the intense scent of thyme fills my nose.

I glide onto the stone border. Barely has my backside touched the stones when the edge suddenly gives way. I lose my balance and land on the ground with a few pieces of rock. Cement, the consistency of fine quartz sand, trickles onto my head.

Ouch.

I massage my wrist, which cushioned the fall. Hopefully, nobody saw how clumsy I was again. Embarrassed, I look around—and freeze.

Over there, leaning against the house wall, is the attractive surfer guy who woke me up in the car earlier.

Oh no. Please, not him.

Embarrassed, I shrug my shoulders. He doesn't grin, but he should. Anyone else would make fun of my mishap, but he seems lost in thought, distant.

What is he doing here? And why is he looking at me with this strange mix of sadness and nostalgia?

He appears different from before.

Closed off.

But something about him also makes it impossible for me to look away. Even from a distance, I can feel that confusing effect he had on me in the car.

Someone should do something. Or say something. And that someone, of course, is me. Because what my senses are tricking me into is nonsense. I'm just disoriented because he caught me in an awkward situation.

Focus, Hanna. Don't forget, you have to play the businesswoman!

What now?

That he's not Camilla, whose contact details Florian wrote down for me, is obvious. Still, he might be able to help me, so I push myself up from the ground, shake off the cement dust from my hair, and walk toward him.

"Hello, I'm Hanna," I say in Italian, trying to act as if I hadn't just made a complete fool of myself. "I'm waiting for Camilla. She was supposed to show me the estate, but she's not here."

His eyebrows rise. "You're the buyer?"

"Yes, I am," I answer, and because my Italian isn't perfect, I directly lose control of my tongue, making it clear that he has no idea what I just said.

His intrigued gaze prompts me to try again. Slowly, I repeat the words.

"Va bene. Welcome, Hanna," he says, suddenly smiling at me, although his eyes remain guarded. "I'm Vico, and I'll show you everything."

Camilla should have been the one showing me around, as agreed. Should I be suspicious? Would Florian be suspicious? I have no idea. Who knows if he even has anything to do with the estate? Maybe he's just following me and playing a prank. "Where is Camilla?" I ask, crossing my arms in front of my chest.

With a perplexed expression, he mimics my gesture. "My sister is occupied." He indicates a belly the size of a stability ball. "She can't see her feet anymore and

47

shouldn't put any weight on them for more than half an hour."

I want to believe him, but I can't afford to make any mistakes here, as my future depends on this estate. "What's your last name?" I inquire, trying to keep my focus.

With a bewildered look, he copies my movement again. "Olivetta."

He seems to genuinely belong here. And if this Camilla really is his sister, I will soon meet her too. His lie will be exposed then. Maybe I should just let it go, right? A businesswoman would probably focus on her mission, wouldn't she? "Alright, Vico Olivetta, let's get started," I say, trying not to let his odd behavior affect me.

Briefly, a strange flash flickers in his eyes, then they close off again. "Follow me," he says, waving his hand.

Is he trying to throw me off balance? I can't let him succeed, no matter how strange he behaves. With my shoulders hunched back, I march beside him across the courtyard and enter the estate through the creaking double doors.

The first glance inside gives me no reason to rejoice. The plaster crumbles in some places, and I spot a damp stain in the corner of the wide hallway. A crack runs across the ceiling.

Before I can bring up the condition of the building, he opens a door. "This way, please."

I step in hesitantly. The room looks like an abandoned teenage bedroom. Tape residue and tiny holes cover the wall behind the white-painted bed. The wide dresser next to the window is empty, just like the wardrobe with its doors open.

At least I find a bottle of water and a bowl of grapes and oranges on the nightstand.

"This is your room," he says in a strangely controlled tone. "The tour will start tomorrow. Rest up, you must be tired."

Is he alluding to our first encounter?

"Not at all," I reply quickly, not wanting him to notice how much he's unsettling me. "I'll just settle in quickly, and then I'll be ready." Florian's checklist is frighteningly long, and I only have three weeks before Natalie's internship at our inn ends. Even though the sky outside transforms to a pale pink, it would probably be better to start right away.

Suddenly, he looks as if he has a stomachache. "Everything in due time. The bathroom is across the hall, and the kitchen is next door," he says, turning to leave. "It's better if you don't go anywhere else alone. See you tomorrow."

He leaves the room so quickly that I can't respond. What about dinner, for example? *Or when do we start tomorrow?*

He closes the creaking door behind him, and then it becomes conspicuously quiet. He must be on the other side. On tiptoes, I sneak around the room. When I reach the door, I hold my breath.

Yes, he's still here. Just a few inches away, I hear his shallow breath, followed by a rustling sound.

Is he brushing his shoulder-length hair away from his face? Or is he wiping his palms on his worn-out jeans?

Is he considering coming back to me?

"Cursed," he mutters in despair, and then footsteps follow.

I have no idea why, but I start running too. Straight to the window that overlooks the courtyard. With a pounding heart, I peer outside.

"See you tomorrow," I murmur.

Chapter 6

Vico

Just this one day.

That's the sentence I repeat to myself since waking up. And even now, as I approach the mansion, those words echo in my head.

I will show Hanna the estate, the main rooms, the outdoor areas, and even the tool shed if needed. Then we'll be done here, and I'll never have to set foot inside the main house again. Everything that comes after will be easy. In the following weeks, we'll just go through the tourist program. I'll feel much better once today is over and we leave the estate tomorrow.

So much better.

To divert her attention from the house, I hold the Tuscany guide I found in my sister's bookshelf. We won't need to come back here if I play it right. I marked my ideas for accommodations with an exclamation point. Today, she gets an impression of the country estate in fast-forward, which she hopefully buys, and then she plunges directly into the much-vaunted magic of Tuscany.

As I approach the entrance gate, I imagine catching a hasty movement behind the window of my old childhood room. Was that Hanna? Was she watching me?

Lost in thought, I enter the house and walk through

51

the hallway with my head down. That's the strategy for today.

Don't look. And always smile as if everything is perfectly fine.

Just this one day. Then it will get easier.

I knock on Hanna's door. With a focused look, she opens it and greets me in her remarkably good Italian. Once again, her hair is wild and disheveled, the fringe falling irregularly over her eyebrows.

Her green eyes shimmer underneath. Yesterday, they were agitated, but today they seem gentle, perhaps even cautious.

"Buongiorno," I say, trying to sound casual. "Are you ready for the house tour?"

"Absolutely." She grabs the camera on the dresser and slings the strap around her neck. Then she takes out a clipboard with what feels like a thousand sheets and a pen. She stands before me like an eager student with perfect preparation.

"Are my shoes okay?" she asks, pointing at the light-brown sneakers she wore yesterday as well.

To be honest, I have no idea. I don't know what has happened here in the past four years. Even when I left the estate back then, it was in bad condition, and what I've seen so far hasn't been promising.

"Perfetto," I say nevertheless, as it's crucial to present the house in the best light.

She looks at me expectantly. "Then what are we waiting for?"

We're waiting for a lightning strike that would prevent me from embarking on this tour of my past. Nausea rises in me, and I wish I could cancel it right away.

Just this one day.

I take a step back and gesture toward the hallway. "After you," I say.

With an oddly stern expression, she marches past me and walks along the wide corridor with its large stone tiles, forming a pattern of different colors.

"Is this the entrance area?" she asks, although it's obvious. I nod, and she takes notes on her clipboard.

Her jaw appears tense, and she seems nothing like the enchanting woman I met on the country road yesterday. What a pity.

"What is the floor area?" she asks.

I have no idea, so I shrug. "Does it matter?"

Instead of answering, she continues down the hallway. "I'd estimate about twenty yards in length," she says when she reaches the other end, measuring the width in the same manner and jotting down notes. "We'll need to measure it properly later," she mutters tensely. Then she inspects the plaster, once white but now covered in a gray haze. She moves on to the floor-to-ceiling double-glazed window and takes photos of the crack running across its entire surface.

It's a relief that she's focused on her task. It means she doesn't notice the discomfort twisting my stomach. That glass damage has a story, just like everything else here, and I dread delving deeper into the house.

"What's behind this door?" Her question snaps me out of my thoughts.

I glance at her and reply, "Nothing." Cursing myself, I sound panicked, as if I have something to hide. "Just a storage room," I add with a forced smile, hoping she won't enter my mother's room.

That's where she passed away.

Hastily, I guide her to the opposite double door leading to the living room. "This is the largest room in the house," I say with a promising tone and swing open the doors.

"Oh." She freezes like a statue. The clipboard almost slips from her hand.

I follow her gaze and freeze too.

This was our center. The open fireplace, the antique pieces of furniture, and the thick carpets where we used to lie as children while Mother read us fairy tales.

The heavy burgundy curtains we hid behind to avoid brushing our teeth.

The display cabinet with the crystal glasses we secretly sipped from when my sisters forced me to play the prince for them.

None of it exists anymore.

As I see the abandoned seating area covered in plastic, the chandelier draped in cobwebs, and the meager remnants of the ceiling decorations, I struggle to swallow the lump in my throat.

This is in ruins. Nothing is left of the Olivetta family.

At this moment, I know one thing for sure. Even just one day is too much.

I can't do this. I can't walk through this crumbling building and ignore the messages screaming at me from every corner. Maybe my father and my sisters think differently, but they're wrong.

"You know what? I'll get you a map, and you can explore everything at your own pace," I force out with effort.

She doesn't reply.

I turn my head toward her, and immediately I

understand why she's silent. Her expression tells me she's not even here.

She's somewhere else.

Her eyes shine like the sea on a sunny day. I hear her breath flow with a calmness that almost magically transfers to me. Mesmerized, I watch as her lips curve upward more and more. Then she tilts her head, as if she's listening to a melody that exists only within her soul.

I have never seen anything so charming.

Though she doesn't even look at me, she captivates me. She's like a piece of art I want to explore every detail of.

Now she blinks, and moisture clings to her dark lashes.

"Good morning," I whisper, more tenderly than I intended.

Chapter 7

Hanna

His eyes hold something so gentle that I would love to lose myself in them.

"Did you have beautiful dreams?" he asks.

What? No!

Suddenly, I realize what just happened.

How could I?

"Do you want to tell me about it?" he adds with a warm tone. He sounds as if there's nothing he'd like more than to know the world I just woke up from.

Hastily, I take a step back. These daydreams belong to Hanna Daydreamer, and I can't be her. Many years ago, I vowed never to show anyone what goes on inside me when I get lost in my dreams. It was the best decision of my life.

He takes a step toward me, seemingly in a trance. "It was beautiful there, wasn't it?"

He needs to stop asking such questions because I'll never answer them. An immediate memory wells up in me, and my heart becomes heavy. But at the same time, I know how important it is not to forget. Ultimately, it helps me to keep experiencing the consequences of my daydreaming, and today, it's the moment when I stood on the stage in front of the entire school to present my project for beautifying the school building.

Everyone was there. Not just my classmates but also

my family. The neighbors had come and even the priest. Without considering the possible consequences, I lost myself on that stage in my daydreams.

I didn't just talk about blue walls and wild-patterned curtains. In my mind's eye, I also saw colorful cushions where we could sit. And an improvised village shop where we could sell fruits and vegetables while learning mathematics.

I forgot where I was and only saw the image of a school where one didn't have to sit still to receive an education.

The vision in my mind was so vivid that I desperately wanted to share it with everyone. With my eyes closed, I delivered a passionate speech. I not only spoke about what I saw but also about what I heard, smelled, and tasted at that moment. And about how it would feel to learn every day with joy and curiosity.

It was an entirely new kind of school. And it was fantastic.

But it was only fantastic for me.

As I lifted my eyelids after my presentation, a blissful grin on my face, the teachers stared at me in shock. My classmates whispered excitedly to each other and giggled mockingly.

"Hanna Daydreamer," one of them suddenly shouted.

Everyone in the auditorium heard it. Laughter filled the room immediately.

Nausea surged within me. As the "Hanna Daydreamer" chants grew louder, my stomach tightened relentlessly. Seeking help, I looked at my mother. I needed nothing more than a reassuring smile or a loving nod. Just anything that would show me how wrong it was for the others to laugh at me. But all I received was an ashamed look before she turned away, apologizing to the principal for my behavior, feeling embarrassed.

Back then and even now, I swallow hard. That experience seared into my soul, and it was far from the only one. It took a long time, but eventually, I understood how useless and senseless my imagination was.

It's a curse.

As much as I try, I can't turn it off, but I have at least learned to hide it. And today, I must do that more than ever. After all, I want Vico to see me as a businesswoman, not a ridiculous daydreamer.

Not knowing what else to do, I grab my camera and escape from him, taking random pictures. Only when I feel like I have control again do I dare to look at him.

His gentle expression is gone. Once again, he shows me his weary face. I have no idea why, and it doesn't matter. It helps me play my role.

"This will be the foyer." I try to sound matter-of-fact. That's what businesswomen do, I think. "Is there direct access to the outdoor area?"

He clears his throat. "Of course." He points at the glass door leading to a terrace.

I head toward the door, spotting a crooked pergola and dead plants in terracotta pots. But when I try to open it, the handle comes loose in my hand.

Chapter 8

Vico

In disbelief, she presents the broken doorknob to me.

"Come on, let me show you the other rooms," I say hastily. Not just to end the torment for myself but also because Father was very clear yesterday. She must buy the property. The fewer damages she discovers, the better.

"Does the terrace have an external staircase?" she asks, ignoring my request.

With a nod, I signal her to leave this cursed room and lead her up the worn-out staircase to the upper floor. Here we stand now, facing the seemingly endless hallway with ten doors on each side.

I doubt I can show her even a single room without my instinct to flee overwhelming me. "Please, take a look around. I'll wait here and gladly answer all your questions."

Instead of taking out her camera, she eyes me anxiously. Then she taps her shoe on the wooden floor as if it were made of delicate glass. "It looks quite dangerous."

Yes, the estate is a wreck. Is that what she wants to hear from me?

"Do you have a construction helmet? Or safety shoes?" She hastily brushes a strand of hair from her face. "Because of the risk of injury."

Now she's exaggerating. Automatically, my gaze glides over her delicate frame. "It's safe, don't worry."

"But I..." She stops mid-sentence. Then she straightens her back and starts walking.

I watch her thoughtfully. I can't figure out this woman. Sometimes she's this fascinating fairy who captivates me effortlessly, to the point where it scares me. Then again, she becomes a tough, unsympathetic businesswoman.

Just like now. From time to time, she appears in my field of view, inspecting one room after another, taking photos and jotting down notes. Not once do I see that expression from earlier when she seemed unapproachable for a moment. That's a good thing.

I don't want to experience whatever was happening in the living room again. At that moment, something was far more dangerous than decaying floorboards.

Much more dangerous. I wanted to be with her, to feel with her, and to share her thoughts. If she had allowed it, my heart would have been defenseless, and that must never happen.

I use the break to read the message from my coach, Matteo. He informs me that he managed to register me for the main draw in a competition in Bari in mid-April.

Such an opportunity comes only once in a lifetime, he writes, and he's so right. *When will you be back? We definitely need to work on your somersaults.*

Before I can react, Hanna is once again standing in front of me with her ridiculous clipboard. "Is there a cellar?" she asks.

"A wine cellar." But I don't want to show it to her. "Why?"

For a moment, she lowers her gaze to her checklist, as if she could find the answer to my question there because she doesn't know it herself. "I have to see it," she says absentmindedly. "I need to check if it's suitable for events. It's important because of…" Her finger follows a line of text. "The funding opportunities."

Earlier, she mentioned a foyer and now events. What does she have in mind for my family estate? "Are you planning to turn the estate into an event venue?" As I ask the question, a cold shiver runs down my spine.

This is unnecessary. The sale is the right decision. Whatever the buyer does with the property and the land, the main thing is that nothing reminds me of the tragedy that unfolded here.

"A guesthouse," she replies. Shouldn't she be smiling or showing some kind of excitement? Instead, she looks strained. It seems like she's only concerned about the money. "How many guest rooms do you think we can set up here?"

Something inside me resists thinking about this question. I also don't like her cold business tone. "I have no idea," I reply curtly and reluctantly lead the way to the wine cellar.

Clutching her clipboard to her chest, Hanna follows me. I swallow heavily as we reach the massive wooden door of the wine cellar.

"We'll have to figure that out in the next few days. We also need to go through each room and assess the damages," she says.

What?

No. That's not how it was planned.

I can't do this. I can't spend days meticulously digging into the past with her. Who knows what we might uncover!

In my panic, I thrust the travel guide into Hanna's hands. "I have to go now. Explore the rest on your own. Inside, you'll find everything you need to know about excursions and activities," I say, gasping for air. But the air I strain to inhale feels like poison in my lungs. "Come to the red-brick bungalow for dinner at eight tonight."

That's it. I can't do more. She has everything she needs, and I've delivered Camilla's invitation as promised.

Now I just want to get away from here.

Without waiting for her reaction, I turn around and walk down the corridor, heading toward the bright light of the exit. I wish I could escape to my camper, but Pietro took it to the workshop for some necessary repairs. I'll get it back tomorrow, and then I'll be free again.

With trembling fingers, I pull out my phone. *I'll be back tomorrow afternoon*, I type in a message to Matteo and immediately feel relieved.

Tomorrow, I'll set off and leave this crushing piece of land behind.

As terrible as it feels to disappoint my family and as much as I wish I were as strong as they believe, I simply can't do this.

Chapter 9

Hanna

I adjust the grasses of the wildflower bouquet in my hand and then knock on the door of the modern bungalow. Vico's invitation to dinner came as a surprise. After barely smiling the whole time, I was sure he wouldn't want to spend the evening with me. He's peculiar, yet I'm excited.

And who knows, maybe the dinner will turn out to be enjoyable?

The door opens, but it's not Vico who greets me; instead, a stranger with very short dark hair stands before me. "Ciao, you must be Hanna. I'm Pietro, welcome," he says. I return his greeting, and he waves me inside. "Just go straight ahead. Follow your nose."

I step inside, slip off my sneakers, and venture farther into the unfamiliar house.

A delightful aroma of roasted onions, tomato sauce, and a whole herb garden surrounds me even before I enter the large open-plan kitchen at the end of the hallway. A woman with buttock-length corkscrew curls stands with her back to me, stirring a massive pot with a wooden spoon. She chatters excitedly with another woman who takes a stack of plates from a hanging cupboard. When she turns around to face me, I instantly know that she must be Camilla.

As Vico hinted yesterday, she is heavily pregnant.

Curiously, I continue to look around, but Vico seems to be absent. A hint of disappointment creeps in.

"Hey, this is Hanna," Pietro says from behind me, and immediately, both women greet me warmly.

"Hello, everyone," I say, setting down my bouquet and hurrying toward Camilla.

She extends her hand to me. "It's nice to meet you."

"Take a seat in your chair, sister," the curly-haired woman at the stove turns around and grins at me. "I'm Alessia," she says, and I don't even have to ask. Despite their different hairstyles, I can tell right away that they are sisters.

While Camilla settles into the cozy armchair with the help of Pietro, I stand awkwardly in the kitchen. I observe how Camilla and Pietro nuzzle their noses together, locking eyes deeply. He whispers something to her, almost pleadingly. His hand rests on her cheek, and a slim gold ring glistens on his finger.

As if drawn by an invisible force, my gaze searches for Camilla's right hand. There, I find—albeit on her little finger—the same ring. They are married. And soon, they will have a baby and be a perfect family. Immediately, a longing stirs inside me, as I haven't had a real family in a long time. It's just Noah and me, and even that bond has weakened lately. He and Elina are now a unit, but at least I still have Florian, and I hope that soon we'll be able to afford to start a family of our own.

To dispel the rising longing, I ask Alessia for a vase, arrange my bouquet in it, and place it on the dining table. The violet blossoms form a beautiful contrast to the bright yellow broom flowers. "Can I help with the preparations?"

64

Pietro immediately jumps up. "You are our guest," he says, signaling me to take a seat on the sofa next to Camilla's chair. "I'll take care of it."

Alessia's warm laughter drifts over from the kitchenette. "As if you knew how to use the stove."

All three burst into laughter. It's so contagious that I no longer want to be skeptical. Florian's concern was unfounded; the Olivettas are a warmhearted family. Only Vico is strange. Will he still come? It would be a chance to find out what lies behind his impenetrable facade.

Before I take a seat on the sofa, I notice a row of photos on a shelf. Curiously, I step closer and give Camilla a questioning look. "May I?"

She nods, so I study the pictures more closely. My attention is immediately drawn to a slightly younger version of Vico in a photo, with his arms around Camilla and Alessia. But another woman is there. Her wavy hair, styled in an ombre fashion, falls over her shoulders. With her bright red lips and high cheekbones, she looks like a model.

I tap the photo. "Is that Vico's girlfriend?" I ask, wondering at the same time why I want to know.

"That's Aurora. She's the star of the family." A warm smile crosses Camilla's face. "My sister wanted to become a dancer, but…"

So she's not Vico's girlfriend. Interesting.

"She's currently working as a server. In France," Camilla says with a wistful tone.

"Mm-hmm," I reply absentmindedly. Is Vico single?

"I miss her a lot…family is family." She sighs, but I barely register it because I can't help but take another look at the picture.

Vico smiles at me, but his eyes are so sad that suddenly, I wish I could comfort him. Maybe …

"Dinner is ready," Alessia's call interrupts my thoughts.

I whirl around and see her placing a steaming ceramic pot on the wooden table. Pietro invites me to sit down with the others at the well-set table.

"This is Ribollita," Camilla explains, beaming, as she passes me a plate. "A true Tuscan specialty."

As she says it, it immediately gives me the feeling that they prepared the dish today just for me. Touched, I taste a spoonful of the creamy soup, apparently made from beans, cabbage, and loads of vegetables.

A burst of flavors fills my mouth. I taste thyme and marjoram, as well as robust notes of onions and garlic. The tomato base has a pleasant sweetness.

"It tastes fantastic," I say convincingly, bringing a satisfied smile to Alessia's face. "You're a great cook."

"She has to be," Camilla says, handing me the bread basket and gesturing to her sister. "She's studying biochemistry in Rome," she says with such pride that my heart tightens momentarily. "And cooking is just chemistry, too."

I look at Alessia in amazement. "You don't live here?"

Earlier, she seemed as though she did. And even what Camilla just said about the value of family didn't make me doubt it.

Alessia dips a piece of white bread into the soup and takes a bite. "I moved out almost four years ago. But I come to visit whenever I can." She shoots a furtive glance at her sister.

What does that mean? Do they assure each other

that they will always be there for one another? Or is it more of an exchange of secretive information that they want to keep from me?

I'm sure I'm just imagining these strange vibrations, but I still feel compelled to ask a few questions. Florian wants to know if the Olivettas are trustworthy. He'll want evidence. Unfortunately.

"Where is Vico today?" Of course, it's not the most important topic, but it's the only question that's been lingering in my mind all along.

Again, the sisters look at each other. "He had to work," Camilla shrugs, hastily turning her attention back to her soup.

"Does he live here with you?" I ask further, even though it's not really important.

Shaking her head, she reaches for her glass of water. "He wouldn't be able to stand that for a moment." Her grin doesn't match the turmoil in her eyes.

She seems sad. Why? "Why is he so…"

"Enough about us. Tell us what you want to visit while you're here." It's Alessia who interrupted me mid-sentence and now looks at me expectantly with her sharp eyes.

Perhaps she thinks it's a good topic, but it's not. The checklist is endless, and Vico's behavior this afternoon made it clear to me that I'll have to tackle it alone. He probably knew nothing about joint excursions and expert assessments, even though Florian assured me that someone would take care of me and all my questions.

While we enjoy the main course - a delicious fresh dish of squid and chard - I list the points on the list that I can vaguely remember. I'm embarrassed that I've gone through the documents a hundred times and still can't remember everything. Occasionally, I have to search for the appropriate Italian terms, but the longer I speak, the more fluid it becomes.

"Can you recommend any other highlights?" I ask finally and lean back in my chair with a full stomach. The meal was wonderful.

Pietro mops up the last of the sauce with bread. "You have the best tour guide by your side. Vico will show you everything worth seeing."

Ah, so he did know about the arrangement after all? Still, he dismissed me with a quick tour. Did my daydreaming in the living room shock him so much that he wanted nothing to do with me anymore?

His reasons should not matter to me, yet the thought makes me sad. "I'm afraid he won't. He just gave me a travel guide, and then he was gone."

"He didn't do that!" Camilla slams her hand onto the table with an incredulous expression, causing the plates to rattle. "He can't just…" Tears fill her eyes out of nowhere.

Alessia swallows hard too, reaching for her pregnant sister's forearm. "Calm down. Everything will be fine," she says in an imploring tone. "I'll take care of it."

Again, the two exchange an intense look. Again, I don't know what it means.

It's Pietro who saves the situation by jumping up from his chair. "We have Schiacciata dolce," he announces on his way to the kitchen.

Until he returns to the table with the generously fig-topped yeast cake, I dare not ask any more questions. It seems as if there are no innocuous topics here. As if in the Olivetta family, hidden corners and sad spots are everywhere, making them nearly impossible to avoid.

"We still know nothing personal about you. Will you tell us something?" Camilla asks me as the deliciously scented dessert, filled with pine nuts, is placed in front of me.

Even though I'd rather not think about it, I share details about the inn and our guests.

Work. Garden. Sleep. Cleaning.

There's not much else in my life, as I'm responsible for everything except paperwork. The Olivettas smile kindly at me, asking numerous questions, while I secretly glance at the door, hoping Vico might still show up.

Finally, I talk about my future plans with Florian. "After the renovation, we want to host guests here in Tuscany."

No one says anything; only Pietro nods cautiously. "I hope everything works out as you wish."

Camilla and Alessia keep their eyes lowered, and I can't read anything from their gazes. But their slumping shoulders tell me enough.

My words make them sad, almost as if they don't want the property to be sold. They must desperately need the money.

Immediately, I empathize with them. This feeling accompanies me until Pietro serves grappa afterward. From then on, the mood becomes more jovial. When I say goodbye to the Olivettas well past midnight, I feel more lighthearted than I have in a long time.

Both sisters embrace me before parting. "Don't worry, we won't let you wander around Tuscany alone," Alessia whispers, hugging me so tightly, as if she has grown fond of me throughout the evening.

Her words feel so heartwarming, and as I walk back to the estate, I realize that the past hours were a delightful escape from my life. I wrap my arms around myself and catch myself smiling involuntarily.

Chapter 10

Vico

I let the engine roar. The jet ski beneath me is as restless as a horse eager to burst out of the starting gate. The anticipation of the adrenaline rush that's about to come puts a wide grin on my face.

Here I come, freedom.

I release the brakes abruptly, and the jet ski lunges forward. Clinging tightly to maintain my balance, I relish the increasing rush of wind that blows my hair away from my face. I twist the throttle, and the vehicle accelerates rapidly, reaching fourty miles per hour. Seventy now.

I want more.

The jumps, thanks to the waves created by the surf, become wilder, and the moments of floating become longer. The motor roars deafeningly, and the salty water splashes up on my sides. When the speedometer hits one hundred, my mind finally empties.

Adrenaline floods my body, washing away everything that doesn't belong in my thoughts.

Hanna's sea-green eyes, her absent-minded smile, and the dreamy way she looked at the dilapidated remnants of our estate fade into the background.

I am free. Carefree.

This is how life should feel, and I savor it with all my senses until the fuel gauge starts blinking. I wish I could stay out here forever, but without gas, that's impossible. So reluctantly, I return to the shore. With each yard that brings me closer to the beach, reality seeps back into me.

I'm still in Tuscany, just ten minutes away from the place that triggers an uncontrollable flight instinct in me. It's responsible for the promise I made to my coach yesterday to return to Southern Italy today. It's the reason I brushed off Hanna with a travel guide when she needed my support.

I shouldn't have done that. And my plan to run away from here as soon as my van is out of the workshop feels simultaneously right and wrong in a grotesque way. It's as if I'm trapped between the suffocating memories of my mother's death, which are so omnipresent here, and the love for my sisters. My life feels like a labyrinth right now, and I can't find the way out.

How can I stay when all this is devouring me? But how can I leave when my family needs me so desperately?

Today, Camilla told me everything. Over the past few years, she's worked tirelessly to keep the estate afloat. It took her a long time to admit that she had failed and that she wasn't the right person to inherit it, especially with two newborns demanding all her attention. What kind of miserable brother would I be if I left her alone in her condition with Hanna and the burden of the sale?

Hanna.

She is another reason not to stay here. Yet she's the one holding me back from leaving. I don't understand it. It should be simple, but it's anything but that.

With a heavy feeling in my chest, I steer the Jet Ski to the shore and push it onto the beach to return it to the rental place. Beside the wooden pier, I spot Alessia sitting on one of the parked pedal boats.

"Hey," she says in a tone that churns nausea inside me. So warm. So considerate. So full of understanding.

I secure the Jet Ski, unzip my wetsuit, and approach her to give her a hug. "Aren't you supposed to be on the train to Rome already?"

She nods against my shoulder, her curls tickling my cheek. "That's true…"

But I hear the unspoken words in her sentence, yet she doesn't continue. Carefully, I pull away to look at her.

"Hanna needs support. I'll stay," she says, trying to appear carefree, but I know what's going on behind her furrowed brow.

She believes I don't know what it would mean for her academic progress, but she's mistaken. "You'll miss your exams," I say, and she looks surprised for a moment.

Then she lowers her gaze and smooths her overly long skirt. "I can make up for them. No problem."

Oh, it is a problem.

The sea breeze catches in her hair as she lifts her head. "Go ahead, Vico. Camilla and I can handle this."

Yes, I should do that.

We lock eyes. Seagulls fly above us, screeching in their paths.

She nods at me. But I shake my head.

"It's okay, I understand." Her words are almost swallowed by the sound of the sea, yet their intensity weakens my muscles.

Before me stands my little sister, ready to sacrifice herself for me. Not because she recognizes what a coward I am but because she loves the coward in me.

This is not right. I can't do this to her.

Agitated, I run my hand through my hair. "That's kind of you," I reply, my voice hoarse, but then I gather all the courage I have left. "But it's not necessary. I'll stay."

Matteo will have to wait, so will my career. I have to deal with this here, and there is a way I can make it work.

I'll build the walls around my heart even higher. That way, I'll survive the time at the estate. And her proximity as well.

Abruptly, she lifts her gaze, a single tear rolling down her cheek. "Thank you."

She says no more, and it's not necessary. Because I immediately understand where this gratitude comes from—deep inside her, where both of us carry the same wound. Her muscles give way, and she sinks into my arms. I do what I've always been responsible for as her big brother.

I'm there for her.

Chapter 11

Hanna

With my phone pressed to my ear, I gaze into the mirror and adjust my bangs. My eyes appear clearer than usual, and behind me, the broken bathroom tiles glow in a radiant azure blue.

"I've already done a rough tour of the estate. I'll send you the photos today," I say to Florian, who must be eager to get some initial information.

"Have you also contacted the craftsmen?" he asks, sounding strangely absent. I hear the rustling of paper in the background.

Did that even make it to the list? I must have overlooked it or, worse, forgotten. "It's in progress," I reply, not wanting him to think I'm just daydreaming here instead of pushing our mission forward.

"Without cost estimates, I can't estimate the loan amount. The banks want a clear breakdown." He sighs wearily. The creaking of his desk chair suggests that he's leaning back. Is he running his hand through his hair too?

His mood makes me suspicious. He sounds drained. "Is there a problem?"

"I have it under control. Don't worry. The plan will work. I just need the numbers," he answers so gently that it provides some comfort.

Thoughtfully, I grab the towel and head for the

door. "You'll get them as soon as possible." I step into the hallway and hurry to my room. Even though I'm allowed to use the bathroom here and the part of the kitchen that's still in working order, I still feel like a stranger.

Florian exhales with relief. "Thank you, Hanna. You're amazing." Just from the sound of his words, I could swear he's smiling now.

Suddenly, I halt in my movement. My cheeks flush, and my lips turn up on their own. No one has ever shown me as much appreciation as he does. He is proof that the new Hanna is lovable. And that my decision to hide the daydreaming Hanna is the right one. "Oh, it's nothing special."

"For me, it is," he says, then clears his throat. "I have to get back to work. The intern is a bit… clumsy. She needs support."

I stroll over to the window and pull aside the thin white curtain to look outside. I don't know what I expected, but seeing the courtyard empty before me disappoints me. "I understand. Have a great day."

"You too." A voice in the background calls his name. "What are you up to today, by the way?"

"I'm exploring the surroundings," I reply. Probably alone, but that's okay. I can handle it.

"One moment, I'll be right there…" He sounds muffled, as if he covered the receiver with his hand. Then there's rustling on the line. "Is Camilla treating you well? Is everything okay?"

I turn away from the window. "She's great," I answer. Apparently, he has enough of his own worries and doesn't need to deal with mine too.

"That's wonderful, Hanna. I'll talk to you again

tomorrow. Don't forget about the craftsmen, okay?" A thudding noise makes it hard for me to understand his words. "Should I send you a reminder?"

Florian knows me too well. "Sure," I reply, packing my photography gear into my backpack. "But now, make sure you help Natalie." I don't want anything bad to happen.

"Oh yes, I should do that." His laughter piques my curiosity. I've only been gone for two days. Could so much have gone wrong already? What has Natalie done? "Talk to you later." With these words, he hangs up before I can ask further.

I take the phone from my ear and check the time on the display. It's almost noon.

For the past four hours, I've been waiting in vain for someone to come and pick me up. Alessia promised last night that she wouldn't leave me alone. But now, it seems I have to admit that she stood me up.

I fall back onto the bed, staring at the crack in the ceiling and massaging my temples.

A hesitant knock reaches my ears. That must be Alessia. Thank goodness!

Abruptly, I rise from the bed and adjust my T-shirt. "Come in."

The door opens, but instead of Alessia, Vico stands in the doorway. His shoulder-length hair frames his forbiddingly attractive face. He's wearing worn-out jeans and flip-flops, their seams looking like they could come apart at any moment.

"Ready for a little sightseeing?" he asks, as if he hadn't rejected me yesterday, and gives me a tentative smile.

Suddenly, I feel unnaturally warm. "Um…" Oh,

heavens, why am I at a loss for words now? This is so unprofessional.

You're a businesswoman, Hanna, don't forget that!

He raises an eyebrow. "Or would you prefer to explore the area on your own?"

"No," I reply hastily, turning to my backpack. "We can go right away."

"Great." I can't quite place the undertone in his voice.

"Great," I respond, putting on the determined expression of a guesthouse owner on an expansion course. I feel like I'm wearing a mask as I quickly slip into my sneakers and approach him. But it's necessary so he doesn't confuse me even more. "Where are we going?"

He defers to me and closes the door behind us. "Wherever you want."

My checklist is in my backpack, so I have no idea where I want to go.

Chewing on my lower lip, I head toward the exit. "What do you recommend?"

"Everyone knows about the hills, the wine, and the pasta. That's boring," he replies thoughtfully. Then for a moment, his usually guarded blue eyes spark. How charming he suddenly appears. He gestures toward his VW bus. "Climb aboard, please, we'll make your blood boil today."

Did he just say that we boil blood, or did I misunderstand?

Not only his words but also the sight of his van give me pause. Up close, the vehicle looks like it could break down on the road at any moment.

It's probably safe, but my fear has too tight a grip on me to get inside.

I have a talent for constantly injuring myself. It's been like that my whole life. My mother drilled into me to take care of myself until I developed the habit of avoiding every little risk.

It's a bit crazy, but I can't shake off the fear. "Let's just take my car instead," I quickly say and nod toward my red Golf.

A steep crease forms between his eyebrows, and suddenly, he doesn't look charming at all. Still, I'd really like to know what's going on in his head right now.

Did I hurt him? Does he think I'm a snob? Or is he trying to figure out why I'm so confused by him, just like I am?

For seconds, we gaze at each other. Then he closes the door of his camper again. "Okay," he says with a shrug and strolls over to my car.

Never before has someone just accepted a suggestion from me like that. With a grateful nod, I march to the car and slide into the driver's seat.

I start the engine, give it a cautious rev, and steer the car onto the access road. "Where are we going?"

His promising grin is infectious. "It's a surprise. At the exit, turn right for now."

He's not going to tell me, huh? What does that mean?

Well, it's something different and kind of cute. Somehow.

"Okay," I mumble and turn onto the paved country road.

On the way, I focus on the road. Not just because

safety takes precedence while driving but also because something about Vico makes me nervous.

The way he immediately goes for my car radio to turn up the volume. How he sings along loudly as if he doesn't care that he's completely off-key. And the glances he throws my way from time to time. Then he smirks to himself and eventually looks away.

Inevitably, I wonder what he thinks of me. What he thinks he sees when he looks at me. And why he's been acting so differently since we left the estate behind.

Suddenly, he turns to me. "Come on, sing along."

"I don't know this song." I emphasize my words with a dismissive gesture.

"It doesn't matter." Even though I'm not looking at him, I feel his gaze. It's making my entire right cheek glow. "It's all about having fun, after all."

Fun? I raise an eyebrow. That has something to do with letting go. As much as I'd love to let go, it's unfortunately not a good idea at all.

Curious, he leans over to me. "You don't know what this is, do you?"

Um…

"Just give it a try." With those words, he turns the music up so loud that the bass vibrates in my chest and rolls down the car window.

In the corner of my eye, I see the wind gently tousling his hair. His expression is filled with happiness as he sings and moves his feet to the beat. He exudes something that I want to feel too.

Joy. Freedom.

On impulse, I start humming softly. Even though I can barely hear myself, it feels wonderful. Without any effort, my head nods to the rhythm, and my fingers dance on the steering wheel. For a few moments, I enjoy just being in the moment. But soon, the last notes of the song fade away.

Smiling, Vico lowers the volume of the radio. "You can park up there by the hill."

I'd much rather continue cruising through Tuscany a little longer, enjoying the view and feeling the emotions the music stirred in me. But no sooner do I see the parking lot ahead, reminding me why we're here and making me realize I forgot once again. Reluctantly, I put on my business facade and step out of the car.

"Now it's getting hot," Vico teases. Raising his eyebrows, he leads me toward a weathered wooden fence, the kind you'd find in Tyrol around horse pastures.

"I can't see any fire." Besides, no visitors are here, which makes me suspicious.

Chuckling, he raises his index finger. "Not so fast," he says, coming closer. Suddenly, he's so near that the gentle breeze carries the fresh scent of his skin to my nose. "Close your eyes."

With this uneven ground, you'll only stumble and scrape your knees, my mother warns

"Maybe not." Dammit, I sound like an insecure girl. I can't let him throw me off balance like this.

Abruptly, I turn away and walk to the fence. But once I get there, I'm again struggling with myself.

"Wow," I whisper in awe, as before me lies a world unlike any I've seen.

The shades of green on the gentle hills glow in the sunlight while soft cumulus clouds drift lazily across the horizon. I spot houses with terracotta roofs partially hidden behind small forests. On the slopes, vineyards grow. Amid this scenery, mist rises, giving the view a sense of mystery that once again makes me forget why I'm here. The white veils embrace tree trunks and glide along the tall grasses in the meadows.

I'm at risk of getting lost in this spectacle, wanting to surrender and let my imagination take control. I want to hear what music suits this place, see the colors light up, and feel as if I'm a part of this natural paradise.

But I can't do that.

Frantically, I pinch my forearm, realizing too late that Vico watches me. He frowns inquisitively. To prevent him from even bringing it up, I sling the backpack off my shoulder and pull out the checklist. I don't like it, but it helps me now.

I clear my throat. "What's the name of this place?" My voice is clear and sober, just as it should be.

However, Vico doesn't seem to like it. He looks at me as if I've just turned into a monster. Hands in his pockets, he kicks a stone aside. "Sasso Pisano."

While searching for the name on the checklist, I ask the next question. "And where does this fog come from?"

"Geothermal activity."

Geo-what?

This place is definitely not listed on Florian's checklist. Should I call it off? What would Florian do?

"Come on, let's take a closer look." Vico points at a path leading down the hill from the parking lot.

"With these shoes?" I gesture to his feet in confusion.

"I like living dangerously." His inviting gaze meets mine, then he turns around and starts walking.

What else can I do but follow him? Eyes fixed on the ground, I descend the rocky path. I fear I might be wasting my time here, as this place probably isn't what tourists first imagine when they think of a Tuscan vacation.

Suddenly, he comes to a halt so abruptly that I run into his back. Again, his scent fills my nose. So fresh. And so light. He smells like a vacation.

My eyes drop. "You smell like your homeland."

No. I didn't just say that out loud, did I?

In the split second after realizing that the barrier between my brain and my mouth malfunctioned for a moment, his muscles tense up as well. "This isn't my homeland."

My gut tells me he wanted to add something more, but he doesn't. At least he doesn't condemn me for my clumsy collision or my thoughtless words. I exhale in relief and make sure to put some distance between us. "But you grew up here, right?"

As if having trouble staying still, he starts walking again. "I haven't lived here for a long time." The winding path levels out, and even with his mismatched footwear, he moves faster now.

I catch up to him. "Where do you live instead?"

He gives me a meaningful look. "Everywhere."

Everywhere? What does he mean by that? No one can live everywhere. Everyone needs a place to call home, offering them safety and stability.

"It confuses you." It's not a question; it's an observation. And he seems to find it amusing.

Should I admit he's right? Probably not.

"You are…" What was that in Italian? "Senza dimora?" I finally ask, not finding the exact translation.

I can hardly believe he's really homeless. True, his clothes don't suggest he's swimming in money, but he's definitely lying to me. He's testing me to see if I'm a serious businesswoman or just a naive dreamer. Perhaps.

Better not let any uncertainty show.

As we walk, he scans the vastness of the valley that lies before us in all its idyllic beauty. The gentle wind blows his hair into his face. Not for the first time, I wonder what he's thinking. And I can't wait to hear his response.

"Something like that," he replies mysteriously.

Chapter 12

Vico

Her gaze reminds me of a startled rabbit. Does she really think I'm homeless?

"I live in my camper," I correct her before she imagines me sleeping under bridges and warming myself by a fire in a discarded metal barrel.

My answer doesn't seem to reassure her. I can see the "why?" written all over her face. "But…"

The idea that someone could be content with little seems beyond the imagination of a businesswoman.

"I am always exactly where I want to be. I carry my home with me always." I look at her with a fulfilled smile, but she still seems skeptical. "I'm free," I add, and I feel the impact of those words on myself at the same moment.

Since we left the estate behind, the pressure on my chest has disappeared. My shoulders have relaxed with every step. Now, talking about the life I am destined for feels like breathing pure oxygen.

"Nobody is free." Hanna fidgets awkwardly with the clipboard, seemingly unable to let it go even here in the midst of nature.

Unfazed, I spread my arms. "I am."

"But how do you make a living?" she asks timidly as we continue to approach the valley.

As we enter the shade of the trees, their branches

forming a canopy over us, she finally releases the clipboard from her grasp. "Ever heard of freelancing?"

She nods, and she seems at least a little reassured. "In what field?"

"Graphic design." My answer seems to please her, and she probably has all the information she asked for. However, I feel the urge to tell her more about myself. "It's not exactly my dream job, but until I make enough money with cliff diving, I take on just enough freelance projects to make ends meet." And that could be over soon. If only the talent scout would finally get back to me.

She swallows hard. "Cliff diving?" Suddenly, her chest rises and falls as if she were about to take a plunge herself. "That's way too dangerous."

"Not if you do it right." I'm immediately engrossed in thoughts of my passion. I've only been back home for a few days, but I already miss the sport with every fiber of my being. "When you've got the technique down, it's like flying. Adrenaline courses through your veins, and you feel so… alive."

I can't help but beam at her, hoping my enthusiasm will rub off on her.

She can't hold my gaze, as if she sees something in my eyes that terrifies her. Nervously, she tugs at her fringe. "Have you ever been injured?"

I stop, roll up my jeans, and show her the scar that stretches across my calf. "There was a rock in the water."

With an incredulous expression, she reaches her hand out to me. Seconds before she touches my injury, she pulls back abruptly. "One must always take care of oneself," she mutters, but I can barely hear her. I'm preoccupied with pushing away the strange feeling spreading in my stomach.

Now, she looks up at me with a penetrating gaze. "Safety first," she says, her tone serious.

"Safety is dull," I respond, unsure why I'm being so reserved with her. Perhaps because I don't like how she talks about my passion. Or maybe it's my hope to quell the odd tingling sensation.

She straightens up, her disheveled hair and natural look making her resemble a cute woodland elf amid the foliage.

The businesswoman is gone.

"But you also have to think about others. Imagine how your sisters would feel if you seriously got hurt," she says, sounding fearful, and I can't tell if she's truly serious.

Involuntarily, I step closer. "So you'd choose a long life of monotony over a shorter life filled with energy and excitement?"

As if doubting herself, she shrugs. "Safety first," she repeats.

She definitely never indulges herself. All she does is work and sleep; there's nothing else in her life. Tilting my head, I observe her. "You've never experienced an adrenaline rush, have you?"

She presses her lips together and looks around hastily. I can almost see her brain working hard to find a suitable response. Then she continues along the path.

"So no," I answer my own question and follow her. As we emerge from the trees, the sunrays dance on the ground. I catch up to her. "Do you realize what you're missing out on?"

As if finding her lifeline, she raises the clipboard

demonstratively. "Speaking of missing out, what did you want to show me down here?"

How can someone be so controlled? Especially someone who occasionally seems so dreamy, as if her mind is somewhere else entirely? She has two sides to her. Which one is her true self?

I study her facial expressions, but her tense jaw and rapid blinking don't give me an answer. "The geyser behind you," I murmur absentmindedly.

She turns to look at the grumbling water fountain, which she hadn't noticed before due to her stupid checklist. I think she says something, but I'm not listening. My mind is busy envisioning what would happen if I could get her to let go of her control.

Would she let me see the real Hanna? How would she react when the thrill of adventure courses through her body?

It's not my job to show her that. And whether she ever lets me see that fascinating, dreamy expression again or not, I couldn't care less. Yet an idea already starts to form in me, a way to make it happen.

Chapter 13

Hanna

The day began with a throbbing headache and a shrill ringing in my ears. When Vico came to pick me up late in the morning, I couldn't fathom stepping into the glaring sunlight. Even the darkest pair of sunglasses wouldn't have saved me from the burning pain in my head.

Vico had no issue with me canceling our plans. On the contrary, he even asked if there was anything he could do to help, and his gaze seemed strangely intense. As much as a part of me wanted to accept his offer, my headaches only respond to my medication.

Now, in the afternoon, the pills are finally taking effect. With the intimidatingly long checklist in hand and sunglasses perched on my nose, I make my way to the shaded seating area of the estate. The air is pleasantly warm, carrying the scent of grass and a wild mix of flowers. I cautiously test the stability of the wrought-iron chair before sitting down and place Florian's notes on my lap.

Yesterday, I didn't check off any of the items on the list. At least I contacted the craftsmen earlier. I forgot to mark the checkboxes, so I do that now. I manage to make just three measly ticks. Of course, I'm well aware that it's not enough. I need to work faster, even if I have no desire to do so and no one to accompany me.

Vico said he'll handle a client's project first and then go on to do canyoning.

Should I really be worried about him recklessly diving into the torrents?

I shouldn't dwell on it. He should do whatever he wants.

With all the concentration I can muster, I go through the checklist. I shouldn't drive with my condition, so the only option is to visit Collina da sogno. It's a fifteen-minute walk to the village center. There, as noted by Florian, I'll check out the local establishments and see if there are any charming shops for tourists to browse. It sounds like a suitable excursion for the last hours of the day, so I pack my backpack and set off.

Along the way, I can't get enough of the surroundings. The landscape in Tuscany is characterized by rugged cliffs and pointed firs. It's rough and wild. But here, gentle beauty dominates the panorama. The oaks and chestnut trees sway gracefully in the wind. The unspoiled nature is intermittently interrupted by wheat fields and olive groves. Spring is already nearing its end here, and soon, lavender and poppies will open their intensely colorful blooms, enriching the green world with their splashes of color.

I take deep breaths, one after the other, allowing the idyllic surroundings to wash over me. Still, I don't stop, afraid to get lost in daydreams and forget my mission. Besides, the village is already in sight. The bright terracotta roofs and ancient stone facades glisten in the afternoon sun.

Shortly after, I leisurely stroll through the historic village center. A cobbled square with a fountain adorns the heart of the village. There are indeed several small shops here, their facades overgrown with wild vines and ivy. In front of the café, wrought-iron chairs and tables with stone mosaic tops stand invitingly. Everywhere, I discover charming details—the rustic wine barrel converted into a high table, the ground cover with tiny white flowers peeping through the cracks between the cobblestones.

This place looks like something out of a fairy tale—enchanted and beautiful.

Inevitably, I imagine what it would be like to explore the village with Vico. I'm sure he could tell me a lot about its history and inhabitants. Or about himself. And his life.

Wait a minute, what am I thinking?

Startled by my strange thoughts, I pause at a specialty shop and focus on its display window. Bottles of olive oil, jars of pickled olives, pasta, pesto, and honey are lovingly arranged on upturned wooden crates. Italian pop music drifts out from the open door. The shop is so inviting that I want to step inside.

A petite elderly lady nods at me friendly from behind the counter. "Ciao, Signora. Come sono?"

"Very well," I respond to her inquiry about my well-being in Italian, and at that moment, I realize that my headache has completely vanished. "And how are you?"

Her smile reveals a gap between her upper front teeth. "On such a wonderful day, I'm always happy," she says with exuberance. "May I show you something, or would you like to look around on your own?"

I would love to browse this store for hours. Not just the Italian specialties, but also the soaps and souvenirs stacked on the shelf next to the sales counter, catch my interest. But unfortunately, I don't have hours, so I point at the table with the spices. "Tell me about these."

She grins mischievously. "You're from Austria, right? Your Italian is excellent." I nod in agreement, and then the lady with the wide smile peels herself off her stool and waddles toward me. "These are a selection of Tuscan herbs. Look here, this is oregano. If you want to prepare a real Italian pizza at home, this one is a must-have."

Even though I'm already familiar with the herbs, I still enjoy listening to her talk about their cultivation and harvest and what makes their unique flavor. Then she moves on to the shelf with olive oil and takes out a slim bottle.

"This here is a special treasure," she says, handing me the tiny bottle, the price of which makes me break into a sweat. Twenty euros for two hundred milliliters?

I take it with utmost care. "What makes it so special?"

"It's pressed from olives of the Leccino and Moraiolo varieties, making it exceptionally aromatic." Her rapturous expression captivates me. "Would you like to taste it?"

I quickly shake my head. "It's far too valuable for that."

"But why! Life is meant to be enjoyed," she responds gently, smiling, and takes the bottle back from my hand to open it. "Smell it."

Hesitantly, I sniff at the opening, and an intense blend of bitter and oily notes enters my nose. It smells like everything I've experienced so far here in Tuscany. Like the warmth of the sun and the green of the rolling hills. I feel my lips curling into a smile.

Beaming, I look up at the saleswoman with her salt-and-pepper hair. "This is wonderful."

"A true treasure," she says, lovingly caressing the dark bottle's exterior.

"I'll take one," I hear myself say, even though I don't have any money to spare. But I feel compelled to do something nice for her. When she looks up at me, I know what it is.

Her eyes are suddenly filled with wistfulness. "With pleasure," she says, blinking rapidly.

Curiously, I tilt my head. "Is everything okay?"

She gives me a pained smile. "Of course. It's just…"

"Yes?" I nervously shift from one foot to the other, although there's no reason for it.

"Treasure the oil. Savor every drop. Promise me that?" she asks, her voice hoarse.

With that price, I'll definitely cherish it. "Of course."

With the bottle in her hand, she walks over to the sales counter. "They no longer produce this, you know. The olive farmer has given up his agriculture." She reaches for a sheet of brown paper and places the olive oil on it. "For over two hundred years, the family has cultivated the olive grove and produced the finest oil in the region. It's such a shame."

I'm not sure how to react. The end of the business clearly saddens her. "Why does the farmer want to end the tradition?"

She sadly shrugs her shoulders. "No one has seen him in the past few months. He's apparently ill. Too ill to continue his life's work any longer."

Her pain is so palpable that I can't quite believe the time-honored agriculture is coming to an end. "But there must be children who can step in, right?"

"Some cannot, and others do not want to," she says, her fingers caressing the bottle with a wistful smile. "That's the way of time. Everything changes. Even things that were so good that they should never have ended."

What a sad story. "But family is the most important thing," I inquire again. How can the children be indifferent to the family tradition? Don't they realize how fortunate they are?

She pats my hand. "It is, dear. It is." A heavy sigh escapes her lips. "Can I help you with anything else?"

Actually, no. But this little shop has such a cozy atmosphere that I want to savor it a little longer. "I'll continue looking around, if that's alright."

She gestures toward the shelves. "Of course. Call me if you need assistance," she says. Immediately, she settles back into her stool and picks up a half-finished knitting project.

I first look at the souvenirs and then move on to the hand-painted vases. The colors are vibrant, and the gracefully curved shapes make them look exquisite. They would certainly look great in the guest rooms of the inn, with a pretty flower and some grasses—a welcoming gift for the guests.

At the next table, I discover bottles of various sizes with swing caps. *Acqua di fiori d'arancio* is written on the lovingly designed labels.

Orange blossom water?

"Feel free to smell it," I hear the saleswoman call from her seat. "It's heavenly."

If she's praising it that much, I must at least open the bottle. An intense orange fragrance creeps into my nose, transporting me to another world where orange blossoms fall from the sky. They land all over my body—in my hair, on my shoulders, and in my outstretched palms. Softly, they caress me, and a gentle melody reaches my ears. On my tongue, I taste the pure essence of sun-ripened oranges—fruity, sweet, and refreshing.

"Heavenly," I repeat her description from earlier because there's simply no other way to express it.

Suddenly, the elderly lady stands next to me. "You can use the water for baking. I have a recipe if you'd like," she kindly smiles, her cheeks taking on a rosy hue. "Or you can enhance your beverages with it."

I would love to buy a bottle, but I should have refrained from the olive oil already. Struggling with myself, I close the bottle again. Just as I'm about to reluctantly put it back in its place, the saleswoman places her hand on my forearm.

"Keep it," she says with a loving tone and nods eagerly. "It's a gift from the house."

She shouldn't be giving me anything. "That's kind, but…"

"A refusal is not accepted," she quickly replies, taking the orange blossom water from me and wobbling back to the counter with it. "Or have you forgotten already? Life is meant to be enjoyed."

Life is meant to be enjoyed, echoes within me.

Inevitably, I smile as I follow her to pay for my purchase. She prepares both bottles for wrapping and turns to the shelf behind her to grab a paper bag. At that moment, the golden sticker on the back of the olive oil catches my attention.

Famiglia Olivetta, it reads in small letters on the label, along with the address of the estate. It's clear now. The traditional family business that until recently produced the region's finest olive oil is owned by the Olivetta family.

Is this the secret that the two sisters kept from me during dinner? Why did they do that? And why didn't Vico say anything when he showed me around the estate?

Confused, I watch as the saleswoman puts the bottle into the paper bag.

Even though I can hardly gather my thoughts, one thing is evident: Tomorrow, I must confront Vico and finally get the whole truth. The idea of it makes my stomach churn. Moreover, I realize that I'll only succeed if I don't let myself be distracted by his captivating charm.

Chapter 14

Vico

Hanna's migraine seems to have disappeared overnight. As always, she clings to the clipboard in her hand as if it were a lifebuoy.

"Spiaggia bianche?" she asks.

In truth, I don't really care where we go. The main thing is to get away from here. "Is that a question or your answer?" I reply nonetheless, just to see her smile.

"My answer," she says seriously and immediately marches to her car. There's something different about her today compared to the past few days. This closed offness. And the probing look she gave me since our greeting earlier, as if she were trying to determine whether I have ill intentions.

Whatever it is, it won't stop me from carrying out my plan and giving her a taste of freedom. Perhaps that's exactly what she needs right now. "The beach isn't far from here; we don't need the car," I call after her.

She whirls around and raises her eyebrows. "You want to walk?"

Oh no. I certainly don't want that. "Come with me," I say.

"Where to?" She looks at me with that anxious expression that makes me want to wrap my arms around her.

What is she afraid of? Surely not me? I flash a teasing grin to help her relax a bit. "You'll see."

She doesn't like my answer, but she doesn't have much of a choice if she wants to visit Spiaggia bianche. Once we arrive at Camilla's bungalow, I open the garden gate where my sister and her husband's Vespas are hidden.

"Tada," I announce, gesturing with both hands to the original Italian mopeds. White and Ferrari red, they stand before us. "Today, we'll travel in style."

"No." Her body tenses up.

Really? Does she have absolutely no fun in life? "But you have to try everything the guests can do. And a Vespa tour is precisely what tourists want to do in Tuscany."

She places her hands on her hips. "Oh, really? You don't even live here. How do you know what tourists like to do?"

Because I grew up here. That would be the right answer, but I don't say it. I don't want her to start asking questions about the past. "You have no idea what you're missing," I respond disappointedly, closing the garden gate.

Suddenly, she seems remorseful. "I'm sorry," she says even though she doesn't need to apologize to me for holding back any feelings of happiness.

I wave it off. "No problem. It's your life." As I say the words, I suddenly feel that a part of me doesn't want to accept it. What's the point? Why is it so important to me to tease the real Hanna out of her?

"Shall we take my car?" She points at the mundane Golf that I had planned to leave in the parking lot outside the estate.

"Sure," I say with a shrug, trying to shake off my disappointment about not making her smile. I shouldn't feel like this.

Side by side, we trudge back to the car. But even during the drive, I can't help but secretly observe her. My gaze lingers on her lips. Way too long. They look soft.

Now they move. "There it is, right? Vico?" She turns to me. "We've arrived."

A jolt runs through my body, and I startle, opening my eyes wide.

Right, there it is, Spiaggia bianche.

I try to collect myself as Hanna already leaves the car.

What was that just now?

Doesn't matter at all. Now is the time to be myself again.

Maybe we can take the speedboat or rent some Jet Skis. A bit of adrenaline would be just right to prevent these strange feelings from resurfacing.

"I hope you brought your bikini," I say with a deliberately casual tone, slamming the car door shut.

Either she didn't hear me or she's pretending not to. "Where can I take good photos?" she asks with her businesslike voice, and once again, disappointment fills me.

Why can't she forget her stupid camera and checklist for once? We're at the most beautiful beach in Tuscany, and all she can think about is her obligations.

Regretfully, I point to the southern end of the parking lot. "If we walk this way, we'll reach the natural beach. Pictures of that will attract tourists like moths to a flame."

She shoulders her backpack and marches ahead. I look at her in bewilderment. Just two days ago, I got her to be a bit more relaxed in the car and even hum along to the radio. Today, she's acting even stuffier than ever.

It's better this way anyway, I remind myself, catching up to her and walking silently beside her until the beach comes into view.

In radiant white, interspersed with some dune grass, it lies before us. Only a few brightly painted beach huts line this stretch, which is still deserted in March.

"Beautiful, isn't it?" I ask Hanna, who stands next to me.

"Mm-hmm," she simply says, letting her gaze wander several times over the scenery. Her expression is now a little softer, and I catch glimpses of her enchanting beauty.

Everyone feels the same way when they see this place for the first time. No one expects to find a beach like this in Tuscany, where you feel as if you're in the Caribbean. The extremely light seashells and the turquoise sea gently lapping at the shore create such an exotic atmosphere that only palm trees are missing to complete the illusion.

Suddenly, she slings the backpack from her shoulder. "The water is fantastic. Truly amazing." She pulls out her camera and takes several photos.

"Ciao, Vico!" someone calls from a distance.

I know that voice. I look around and spot my best buddy from my youth standing in front of one of the huts, waving. Adriano hasn't changed much. His jet-black hair is cut shorter, but his wide grin is still the same. He's already coming toward me, ready to give me a big hug.

I can't help but smile. "Hey, stranger."

"Man, Vico, I had no idea you were here," he says, patting me on the back several times before releasing me from his embrace.

"Just arrived a few days ago. I was going to get in touch, but you know how time flies." In the corner of my eye, I notice Hanna giving me a penetrating look.

Adriano, already tanned by this time of year, waves it off. "Doesn't matter, we're here now." His gaze shifts to Hanna. "I had no idea you… but I'm glad. That's… wonderful."

Both Hanna and I raise our hands at the same time.

"I'm just showing her around and introducing her to the area. Nothing more," I say, trying to appear as cool as possible.

"So you're the one," he responds with a sympathetic look. "I heard about it. Must be tough, man."

He knows. Of course, he knows. Collina da sogno is a cursed village; there are no secrets here. While I strain to think of a way to quickly end the conversation, Hanna takes a step forward.

"What's tough?" she asks with anxious curiosity.

"Nothing," I hastily reply before Adriano can say anything, giving him a meaningful look. Hanna must not learn about my family history. Besides, complaining won't change the facts.

For a moment, Adriano glances between Hanna and me, then he forces a smile. "I'm sorry, but duty calls. I should…" he says with a questioning tone, which Hanna surely can pick up.

Great.

I nod. "It was nice meeting you."

"Keep in touch." He gives me a quick hug again before striding back through the sand to the blue-and-white-painted hut with a corrugated tin roof.

"That was strange," Hanna comments and puts her camera back in her backpack. "What's so tough?"

"He's just upset because I didn't get in touch," I say, relieved that this excuse came to me so quickly, and I grin at her. "So what about your bikini? Did you bring it?"

As if I suggested swimming with sharks without a cage, she freezes. "I…"

Her reaction to riding a Vespa was somewhat understandable, but what's the issue with a little water? "Can't you swim?"

Anxiously, she shakes her head.

Something in her expression compels me to ask further. "Why not?"

Her lower lip disappears into her mouth, and her fingers fidget nervously. She takes a deep breath and looks out at the sea, as if seeking the answer. "I never learned properly," she finally says.

"Are there no lakes in Austria? Or swimming pools?" I signal her to walk a few steps along the beach with me.

Hesitantly, she takes off her shoes and joins me at the water's edge, where the sand is moistened by the gently rolling waves. "Of course, we have them."

"But Austrians only learn to ski as children, right?" I inquire, kicking my flip-flops aside so the sand doesn't rub between my skin and the fabric.

Silently, she shakes her head.

It's none of my business. And I don't want to know

either. "You're afraid. Afraid of so many things," I say anyway. "Tell me why."

Her gaze flickers to me as if she's trying to assess if she can trust me. On an impulse, I nod. It takes what feels like an eternity before she opens her mouth.

"When I was six, I nearly drowned." She looks at me apologetically, and suddenly, nothing remains of the controlled businesswoman she showed me so often in the past few days. The subtly accusing expression has vanished into thin air as well.

"That must have been terrifying." No wonder she's so afraid. Now I feel bad for not taking her panic seriously earlier.

"I had just learned to swim, and I thought I was good. In the public pool, I could swim several laps without any problem." She tucks her hair behind her ear and gazes into the distance. "I was confident that I was ready to try it in the lake." Her voice falters.

I can barely contain the urge to wrap my arm protectively around her delicate body. Instead, I clear my throat loudly to dispel this inappropriate thought. "What happened?"

She shrugs. "I swam out. And the next thing I remember is lying on the shore, coming back to my senses. With the taste of lake water in my mouth."

Now it's my turn to say something. But I have no idea what could comfort her. "I'm sorry for pushing you earlier," I mumble, feeling like a complete idiot.

"You couldn't have known," she replies with a smile.

"Tell me more about yourself," I find myself saying. "Why are you afraid of motorcycles?"

As soon as the words leave my mouth, I realize it was a mistake. The less I know about her, the better.

That way, we won't get too close, and that's all that matters. She evokes a feeling in me that I already experienced during our first encounter. A warm glow that I must not pay attention to if I don't want to end up like my father someday.

Chewing on her lower lip, she crosses her arms over her chest. "Because I get hurt with everything, even if it's not as dangerous as riding a motorcycle. The incident in the lake wasn't the only one that terrified my parents."

In my thoughts, the scar I noticed under her chin during our first meeting resurfaces. Who knows where else she may have suffered injuries. Can someone really be so clumsy?

"So you've started taking good care of yourself," I continue her earlier words. "Maybe a bit too much?"

She shakes her head with effort. "My life is fine. I lack nothing. I am healthy, and no one needs to worry about me," she reassures.

Fine is not enough. "But if you never allow yourself to do something outside of your comfort zone, you risk missing out on so much," I counter. Although I now understand better why she behaves this way, it's still hard for me to see how much she locks herself away.

"Each of us can only live one life," she turns her head to look at me. "We choose one path and will never know what the other might have brought us."

Maybe that's true. "But how do you know if you've chosen right?" I inquire.

The corners of her mouth lift, and her expression takes on that dangerously dreamy charm. "Perhaps with the heart," she says so softly that my knees suddenly feel weak.

Chapter 15

Hanna

With a clearing of his throat, he turns toward the sea, the waves crashing dangerously against the shore. Our eye contact breaks, and I instantly realize that I've once again lost control for a moment.

My goodness, why did I tell him all of that? I don't let anyone else know such personal things about me. How did the conversation even take this direction when I'm here to explore the beach?

Silently, we walk a few steps side by side. I take in the salty sea air, smell the seaweed, and feel the sun rays on my skin. But most of all, I'm aware of Vico's presence, which gives me a warm feeling in my chest that shouldn't be there. I can't forget my mission here and must do what needs to be done.

I blow my bangs out of my face. "Can I ask you something?"

"Sure." His hands casually slide into his pockets.

We pass by two seagulls resting on driftwood, undisturbed by our presence. "What happened to the estate?"

For a moment, he holds his breath. "What do you mean?" he asks, evading the question.

My intuition tells me he understood my question well. "What led to its decay?"

Silently, he shrugs. I sense his unease and would

love to end the conversation immediately, but Florian won't let me get away with it.

"I know about the olive oil," I say cautiously.

Instead of responding, he presses his lips together and turns his head, letting the sea breeze ruffle his hair.

As little as I could read him before, I can now clearly see what's going on inside him. Though I can't see his expression, his tense posture reveals that he's struggling.

This topic hurts him.

"My mother passed away five years ago," he suddenly says so softly that I can barely hear it over the crashing waves. "Father never recovered."

"He loved her very much," I say wistfully, my heart painfully tightening. Can there really be such great love? And what would it do to a person who loses their soulmate too soon? "I'm so sorry."

Vico nods absentmindedly. "He wanted to carry on. Despite his grief. Work was supposed to distract him."

In my mind, the story continues to unfold. "But he couldn't make it," I add, and I have to swallow hard. What if he kept getting worse and worse? What if he's at risk of dying from his broken heart?

"They say time heals all wounds." He scoffs, his voice tinged with bitterness. "But for my father, time has only done one thing. It's made his wound open up more and more."

My goodness, how terrible. I look down at the ground, where the waves' tendrils coolly touch my toes. "Is he suffering from depression?"

"He has lost all motivation," he confirms, kneading his hands as if trying to release his tension.

So this is the illness the woman at the village store

spoke about. And that's also why I've never met him, and Florian has only had contact with Camilla.

I want to embrace Vico. Tell him that I empathize with him and would gladly share his pain to make it a little smaller for him.

"What about you?" I ask in a hoarse voice. " Do you miss her so much too?"

His jaw clenches. "I'm coping."

I suppress the impulse to reach out my hand to him. A thousand questions swarm in my head, but I don't dare to ask any of them.

"Even when Mother got sick, the estate started to decline. We needed the money for her treatment." He takes a deep breath. "After her death, it fell into further disrepair. Camilla did her best to take care of the property and Father. She was too proud to ask for help. But her pregnancy showed her she couldn't handle the estate," he continues in a controlled tone. "And once the twins are born, she won't have time for anything else."

Life is meant to be enjoyed, I suddenly hear the village store owner whisper inside me. What does she mean by that?

He clears his throat for a noticeable length of time. "It's good that the estate is being sold. My father needs closure."

"But our roots are the most important. Family, security, and—" I stop myself because speaking those words only reminds me of what I don't have.

His first reaction is shaking his head. "That family doesn't exist anymore." His tone brings tears to my eyes.

Was their mother the glue that held them together?

After her death, did not only the estate but also the family break apart?

"That's terrible," I find myself saying in a hoarse voice, and before I understand what's happening, I put my arm around him.

He swallows hard. "It is what it is. We look forward because we can't change what's behind us."

I scrutinize his face, but I don't see any indication that his own words hurt him. He truly believes it's best to put an end to everything.

"Why don't you take over the business?" That could save the family. They wouldn't have to sell if someone would invest time and love into the estate, restoring it to its former glory.

As I wait for his response, I realize what I'm doing.

I'm hugging a stranger. More than that, I'm caressing his arm and feeling closer to him than to anyone else before.

It's wrong, yet somehow it feels right.

Strange.

"Do you see that hut up there?" he asks out of nowhere, pointing at a small wooden structure with a white awning and a sales counter. "They rent picnic baskets filled with Italian specialties. That could be something for your guests."

He doesn't want to tell me. Perhaps we're not as close as I thought we were just a moment ago.

Disappointed, I release my arm from his back and try to collect my thoughts.

Is it even important why he doesn't want to stay here? The estate is being sold because his father can't manage it anymore, and apparently, none of the children can provide enough support. I have the information I need. I don't need details, so I should be content. Yet Vico's story tugs at my heart.

Are Florian and I doing the family a favor by buying the estate? Vico seems certain about it, and it suits me just fine. I should refocus on my mission. At the same time, I feel something that I can hardly deny.

Something has happened between us in the past few minutes. Vico is no longer just the seller of the estate. And I am no longer just the interested buyer.

We are… something else that I can't grasp.

"Alright, let's see the offer," I say, for his sake, and smile to let him know that he won't face any more questions from me.

He smiles back. And I think I even see gratitude in his eyes.

Chapter 16

Vico

Two days ago, we sat on the beach for hours, emptying the picnic basket filled with the finest Prosciutto crudo, Pecorino, and Chianti. We laughed together, gazed at the sea, shared moments of silence, and simply enjoyed life without dwelling on the heaviness that often surrounds it.

Since then, Hanna seems different. Even though the clipboard with the checklist remains her constant companion, she showed less of her businesslike demeanor during our trip to Siena yesterday. Surprisingly, that helps me to withstand the pressure the estate imposes on my chest a little better.

On all fours, she inspects the mosaic tiles in the kitchen. "We'll need to renovate the floor here. What kind of craftsmen do we need for that?"

"Perhaps a stonemason?" Although that was more of a question than an answer, she immediately jots it down in her notes. A contented smile plays on her lips. "It will look amazing."

Suddenly, I'm in my childhood memories. Back then, when Aurora and I painted the floor with chalk colors. Over there, in the corner next to the spacious kitchen island, we lay on our bellies and sketched our family as scribbled figures. Father, mother, children. Sun, trees, butterflies. A perfect picture.

Suddenly, I feel someone gently touching my arm. "Can you help me, please?"

"Sure," I reply, doing my best to shake off the memory. The less I let it resurface, the easier it is for me to spend time here. "Should I take the checklist for you?" I can't resist winking at her.

"Very funny." She grins amusedly. "I need you to hold the flashlight so I can see better." She opens the cupboard under the sink and motions for me to come closer before kneeling again. "Shine it in here, please."

I grab the flashlight and turn it on as she bends into the opening. My gaze inevitably lands on her curves.

"Where's the light?" her muffled voice asks.

What light?

Ah yes, the flashlight. Quickly, I direct it toward the under-sink cabinet. "How do you know about plumbing?" I ask, just to keep my thoughts from wandering again.

The click of a camera is heard, then she pulls her head out of the cabinet. The hair is even more tousled than usual, and dust clings to the crown of her head. "I don't," she admits with a guilty look. "Hence the photos."

When she only showed me the tough business lady, I was not able to recognize it. But now it's becoming clearer to me that the true Hanna—the one with the captivating smile and the dreamy gaze—might not know quite so much about certain things after all. "Wouldn't it be easier to call a plumber to check the pipes on-site? It will be necessary for a cost estimate anyway."

She checks the pictures she just took. "Later. First, Florian needs to see it."

"Who is Florian?" I peek at the camera's display. The images only hint at what's under the sink.

"My partner. We want to buy the estate together," she explains and opens the next kitchen cupboard. "Oh man, is that mold?"

"Business partner or…" Wait, why am I even asking? It doesn't matter who this Florian is.

Her cheeks suddenly turn bright red. "Both."

For a moment, I'm lost for words. I have no idea why. I fear that I might be staring at her.

"I'll take a picture of the mold, then we can tackle the rooms upstairs again," she suddenly says hastily, disappearing up to her shoulders in the under-sink cabinet.

She's in a relationship?

"Can we?" Suddenly, she's next to me. How did she manage that so quickly? She tilts her head to the side, looking inquisitive. "Are you okay?"

"Sure." There is also no reason at all why it should be different. "Where do we go next?"

Her forehead wrinkles. "I already said. Upstairs."

"Alright. Don't forget your checklist." I force my lips into a smile, but they feel heavier than usual. Then I gesture for her to lead the way.

She immediately sets off. I stay for one more breath to get my thoughts in order.

That she has a boyfriend is not a big deal. Not a big deal at all. After all, she's just the buyer, and I'm just the owner's son showing her around, soon to leave and do the one thing that means the world to me. Everything else is unthinkable anyway.

Overwhelmed by a sudden fatigue, I follow her leisurely. When I reach the landing, she leans against the doorframe of the first room. However, instead of taking notes, she simply stands in the light of the setting sun, which makes her hair shine. I step up behind her, trying to discern what's distracting her from her work.

There is nothing. Just dust particles floating through the room as if moved by an unseen force. A crooked wooden floor, an old-fashioned lamp covered in cobwebs, and an armchair with velvet upholstery, which mice have undoubtedly made their home in. Yes, definitely. The dark pellets next to the lion's paws where the chair's legs meet are a clear indication.

"We used to accommodate seasonal workers here," I say because I feel embarrassed about the room's dilapidated state. I wait for a response in vain. Cautiously, I lean forward. "Hanna?"

She doesn't answer, but now that I'm so close to her, I can hear her humming a melody. And she has that look on her face again, as if she's seeing something so wondrous that it almost brings tears to her eyes. In a trance, she tilts her head to one side, then the other. The gentle light makes her skin appear soft, and her eyes are… so full of magic that I can't get enough of looking at them.

On the contrary, I want to examine them more closely. I yearn to discover what hides within the delicate sea-green pattern.

I cautiously touch her arm. "Hey."

Startled, she flinches, then looks around as if having difficulty realizing where she is.

"What were you dreaming about?" I ask gently.

Despite all my caution, she widens her eyes, turns away in shame, and forcefully pinches her forearm.

Chapter 17

Hanna

It happened again. Once again, I lost control of myself. And that's not all.

Vico saw it.

He knows that I was lost in my thoughts.

"Will you tell me where you were in your thoughts?" His hand rises, and for a split second, I'm sure he's going to stroke my cheek. But nothing of the sort happens.

Clutching my forearm tightly with my fingernails, I shake my head. No one can know. Especially not him.

"Why not?" He steps closer, looking at me with open curiosity.

There's something in that gaze that makes me hesitate for a moment. I don't know what it is, but I feel a part of me giving in.

"Is it so terrible?" he asks softly, taking another step. Then his expression softens. "I don't think so."

He shouldn't do that. He shouldn't make me feel like my daydreams are okay. Because they certainly are not.

They're ridiculous, nothing more.

My gaze shifts to Vico, who is now so close that I can feel his warmth. He still looks at me, and now he even nods. How would he react if I explained that the run-down room turned into a dreamy bedroom before my eyes? That I could see airy curtains in a delicate lemon yellow adorning the windows? That I knew which paintings should hang above the wrought-iron canopy bed and that a shabby-chic dresser with a candlestick and a bowl of fresh fruit would give the room a cozy atmosphere? All of it was so real to me that I could even smell the apples.

So many times I had the feeling that Vico was different from every person I had ever met. What if he could understand my dreams a little?

I could take the risk. And find out if he truly is different or if I had only imagined it so far.

"It's okay if you don't want to tell," he says, adding to my confusion. But his expression remains attentive, as if afraid to miss something. " But it would please me very much."

I can't do it. No matter how much I want to share my secret with him, I can't. He'll laugh at me, just like everyone else before him.

"It was just my absentmindedness, nothing worth mentioning," I say hastily, lowering my eyelids. As much as I dislike the checklist, at least it helps me focus now. What was I supposed to note about the rooms again?

While I frantically search for instructions, I can practically feel Vico's gaze on me.

Please, don't say anything. Let it be.

"I don't know… It looked like there was more to it than—"

The ringing of my phone interrupts him. With an apologetic smile, I take my phone out of my pocket. As I see the caller ID, reality comes crashing back.

I feel like I was just drunk a moment ago, but now

I'm sober again. "It's Florian. I have to take this," I murmur and turn to leave so that Vico doesn't overhear our conversation. I don't know how well he speaks German, but my feeling is that Florian wouldn't approve either way.

Once I reach the landing, I answer the call. "Hey, my love." Florian's voice sounds tired, and his long exhale tells me he's worried about something.

This can't be good. "Is there a problem?"

"No," he responds quickly from the other end of the line, but I can tell he's not being entirely truthful.

Why? What is he trying to protect me from? Is he having trouble securing the loan, or is the intern still overwhelmed? Instantly, guilt washes over me. I realize that I haven't thought much about him and the challenges he's facing back home since our last call.

Of course, he misses me. After all, running the inn keeps him busy, leaving little time for anything else. And without my support, he has to bear the full weight of the responsibilities.

"How is Natalie doing?" I ask cautiously, not wanting to overwhelm him. I don't want him to think I doubt his ability to manage without me.

He clears his throat. "She's settling in well," he responds conspicuously controlled. "But that's not why I'm calling. I'm calling about the photos of that beach you sent me yesterday."

Automatically, I straighten my back. "Yes?"

"They are…" Uh-oh. He doesn't like them, and now he doesn't know how to tell me. Maybe I should finish his sentence for him. "Not good enough?"

"Sure, you tried your best. But I can't use them for the promotional brochure or the website." He types frantically in the background, as if he's stressed and multitasking.

"I'm sorry." I press my lips together, leaning against the cool stone wall of the hallway, supporting my head with my hand. After all he's done for me, I can't let him down.

"I just sent you a few sample images. We need something along those lines," Florian insists.

As I look through the photos in my inbox, I see endless wide beaches with white umbrellas and grasses stretching toward the warm light of the setting sun. There are detailed shots of a chic pool area, children enthusiastically jumping on trampolines, and a couple gazing lovingly into each other's eyes against the romantic backdrop of a vineyard.

"What do you think? Can you handle this?" Florian asks while a sense of unease churns in my stomach as I go through the images.

A professional must have taken these photos, and the people in them look like models. How am I supposed to pull this off?

"It's really important, Hanna. If the marketing isn't right, the expansion won't be successful," Florian says, sounding logical. The images will be the first thing potential guests see.

"Of course," I reply. "Maybe we should—"

"You'll figure it out." He interrupts me before I can suggest hiring a photographer.

"Yes." I nod as if trying to convince myself too. "I'll manage. I'll do some research on the internet. There must be tips for great photos. And if that doesn't work, I'll recreate the most beautiful pictures I find." I try to sound more confident than I feel, not letting on that I'm not entirely sure I can pull it off. Florian doesn't need to worry.

"Thank you, those are great ideas. I'm sure you'll do it," he says, trying to sound encouraging, but there's an underlying pressure in his words. Once again, I sense there are issues he's keeping from me for my sake.

"I'll send you new photos by the weekend," I assure him, though less certain than I let on. Our financial security, which we'll finally have with the estate, will be the foundation for a family—the thing I've been longing for.

"How else is it going? Have the craftsmen been on-site? And most importantly, have you found out if we can trust the sellers?" Now he's back to being the focused, driven person he usually is, his voice filled with fervent motivation.

"I'm on it," I say, feeling the need to tell him about the Olivetta family's reasons for selling, and how Vico reacted oddly when I asked him two days ago at Spiaggia bianche why none of the children wanted to take over the estate. But something holds me back from doing so.

"Good. Time is running out, you know?" he insists. "March will be over soon. The sale must be finalized by mid-April."

Right. I momentarily forgot that. I should try again with Camilla. Maybe that will finally give me clarity about the Olivettas' motives.

"The clock is ticking. Understood," I reply, feeling uncomfortable. To make matters worse, Vico's face now appears in my mind. He smiles at me with such longing that my heart suddenly feels heavy in my chest.

Chapter 18

Vico

Hands buried in my pockets, I shift from one foot to the other. It's been ten minutes since Hanna left me alone up here to talk to her Florian.

I wonder what they're discussing. It must be something I'm not meant to hear. I saw it in her expression and her hurried movements when she practically ran away from me to take the call.

Since she's been gone, the tightness in my chest keeps increasing. It's as if the old walls, with their dampness, are suffocating me. I'd rather run away right now. Go bungee jumping or walk a highline. Anything to drown out this feeling that's making it hard to breathe.

But I can't leave Hanna alone here. Yesterday, my father reminded me how crucial it is that the purchase goes through. He looked at me with so much desperation that I couldn't help but promise him I'd do my best.

I wander along the hallway, the wooden floorboards creaking dangerously loud under my feet. The movement helps; it's better than standing still and letting memories take over my mind.

Too quickly, I reach the window at the end of the corridor, giving a view of the overgrown olive grove. The individual trees are barely visible, hidden beneath the tall weeds. There's no sign of Mother's oleander bushes.

Did Father get rid of them because they reminded him too much of her? Or did he just leave them, like everything else here, to their fate, including himself?

Whatever it was, I can't dwell on it. I shake the questions from my mind and turn away. At that moment, I notice that the door to my parents' former bedroom is ajar. I step closer and tap the warped wooden door with its carved ornaments. It squeaks open, and I immediately regret giving it a push.

The other rooms in the house have either been cleared out or roughly taken care of. But here, everything remains as it was.

The simple double bed with its tall leather headboard. The fur rug. The closets with the mirrored fronts.

A spider scurries across the blue-gray painted wall. The dresser is covered in thick dust. And right where the breeze from the drafty windows gently stirs it up, I spot our family album. Even though it's covered in cobwebs and dust, I instantly recognize it.

My stomach tightens, but I still approach the dresser. Ever since our conversation at Spiaggia bianche, something has changed within me as well. The way she spoke to me about the value of family lingers in my mind. And especially the way she looked at me while doing so.

I take the album into my hands and touch the leather cover with my fingertips. Dust rises and fills my lungs. *La famiglia Olivetta* is embossed in golden letters on the front.

La famiglia Olivetta doesn't exist anymore.

I told Hanna that, and it's the truth. Wishing for something else wouldn't make any sense.

Opening the album now and looking at the pictures from long-gone happy times wouldn't change anything either. In fact, it would only make things worse. I should put the album back. That's the best thing to do.

"What did you find?" That's Hanna. She sounds so close, as if she's standing right behind me and could easily reach out to see for herself what I'm holding so tightly.

"Nothing." There's a cold detachment in my voice. Quickly, I place the album back and turn around. "Did you manage to sort everything out?"

She tilts her head and looks at me curiously. Then she nods timidly.

"Good, let's continue." I want this to be over as quickly as possible so we can leave.

To a place where we feel free. Where it's just the two of us.

Her gaze briefly flickers to the album, and then she smiles faintly. "Sure."

Together, we leave the room, and I close the door behind us. I check multiple times to make sure it's really closed even though I feel a bit ridiculous doing so. I'm acting as if the album could come alive and haunt me in my sleep if I don't lock it away.

"May I ask you something?" Hanna wants to know as I turn to leave. She's kneading her fingers as if she's nervous.

I would prefer to decline because I can imagine what she wants. She saw the album. And who knows how long she's been standing behind me, observing my reaction to that stupid thing.

"As a graphic designer, you must have a good eye for perspective," she says, even though I didn't ask to. She can barely look at me. Instead, she quickens her pace. When I nod, she lets out a long breath. "Could you help me take beautiful photos of the landscape? The ones I've taken so far are unusable." An apologetic smile forms on her lips, her eyes filled with sadness.

Ah, so that's what she talked to her boyfriend about earlier. "Did this Florian say that?" I blurt out even though it shouldn't matter to me at all.

"We both think so," she says, raising her hands in a placating gesture.

Despite her casual demeanor, something about her expression is downcast. She seems hurt, and there's only one explanation for that. He's to blame.

"Let me see, I'm sure they're beautiful." I reach out my hand to her.

Immediately, she shakes her head. "They're bad. Seriously."

She sounds convinced. However, I'm sure this opinion didn't come from her. If it did, she would have asked for my help much earlier. Surely, Florian convinced her of this. And she let herself be convinced.

What kind of relationship are they in, anyway?

Until today, she hasn't mentioned him at all. And when she talked about him earlier, she seemed quite detached. It's strange. What binds them together? Could it even be love?

"So will you help me?" Hanna nudges me from the side.

I thoughtfully push my hair back. Helping her also means helping this Florian. It should be irrelevant to me, but everything in me resists.

Hanna's expectant gaze disappears, and she lowers her eyelids. "It was a dumb idea. I'm sorry."

"No," I suddenly hear myself croak, "I'll help you, of course." My voice fails, and I have to clear my throat several times. "That's no problem at all." Why am I doing this, dammit?

"Thank you," she breathes out in relief. "Can we start in Val D'Orcia tomorrow morning? It's supposed to be picturesque there." A faint smile appears on her face, and at that moment, I feel as if I'm looking at the rising sun.

My goodness, what is happening to me?

The estate. The memories. And now Hanna with her talk about family. All of it is slowly driving me crazy.

It has to stop now. "Sure. Do we continue here or call it a day?" I ask hastily, clapping my hands to dispel these absurd feelings even though I already sense that won't help either.

Chapter 19

Hanna

Nervously, I turn the Olivettas' family album in my hands. I can't believe I did it. But when Vico left, I couldn't resist going back upstairs to retrieve it. Carefully, I cleaned it from dust, cobwebs, and dirt, restoring the golden inscription, though the chewed corners remained untouched. It's not my place to look through it, and I have no intention of doing so. I just wanted to save it. If it had been left there, it might have been lost during the renovations. It's probably filled with beautiful memories, deserving of a special place.

Not with Vico, who probably cares little about family. But maybe with Camilla, whose house I'm heading for right now.

I find her on the Hollywood swing in the shade of the bungalow. She's fanning herself with a magazine, and her belly appears to have grown even more.

"Hanna, how nice of you to come." She waves me over. "It's terribly boring just sitting around." Her rosy cheeks rise.

Instinctively, I hide the album behind my back and take a seat beside her on the green-and-white-striped cushion of the swing. "How are the babies doing?"

"I think they're doing well." She lovingly strokes her belly.

That's great news. "You must be excited," I say.

"Mainly, I can't wait to see my legs again." A bright laugh escapes her lips, then her gaze softens. "I can't wait to hold the two little ones in my arms."

I can't help but swallow hard. There's nothing more beautiful than a stable family, where everyone supports and stands by each other. Since my disastrous incident at school, I've yearned for it. But the way my mother was ashamed of me changed our relationship. And because I refused to give up my daydreaming for far too long, we drifted further apart until we barely knew each other.

I shouldn't dwell on that now, so I force a smile. "When's the big day?"

"In three weeks. But I really hope they come out a bit earlier." She reaches for the glass on the side table and takes a sip. "Would you like something to drink too?"

Quickly, I shake my head. She should rest instead of entertaining me. "I wanted to talk to you about something." After all, I'm here for a specific reason.

Her brow furrows. "Did Vico let you down again?"

"Don't worry, he's…" Yes, how is he, actually? An exciting mix of aloofness and free spirit is the first thing that comes to mind. Of course, that's nonsense. "He's doing a great job," I say. Before she can respond, I take out the album. "He found this."

For a moment, she freezes, then with a tender smile, she reaches for the album. Lovingly, her finger traces over the inscription. "Where was it?" she whispers reverently.

"Upstairs. Second-to-last room on the right side of the hallway."

As I speak, she turns her head toward me. "Vico

125

entered that room?" She looks at me in disbelief. "Unbelievable," she murmurs so softly I can barely hear it.

Now I should ask her. But her wistful expression holds me back. "I thought you might like it. For the memories."

Suddenly, her eyes well up with tears. "Yes. Thank you, Hanna. This is really…" She clutches the album to her chest, tears streaming down her cheeks.

I move closer to her and wrap my arms around her. "I'm sorry. I didn't mean to…"

"It's okay," she presses out, followed by an extended sniffle. "It's not your fault."

Helplessly, I stroke her back until she calms down a bit. "Family means a lot to you, I understand that all too well."

She nods against my shoulder. "It comes first. Our roots define us, after all."

"Like this estate is one of your roots." It hurts to say the words because suddenly, I know they're true. No one here wants to harm me. I should trust my instincts more than Florian's fears and not be so suspicious. "Why do you want to sell your home?"

"We don't want to," she replies with a trembling voice, "we have to."

I hear how much this fact torments her. I see it in her expression. And I feel it in my heart. Even during our dinner together, I noticed the deep sadness the sisters carry within. Now I finally know for certain what their silent glances meant.

"Why can't any of you save the estate?" I ask but not to report back to Florian.

At this moment, I wish for nothing more than for

this family to continue their tradition. Camilla wriggles out of my arms and sets the swing in motion. Her gaze wanders into the distance, over the tall meadows and the cypresses rising on the horizon.

"We all have obligations that make it impossible," she replies.

I nod absentmindedly. Vico hinted at it too. "You have your babies, who will soon keep you so busy that you won't have any time."

"Besides, Pietro has been urging us to move to his hometown for a long time. He wants to be closer to his family, and it would be better for the little ones inside me too." She gently strokes her belly.

Of course. Twins are a challenge, and here she has no support. Her sisters live elsewhere, her father is sick, her mother deceased. And her brother…

"Alessia is our genius. One day, she will have developed a treatment for brain tumors and win the Nobel Prize for it." Pride resonates in her voice. "She can't give up on that dream." Camilla strokes the cover of the album.

"I understand," I say, and I truly do. I know what it's like to constantly have to bend, because for years, that's all I've been doing. Maybe you can learn to be content, but you're never *truly* happy.

She exhales with a strained sigh. "Aurora knows nothing about farming. No plant has survived under her care for more than two weeks."

"And what about Vico?" He could stay here. He is free, or at least he claims to be.

"He was supposed to take over the estate one day." She lifts her shoulders sadly and lets her gaze wander. "But none of this holds value for him." Tears once again stream down Camilla's face as she gazes into emptiness. "I even believe he's glad it's being sold."

I search my pockets for a tissue but find none. "Do you really think the family means nothing to him?" I shouldn't ask, especially not in such a hopeful tone.

She shrugs. "I can't imagine that."

Did I just say that out loud? And with a conviction I shouldn't have?

Surprised, she looks at me. "Has he said something?"

"Not exactly." But I want to believe that behind his facade is more than he shows us. Because sometimes, when he thinks no one is watching, a wistful expression crosses his face. He longs for something, but whether it's actually family, of course, I don't know.

"Vico doesn't like attachments. Not to people or things. He wants to be free. Independent." She wipes the tears from her cheeks.

I feel a pang in my heart that doesn't belong there. "But the most important thing you need to know about Vico is that I love him. Very much."

"That's why you surely won't force him to give up his freedom," I continue her thoughts.

Camilla is such a strong woman. I glance at her from the side, observing her high cheekbones, her strong hands, and the broken expression in her posture. She would do anything for her family, even if it means she might shatter in the process. "What do Alessia and Aurora think about what has happened here in recent years?"

Suddenly, she looks straight at me. Seconds pass without her saying anything. Then she clears her throat. "Our mother's death hit us hard, but we learned to live with it. But now, we're losing our home. The place we thought we could always return to if we lost our way in life."

Now, I'm also fighting back tears. What's happening here feels wrong. The sale. And the final breakup of the family it will bring about. It's not right.

"Can't anything be done about it?" I whisper helplessly, locking eyes with her.

Instead of answering, she just shakes her head.

***

A night later, Camilla's expression continues to linger in my thoughts. It's hard for me to push it away, but I force myself to do so.

Florian has given me a task. He relies on me, and what kind of partner would I be if I were to disappoint him? Besides, it's my goal too, the reason I'm fighting here. We won't have financial worries anymore. We'll be secure. Isn't that worth the effort?

Or is it?

Even though it's still dark outside, I get out of bed and pack my camera. They say the most beautiful photos can be taken in the gentle light of the rising sun, so I have no choice. My pictures should impress Florian. Not just him but also our future guests; they should long for Tuscany immediately.

A sense of bitterness fills me as I shower and get dressed. The thought that soon nothing in this building will be as it was saddens me.

I do my best to ignore it and finally head out with all my equipment.

The soft dawn is already visible in the sky. I cross

the courtyard. Only the crunch of gravel under my feet and the cheerful chirping of birds can be heard as I walk along the long driveway until I reach the spot where Vico parked his VW van.

I gently tap on the window, but there's no movement inside. "Vico?" I knock again.

Suddenly, his angular face appears at the window. He opens the door, and only then do I notice he's only wearing boxers. What a torso …

"Is something wrong?" he asks, unsuccessfully trying to tame his tousled hair. His shoulder muscles are prominent.

I quickly look away. I need to focus. "We were supposed to take photos."

"What?" Did he forget?

"Yesterday, we discussed starting early today," I add, feeling uncertain due to his confused expression.

He peers into the darkness behind me. "Now? Are you serious?"

"On the internet, they say—"

He raises his hand to stop me. "You want perfect photos, I get it," he says with a disparaging undertone on the word *perfect*.

"That's why we need to leave now," I say even though doubts start creeping in. Is it right to claim him like this? Should I have explained more clearly what I meant by *tomorrow morning*? Or did I accidentally use the wrong Italian words?

Suddenly, he looks at me so intently that I feel a rush of heat. "Did Florian tell you that?" he asks.

"Um… no." Why does he want to know? Even if he did, it wouldn't matter. "I thought it was a lovely idea." In my imagination, it was, at least. Maybe I was wrong.

"If it's too early for you, we can leave later. That's fine too." I try to sound nonchalant, but I'm not sure if I succeed.

"Alright then, work can wait," he says, pulling out a T-shirt and putting it on. "Do you want coffee?" he asks, turning away from me.

He even has a coffee maker in there? I discreetly peek around the corner. Indeed, I spot one of those old-fashioned stovetop espresso makers on a plate next to the mattress that serves as a bed. Right behind it, his laptop is open. So this is how he lives.

"Sure," I reply absentmindedly.

In my mind's eye, an image of us sitting on the floor, legs dangling outside with the door open, watching the sunset over the coast, flashes before me. I rest my head on his shoulder, smiling dreamily.

"Here." Suddenly, a coffee mug appears in front of my face, snapping me out of my inappropriate daydream.

Focus, Hanna, I sternly remind myself as I take the mug. I do everything in my power to keep my thoughts in the present moment as I head back to the car.

We leave the estate. "Where can we get the most beautiful shots? Val D'Orcia is said to be breathtaking," I say.

He puts his hand on his chin. "We won't make it there by sunrise. Just five minutes from here, there's a vineyard with hills directly bathed in the morning sun."

That sounds good too. I steer the car in the direction Vico indicates, and once we park at the foot of the hill, I reach for the camera.

"We can take the first shots over there." Vico points to an area where grapevines are neatly lined up against trellises.

I step out of the car, thinking I can already see the first rays of the sun on the horizon. "Among the plants? Is that allowed?"

"Sure, why not?" He grins mischievously and strolls ahead. "Come on, the sun won't wait."

With a few quick steps, I catch up to him. "Not that we'll get into trouble," I reply, though it's probably too late for that. Vico has already stepped onto the soft soil of the vineyard.

Shaking my head, I follow him between the grapevines. "Only Austrians are awake at this time."

"And Italians who are forced to by Austrians," I say, now also smiling. Back home, I would never dare to do this, and even though Vico is so laid-back, it feels like I'm doing something forbidden.

Nevertheless, I'm not afraid. On the contrary, the excitement that spreads in my stomach is beautifully thrilling.

So beautiful that I forget to watch where I'm stepping. The soft ground under my sneakers gives way. I stumble, but Vico catches me.

For a slightly too long moment, he holds me in his arms. We gaze at each other.

He clears his throat. "Over there is good."

Abruptly, he releases me, moves a few steps away, and stretches both arms to the side. The warm light of the morning sun softens his features.

I would love to photograph him just as he stands amid nature, exuding that Italian Dolce Vita spirit that captivates everyone.

"If you give me your camera, I can check the settings," he offers.

I hand him the device and watch as he adjusts the knobs and takes a few test shots. The surroundings grow brighter around us, the green of the vine leaves begins to glow, and I even imagine I can smell the earth more intensely in the gentle breeze.

Suddenly, he looks up at me. "Are you ready?"

Reaching for the camera, I let him direct me to a specific spot. All at once, he is standing behind me.

"Do you see how the rows stretch over the hill in front of us?" he asks in a hushed tone, as if in awe of the sight.

I nod. I can't speak. Not when I feel his chest so close to my back. And especially not when he leans forward to have the same perspective as me. His cheek is so close to mine that I feel the warmth of his skin.

"The upper edge of the grapevines is the baseline for your picture," he explains softly. "For a good photo, you need to crouch down."

His legs gently touch the back of my knees as I lower myself at his pace.

"Stop." His hand finds my upper arm. Warm. Gentle. "Can you see it?"

I blink hard because I can barely see anything except him. "Yes."

He wraps his arms around me from behind and reaches for my hands, which hold the camera. He guides them upward.

I stare, mesmerized, at the frame that appears on the display. Between the grapevines, gently lined up in the image, individual rays of the morning sun gleam. Bright circles with a rainbow-like shimmer seem to appear out of nowhere, enchanting the scene in a way that defies description.

"Perfect," he whispers and guides my finger to the shutter button.

Yes. That's it. Perfect.

I can barely hear the soft click because I feel like I'm about to lose myself. With Vico so close behind me, it's as if he's catching me. I should stop it, but I yearn to let go and surrender control to the fantasy in my mind.

Life is meant to be enjoyed, my inner voice whispers suddenly.

I don't want to pretend anymore.

I just want to be.

So I close my eyes, lean against his chest, and sink to the ground. All my tension melts away. His scent is like lilac. His voice, a lonely playing cello. I breathe in his presence, and a new world emerges behind the flickering light on my eyelids.

It tastes like oranges.

A contented sigh escapes my lips.

Something moves by my ear. "Tell me where you are."

There is longing in the song of the cello. The world turns blue.

Chapter 20

Vico

She doesn't answer, and I don't know if I should be disappointed or relieved. Her lips twitch, and she nestles even closer to me, humming a melody. I shouldn't want her proximity, but at the same time, it feels beautiful. Her hair carries the scent of fresh herbs, and her dreamy expression makes my heart race.

It would be better if I woke her up. So we can put some distance between us. Because one thing is clear: Wherever she is in her thoughts right now, if I let her go, she'll lose her anchor.

Her hand sinks to the ground. Quickly, I grab it and take the camera from her fingers to save it from the damp soil. At that moment, her muscles tense, and her finger bones turn white.

"What are you doing?" she asks, still half-asleep, and turns in my arms to face me.

I do the same, and I shouldn't have.

We are too close to each other. With just a little sway on this uneven ground, our noses could touch. I involuntarily hold my breath.

"I…" What was the question again?

She blinks, and whenever her sea-green eyes disappear for even a fraction of a second, I already miss them.

"Tell me where you were just now," I implore again,

because no matter how wrong it is, I simply have to know.

An anxious expression flits across her face, and her fingers grip her forearm. I prevent her from pinching herself by placing my hand over hers.

"There was music, right?" Yes, she was humming to herself.

She nods hesitantly, then lowers her eyelids as if embarrassed.

But she shouldn't be. It's rather charming. "What music?"

"A cello," she whispers so softly I can barely hear her. Her cheeks blush.

I should be grateful she's not looking at me. I should get up and leave. I shouldn't inquire any further. But I can't resist.

"Wow. That's…" She hears a melody that isn't there? Only through the power of her thoughts? "What else?" I ask, filled with admiration.

She presses her lips together, then her muscles suddenly relax. "The scent of oranges." She looks enchanting, almost liberated.

"You're the most fascinating person I've ever met." The words escape my mouth unfiltered. I can't help it, and even though I'm probably talking nonsense, she smiles at me.

My fingers move on their own over the back of her hand. She doesn't pull away. There's no trace of fear or defense in her expression. Instead, I see a mix of disbelief and relief in her gaze.

"You don't find it abnormal?" she whispers, almost toneless.

"Never." No one would draw such a conclusion.

Clearly, she possesses a unique talent, but her question reveals that she doesn't see it that way.

Suddenly, the puzzle pieces fall into place for things I couldn't fit together before. She wanted to pretend to be the structured businesswoman when, in reality, she has a dreamy artist within her. Because someone, probably this Florian, made her believe she had to pretend.

"Anyone who says otherwise is just jealous," I quickly add.

Hanna furrows her brow as if she's pondering what I just said. "Maybe." She gestures to the camera in my hand. "We should continue."

"We should," I confirm, but my arms don't let go of her.

"Then… you'd have to…" She stammers awkwardly, and I could swear she doesn't really want to ask me what she's about to.

Her gaze lingers on my lips.

My pulse quickens. I forget to breathe.

There's not a hint of adrenaline in my body, yet I feel intoxicated.

Oh my God, what's happening here?

This has to stop. I need to get ahold of myself before it's too late!

Suddenly, she's the one who abruptly turns away from me. And with the coldness that her absence leaves behind, I realize what almost happened here.

In my mind, an image of my father appears. He holds my mother in his strong arms and smiles at her lovingly. Everything about him radiates, but the picture changes rapidly. The eyes lose their sparkle, the skin turns pale. The corners of the mouth droop, the collarbones protrude. Within seconds, nothing is left of the man he used to be.

I can't let that happen to me. Under no circumstances can I allow myself to end up the same way one day.

"Where else can we find beautiful subjects?" Hanna rummages through her backpack.

"We'll just drive around and keep our eyes open," I say hastily, exhaling heavily. I need to get away from here. If we get close to each other again, I don't know what will happen.

I quickly turn to leave, but before I can make my way, a siren sounds in the distance.

Searching, I let my gaze wander.

"There, ahead." Hanna points at the horizon where an ambulance appears, rushing past us with its flashing blue lights.

Before reaching the next hill, it slows down. With growing unease, I realize that it's turning.

"My God, it's heading for the estate!" Hanna suddenly stammers.

Chapter 21

Hanna

Everything happened so fast that I had no time to think. We ran to the car. Buckled our seat belts as we were already driving. We raced as if we were the ambulance itself even though my mother's voice inside me had warned me not to.

Yet we were too late.

When we arrived at the estate, all we could see was the paramedics closing the doors of the ambulance. I could only catch a brief glimpse of Camilla, clutching her stomach and groaning. Her pain-stricken face was covered in sweat.

Vico and I just looked at each other. And we both knew what we would do next.

Now we sit in the neon light of the hospital corridor and wait. It feels like an eternity has passed since Pietro rushed past us toward the operating area. But the loudly ticking clock on the opposite wall tells us that it has not been ten minutes. Only he is allowed to be present during the emergency C-section. Vico and I are condemned to wait. We don't talk much, probably too busy hoping that Camilla and the babies will be well.

I lean back in the plastic chair and massage my neck. Vico types on his phone.

"Alessia is coming tomorrow, and Aurora is trying

to get time off. She couldn't confirm if it would work out, but she's doing everything to be here soon," he says, tucking his phone back into his pocket and rubbing his hands on his jeans. His fingers tremble, and his breathing is strained.

I smile encouragingly at him. "Camilla is strong. She can do this."

"Vico Olivetta?"

We both look in the direction of the female voice. A young doctor with her hair tightly tied up in a bun and pearl earrings stands before us. The double doors leading to the operating area close behind her. Her expression reveals no emotion.

Vico immediately rushes toward her. "How is my sister?"

She takes a pen from the breast pocket of her blue surgical gown and taps it on the medical file in her hand. "Due to the premature placental abruption, she lost a lot of blood. Her condition was critical, and the babies were also undernourished for a while."

My God! I cover my mouth with my hands.

"We were able to deliver the babies in time and address the bleeding," the doctor says, looking meaningfully between the two of us. "It was a last-minute rescue."

Vico responds with a deep sigh of relief. And I also feel like I can finally breathe again.

"Thank you, Doctor," I say, as Vico seems unable to react. "Can we see her?"

"Not yet. She needs rest now," she replies firmly, tucking the medical file under her arm. "But the babies are healthy and lively." A warm smile appears on her previously serious face. "Would you like to see them?"

"Absolutely!" I say eagerly, picking up my handbag from the waiting chair and following her. I can't wait to see the little ones, smell their scent, and hear their first sounds. My cheeks glow with excitement.

Vico stays behind, as if he needs to consider whether he really wants to come along.

In my overflow of emotions, I rush to him, hook my arm under his, and pull him with me down the hallway. "Don't tell me you don't want to see your nieces. Babies are something special."

He mumbles vaguely, and there's no time for more because we've already reached the hospital room. The doctor opens the door and signals us to enter.

On tiptoes, I sneak into the room. My eyes immediately fall on the two small cribs with the pink blankets. Between them, Pietro sits on a chair in his sweat-soaked shirt, holding both babies in his arms.

"Allow me to introduce them. Meet Stella and Francesca," he says proudly.

"Congratulations!" I step closer and squat in front of Pietro. He nods at me kindly, and in his brown eyes, I see exhaustion but also sheer bliss.

I look at the babies. Their tiny faces are wrinkled. One of the girls has dark fuzz peeking out from under her cap. Contentedly, she snuggles against Pietro's chest and makes a smacking sound. The other has a star-shaped birthmark on her chin. She yawns widely and clumsily forms a fist.

"They're beautiful," I say, deeply moved. I have never seen anything as adorable as these two. I blink back tears and look at Vico. "Aren't they?"

He only takes a hesitant step forward. It's as if he's afraid of two innocent newborns.

"Do you want to hold them?" Pietro asks softly.

"Oh, really? Can we?" I can hardly believe that he's giving us the chance. I quickly sanitize my hands and pull two chairs for Vico and me.

Pietro laughs. "Of course. I really need to disappear for a while." He hands me the little one with the funny hair and then gently places the other girl in Vico's arms. He accepts her hesitantly, swallowing hard. "Take good care of them. I don't want the ladies to complain," he says with a raised finger before leaving the room.

Now we're alone again. And although we were alone in the hallway before, something feels different now.

The worries about Camilla and the babies no longer dominate my thoughts, and instead, what was on my mind before the emergency returns.

Since Vico touched my hand, more than half an hour has passed. Yet I still feel his touch unchanged on my skin. A gentle tingling remains, and my intuition tells me that it won't disappear quickly. Just the memory of it brings a blush to my face.

How could I let myself go like that?

And feel so incredibly comfortable doing it?

I sneak a glance at Vico, but he seems so captivated by his niece that he wouldn't even notice an earthquake. With a blissful grin, he holds out his little finger, which she immediately grabs with her tiny fingers. They look unbelievably adorable together.

"Hello, cutie," he babbles repeatedly. There is so much love in Vico's expression.

I shouldn't be looking. I shouldn't feel like I'm carrying sparklers inside me. And I definitely shouldn't think about whether Vico would be a great father. With great effort, I manage to lower my eyes. As soon as he's out of my sight, my stomach knots up despite the adorable baby in my arms.

How can I sit here and stare at Vico while Florian is at home missing me?

What kind of partner am I, cuddling up to another man's chest among vineyards at sunrise and telling him about the daydreams I hide from Florian?

This is wrong in so many ways that it can never be right. Yet I find myself staring at him again.

Chapter 22

Vico

How tiny she is. So delicate and fragile. And how she smells! I absorb the scent, unable to get enough of it. She lets out a squeak.

I hold her gently, supporting her little head so she doesn't hurt herself during her little cries. "You're quite active, little lady," I say.

"That must run in the family," Hanna says.

My gaze lands on her face. A mixture of longing and unease is evident in her expression. And suddenly, I realize what I'm doing here.

In my arms lies a baby. And I haven't just admired her, but I've genuinely cherished our connection. She's an Olivetta, just like me. We are family.

Panic surges within me. Why am I thinking this way? Where are these feelings coming from?

As my chest tightens rapidly, Pietro enters the room, whistling a melody. "Well, have the little ones behaved themselves?"

I quickly rise from my seat and place his daughter back in his hands. "They were exemplary," I manage to say with effort. "But now, I must… go away."

Urgently so. My gaze flicks to Hanna, who stares at me with incomprehension. I can just make out how her expression hardens before I turn away and rush out of the room. Of course, she judges me for valuing my freedom over family. But I have no choice. I race through the corridor, push open the door to the outside, and take a deep breath.

Unchanged, I feel as if a giant snake has me in its grip. What is wrong with me? First, I can't tear myself away from Hanna, and now I lose myself in the sight of a baby.

I'm losing my mind.

Yes, that must be it.

I'm going crazy.

It's time to pull the emergency brake. So I fish my phone out of my pocket and message my coach that I urgently need confirmation from the talent scout for sponsorship. I need something to hold on to. Too often in the past few days, I've forgotten what matters most in my life. I was distracted, but a professional career as a cliff diver remains my greatest dream.

Next, I dial Adriano's number. "Feel like grabbing a beer?" I ask him directly when he answers.

His response is a warm laugh. "Have you looked at the time?"

Right. It's only nine o'clock. "Then how about breakfast at Caffè delle Arti?"

"Sure thing. I'll just start work later today," he says with an amused tone.

He's putting his job on the back burner. Even though we haven't seen each other in years, he's still the same old Adriano. "I'm looking forward to it."

We say our goodbyes, and I start walking. It's about a fifteen-minute walk to the café, and when I arrive, Adriano is already waiting for me. A pair of sunglasses casually rests in his short hair, and the first three buttons of his white shirt are undone.

"It feels so good to see you again," I say, giving him a brief hug as a greeting.

We sit at the bistro table outside the café and order espressos and cornetti. Even before the cups are placed on the brightly painted table, Adriano leans over to me. "So tell me, how's the wild life of freedom?"

That's the perfect topic. "There's a competition in Bari in mid-April. My coach thinks I have a chance." Well, after not returning to training as planned, he was a bit less enthusiastic. But there are still six weeks until then. Hanna has been here for almost two weeks; surely, she'll have everything sorted out soon. And once she leaves, I'll be free again.

Hopefully.

"You're positively brimming with enthusiasm," Adriano says in a sarcastic tone.

I quickly turn up the corners of my mouth. "No, it's great. It's just that being stuck here is a problem." And not just because I can't train.

His expression turns serious. "You have to be the rock in the storm here," he says sympathetically.

I wave it off. "That's not a problem."

He looks at me searchingly. But before he can say anything, our breakfast is served.

I take a sip of coffee and search desperately for another topic of conversation. "And what about you? When will I hear one of your songs on the radio?"

Laughing amusedly, he tears off a piece of his cornetto. "Oh, that. That's ancient history."

"You're not playing anymore?" I place the coffee cup down incredulously. This can't be serious. "Music was your big dream. What happened?"

"Life happened." With a happy expression, he pops

146

the sweet pastry into his mouth. Then he raises his index finger and rummages in his wallet with the other hand. He opens it and places it on the table in front of me. "This is Paola," he says, tapping on the photo of the woman with the bright smile, held in his arms.

I can't help but smile amusedly. "You have a picture of you and your sweetheart in your wallet? I simply can't believe it."

Undeterred, he opens the next compartment of his wallet. The snapshot of a little boy catches my eye. "And this is Tommaso."

No! "You have a family?" slips out of me in shock, even before I can gather my thoughts clearly. Adriano, the wild one. Invincible rock star and fighter for freedom, has turned into a dutiful family man? Resistance builds within me. "Why?"

He shrugs nonchalantly. "People change."

Nonsense. He's been lulled into this. And now he's stuck with two people he loves too much. One day, he'll pay the price. The pain will consume him.

"Don't look at me like that, Vico." He shakes his head, putting away his wallet and crossing his arms in front of his chest. "I'm happy."

Yes. Now. But one day, it'll be over. That's a fact. No one can defy death! "I… I'm just surprised, that's all," I manage to say.

For a moment that lasts far too long, he fixes his gaze on me. "What happened to your mother was terrible. I understand that you…"

"Everything's fine," I hurriedly interrupt. "That's not what this is about."

He doesn't release me from his gaze. "Oh, no? Then what is it about?"

147

"About you, of course. You wanted to fill the biggest concert halls in Europe. You dreamed of signing autographs, composing songs late into the night, and living an extraordinary life." And now, he's sitting across from me. The decent family man. He's probably taken on some boring job and dutifully mows the lawn every weekend.

The accusatory tone of my words bounces off him as if he's wearing a protective suit. "No stage in the world could ever give me the feeling I have when I see my son laugh."

In my mind, the image of my niece I held in my arms less than an hour ago appears. Her tiny nose. Her round eyes. And again, there's that feeling I had during that moment, mixing with the memory of when my arms refused to let go of Hanna, even though my mind protested.

Dammit.

The meeting with Adriano was supposed to distract me. It was supposed to remind me that a life of freedom is the best life one can have. It was supposed to make these feelings vanish from me.

Now, he leans over the table to me and pats my hand. "Those who love can lose. But those who resist love have already lost."

I haven't lost anything. I have everything I ever wanted. Even my breakthrough as an athlete is closer than ever before. That's the only thing missing for my happiness.

Struggling to compose myself, I pull my hand back from under his. "Thanks, but I'll stick with cliff diving." As the words leave my mouth, I taste the bitterness they leave on my tongue.

Chapter 23

Hanna

With fumbling movements, I open the bag of brioches and place one on the plate. The night was exhausting. Images of Vico kept appearing in my dreams, images that shouldn't even exist.

Images of him whispering tenderly in my ear. Caressing my hand. Cradling the baby in his arms.

The coffee machine hums, and I take a cup from the upper cabinet. I don't even have to open the door because the glass panel is missing. No one replaced it, even though the Olivettas seem to love this estate wholeheartedly. At least everyone except Vico.

The ringing of my phone pierces my ears. It must be Florian. His name indeed appears on the display. Immediately, guilt grips me. "Buongiorno, mio carissimo."

"What?" he asks bewildered.

"I wished you a good morning, my dearest," I explain in German because the feeling nags at me that today I need to put in extra effort to show him my affection.

The creaking of a chair is heard. "Are you okay?" He sounds suspicious.

"Of course." I pour the coffee into the cup and carry it to the oversized wooden table, the center of the kitchen. "And you?"

His response is a grumpy murmur. "Have you received any updates? Are there any cost estimates?"

Yesterday, the first quotes from an electrician and a plumber arrived. "No," I say, even though I don't understand myself why I'm lying to him. "In Italy, these things take a little longer," I add apologetically.

"Then you need to push them, Hanna. We can't wait, you know that." I can tell he's trying to control his voice.

He's not happy with me. I lower my gaze to the worn stone-tiled floor. I could have told him the truth. No, I should have forwarded the quotes to him directly. "I'll do that."

"I know you're doing your best."

Oh God, no, I'm not. Quite the opposite!

My throat tightens, my stomach clenches. I place the brioches back into the bag.

"It's really important that you stay focused," he continues. Thank goodness there are hundreds of miles between us. If he could see my face right now, he would surely realize what a terrible partner I am to him. "Hanna?" he asks with an accusing tone. "Are you daydreaming?"

"Of course not," I reply shrilly, as if he had actually caught me daydreaming.

For a moment, I only hear his strained breathing. He's probably considering whether to press further. "Alright then. Back to the craftsmen. Call them again today and insist that the quotes must be ready by tomorrow."

Even though I know he means well, his tone puts me under pressure. Nervously, I pace back and forth in the kitchen. "Will do."

"And what about the Olivettas? Have you found out anything about them yet?" he asks next.

My gaze falls on the torn curtain, and the window behind it is covered in a thick layer of dust. "I'm working on it," I say because I simply don't know what else to tell him.

I could never reveal to him how much I've come to feel for the sisters. And I definitely can't voice my innermost wish that they would keep the estate. That Vico would stay here, that their fractured family would find peace, and that they would produce the finest olive oil in the region once again.

"Isn't our future important to you anymore?" A wave of disappointment comes through from the other end of the line.

"Of course, it is!" I respond as firmly as I can. Perhaps I've forgotten it at times in the past few days, but that doesn't change the fact that it's true. "We are building the foundation for a wonderful life here." I swallow. "Together."

"Together, we are strong," he says affectionately. "I need you, Hanna. I can't do this without you. You know that, right?"

My heart skips a beat. "You can count on me," I confirm, as the guilt overwhelms me. Immediately, my migraine returns, accompanied by a ringing in my ears. I squint my eyes and massage my temples.

"Thank you," I hear Florian say from the bottom of his heart. "We'll talk again tomorrow."

"Mm-hmm," I mutter, sinking onto one of the rickety wooden chairs. I urgently need my pills because when I face Vico today, I must have a clear head. I can't allow him to unsettle me like he did yesterday. And not just because I can't afford any further distractions from my mission.

***

Suspiciously, I gaze at the zip line that stretches over the entire length of the canyon. "Are you serious?" I ask.

"Sure," Vico replies, shrugging so casually as if it's the most natural thing in the world to race twenty yards above the ground at who-knows-how-many miles per hour between rugged rocks. "It's perfectly safe. And a lot of fun."

I observe the teenagers daring to try the devilish contraption, only protected by orange helmets, as they cheer with joy. They truly seem to be experiencing something they won't forget easily. "I'll note it on the checklist and we'll take some pictures." That should be enough. Unfortunately.

"But how do you expect to promote the zip line to your guests if you don't even know what it feels like yourself?" He raises his eyebrows, urging me on.

Since we left the estate in the morning, I've been trying to keep enough distance between us. It's not easy at all, even though Vico seems reserved today as well. He constantly crosses his arms and steps back, even when our paths don't come anywhere near each other.

"Look, now it's a child's turn," he points with his finger upward. Indeed, I see a girl about ten years old enthusiastically strapping into the safety harness. "Would they allow the kids to do it if it was really dangerous?"

"Probably not," I admit, kneading my fingers.

You're different from them, Hanna, don't forget that, my mother's voice grumbles inside me.

He claps his hands enthusiastically. "Great, then let's do it."

Once again, I look up at the zip line. The girl pushes off from the platform, spreading her arms jubilantly as she descends.

"You can't get hurt, no matter how clumsy you might be otherwise," I hear Vico say. Not for the first time, it's as if he knows what's going on in my head.

Why is he so insistent on doing something adventurous today? He has tried several times before, but I always managed to convince him otherwise. Could he be craving an adrenaline rush?

Maybe it would be kind of nice…

That's not for you. Better safe than sorry, you know that, Mother interferes again.

"We could also go straight to the restaurant; after all, we need to test it too," I say reluctantly. The sooner we get through everything, the sooner I won't have to deal with what his presence does to me. The tingling in my stomach when he smiles and the warmth in my chest when he looks at me.

Suddenly, he takes a step closer to me. "Come on. It'll be unforgettable. I promise."

He's too close for comfort.

Life is meant to be enjoyed, whispers my own inner voice, as if trying to counterbalance my mother's voice.

I nod hesitantly. "Okay."

Before I can change my mind, I walk to the small wooden cabin next to the starting platform. We receive a safety briefing, helmets, and harnesses, and then join the line of people waiting for their turn. Until it's our turn, we barely speak to each other. Vico is frantically tapping on his phone, and I try to distract myself by observing the surroundings. I didn't know there was a canyon in Tuscany. The rocks are as rugged as those back home, though not nearly as high. A turquoise river winds through the valley below us. Even the vegetation here is different from the rest of Tuscany. There are real forests, and I even spot some fir trees.

"Prego, Signora," the young man with hiking pants and a carabiner in his hand calls me over, but I remain rooted to the spot.

Nervousness wells up inside me. Is it really safe? The ground seems miles away, and I'd have to jump from the platform into nothingness.

If the hook comes loose, you'll plummet into the river. Or worse, you'll land on the sharp-edged rocks of the canyon.

As my mother rages in my head, Vico steps beside me. With a penetrating gaze, he nods at me. "We'll jump together," he tells the employee, preparing for the jump as if he does it every day.

"Bene," the Zip line staff member smiles at me. "May I?" he asks politely.

Two women behind me clear their throats loudly.

"And nothing can happen, right?" I ask Vico again just to be sure. Just because he claimed it earlier doesn't necessarily mean it's true. And just because there's no danger to our bodies doesn't mean it's safe for my heart. Especially not when we're jumping together.

Vico nods decisively. "I guarantee it."

My palms become sweaty. The waiting crowd murmurs irritably. Everything is fine. There's nothing I should worry about. I want to give it a try. I want to enjoy it. Beads of sweat form on my forehead, yet I allow the man to secure me. Afterward, Vico stands behind me, and the employee connects our harnesses together.

"Ready?" he whispers in my ear.

I catch my breath. Not just because of what will happen in a moment, but more so because of what is happening right now.

My pulse quickens. "Ready," I confirm, my voice trembling.

"Fall into the harness and start running," the employee instructs, his words blending with the excitement coursing through my entire body. I feel him gently give us a push, and Vico wraps his arms around me tenderly.

I feel the heat. Almost instinctively, my feet start moving on the ground, and then I lose contact with it.

I squint my eyes shut, and Vico cheers so enthusiastically that I can feel the vibration in his chest against my back.

Faster and faster, we zoom through the air. The rushing wind brushes against my skin, tugging at my T-shirt. I dare not look down and grip the rope tightly. Is the rushing sound in my ears from my blood or the air rushing past? I don't know. But what I do know is that pure adrenaline is coursing through my body.

It tingles everywhere. It's in my head, in my toes, and even in my stomach. It overwhelms me. And it feels incredible.

A scream escapes my mouth, followed by another one. Because letting out my emotions like this is so liberating that I no longer care if anyone judges me for it.

Then I open my eyes.

We're flying.

The view of the world below is breathtaking. The turquoise water, the orange-brown rock formations, the lush green trees. I can't get enough of it all, savoring every second, nestling into Vico's arms, wishing the ride would never end. Here, on this zip line, there's nothing else but the two of us and the feeling of being completely myself. Worries, questions, and obligations no longer exist.

For the first time, as far back as I can remember, I have no fear. On the contrary, I feel a deep strength within me.

Anything is possible.

And even though the end of our ride is already in sight, I want to hold on to this clarity. We race toward the terminal, the speed decreases without any effort on my part, until we come to a stop. I sigh and rest my head on Vico's shoulder, looking up at him.

He beams at me.

Unconsciously, I smile back and turn a bit more toward him.

We draw closer, feeling the magical pull between us, outshining any other emotion within me.

Anything is possible.

With a blissful expression, he opens his arms. Before I comprehend what's happening, I've fully turned to him and press myself against him. His scent surrounds me. My heart races, his breath is fast.

"That was… incredible!" I blurt out, unable to keep it to myself. "Thank you for convincing me."

"You're welcome," he pulls me closer and gently strokes my back.

In no time, it feels like I'm flying again. A lightness envelops me.

"I'm incredibly proud that you dared to do it," he whispers in my ear.

"I owe it to you." I take a deep breath of his scent and surrender to the way he clouds my thoughts. He gave me this moment of happiness, despite my initial resistance.

Inevitably, I think of what Camilla told me the day before on the Hollywood swing, that Vico couldn't handle commitments. But the way he holds me right now, everything within me refuses to believe it.

"You are wonderful," I hear myself say. "Why do you pretend to your sisters that relationships mean nothing to you?"

"Because it's better that way." His voice sounds fragile.

My intuition didn't deceive me. "Your family is important to you. And also your home, right?"

He shakes his head slowly. "It used to be that way. But today..."

"Why?" I ask, although with every passing second, I feel the adrenaline in my veins subsiding. I increasingly realize how wrong it is to be in his arms and feel more secure than anywhere else.

His embrace loosens. "Family just isn't for me. I prefer to enjoy life, do what I'm really meant to do."

Do I hear wistfulness in his tone? Or is it rather resistance, as my questions spoil the mood?

"But family is..." I interrupt myself. This is pointless. Imagining that Vico could be fundamentally different is just wishful thinking. I need to stop seeing things that don't exist. Moreover, this leads nowhere.

Except to guilt, and I already have more than enough of that.

It was wonderful. For a moment when both our realities seemed far away. But now, it has to be over.

I peel myself away from his embrace, release my harness, and try to put on a determined expression. "Shall we test the restaurant?"

Immediately, he takes a step back, running his hands through his hair. "Yes, definitely," he says hurriedly, turning away.

As soon as he puts distance between us, I breathe a sigh of relief. I must ignore the part of me crazy enough to miss his proximity.

Even if I were unattached. Even if I weren't about to buy the Olivetta family estate and thus permanently destroy his family. And even if Vico wanted a relationship—with a daydreamer like me. Vico and I, that can only end in disaster.

Chapter 24

Vico

I press my hand against my stomach.

Not again. Please. Not again.

But my stomach doesn't care. It cramps so hard that I curl up in pain on the mattress of my van.

Oh.

My.

God.

When it finally subsides, I reach for the bedsheet. I have no strength left, but that's no surprise. This has been going on for half the night already. With effort, I pull the sheet up to my nose.

"Hey, sleepyhead," Hanna's soft voice reaches my ear. "We were supposed to meet for departure an hour ago. Where are you?"

Sleepyhead, my foot. I let out a whimper, as that's all I can manage.

Suddenly, the mattress sinks behind me. A moment later, her face hovers over me, a crease forming between her eyes. "What happened?" she asks, resting the back of her hand against my sweaty forehead. "You have a fever."

Oh no, the opposite is true. I'm freezing! "Mm-hmm," I reply anyway, lacking the energy for a retort.

"Where does it hurt?" Her gaze travels down my

body to where I'm pressing my forearms against my stomach. "Could it be that the fish yesterday tasted strange?"

"I don't know. It was so heavily spiced that I..." Another cramp builds up in my body. "Oh God."

Her hand gently touches my back. "I'll get help."

"Not necessary," I reply, but without strength.

"Hold on," she says, caring. "I'll be right back."

Before I understand what's happening, she's gone. I close my eyes and try to breathe evenly until she returns. Why did I order the fish? Hanna had even warned me not to eat something in an empty restaurant that might have been sitting in the fridge for days due to lack of guests. I thought she was crazy. And now I pay the price for it.

"We need to get him inside the house," Hanna says, climbing into the van and gripping my shoulders. Behind her, the concerned face of Pietro appears. "Can you walk, Vico?"

I nod, and with Hanna's help, I manage to sit up. As soon as we leave the camper, Pietro takes over. Leaning on him, I drag myself to Camilla's bungalow.

"Shouldn't you be in the hospital?" I ask my brother-in-law. "Or at the workshop?"

He shakes his head with a smile. "Don't worry, I'll be gone in a moment. Camilla and the little ones are allowed to go home today, and of course, I'll pick them up."

"How wonderful!" Hanna says with that delighted tone in her voice she had when she first saw my nieces. "Can I prepare something for them?"

"I think it's enough if you take care of our patient here," Pietro directs me toward the house.

Once inside, I sink onto the sofa bed in the guest room and close my eyes, utterly exhausted. I've only covered a few yards, but they have drained all my strength. I feel something cool on my forehead and wrists. Then I fall into a blissful twilight sleep.

***

A soft voice hums a gentle melody, and a feeling of comfort envelops me.

"It will be okay," says the voice now. A hand brushes back my hair, and a gentle breeze grazes my skin. Then the humming starts again.

A sigh escapes my lips. The knot in my stomach feels looser, and I no longer shiver.

"He had bad fish. But by now, he's probably overcome the worst," says the voice later. It must be Hanna's voice.

"Hopefully." Something heavy and warm rests on my upper arm. "He looks pale." Is that Alessia speaking?

"It will be fine. I'll take care of him, no problem."

No problem. How lovely.

"Go and see the babies. They are adorable."

Yes, they are. Adorable little beings with even more adorable tiny fingers. I can picture one in front of me, opening its eyes.

Their eyes are sea green.

Now I hear footsteps. They sound muffled and hollow. "Call me if you need me." A door is opened.

"I will, Alessia. Thank you." A chair squeaks softly as it's moved, then creaks. The humming returns.

So melodic. So pleasant.

Could it be Hanna singing? I lift my eyelids, just for a moment.

Indeed, she's sitting right next to me, looking at aerial photographs of our estate on the wall. She appears content. The image fades to black, but I won't allow it. I open my eyes again.

There's that fascinating twinkle in her eyes. It's so serene that it makes me forget my pain. I turn to get a better view of her, and the sofa squeaks.

Immediately, she turns her head toward me. Even in my dazed state, I see her pinch her own hand.

She shouldn't do that. Why does she constantly punish herself for getting lost in her imagination?

"Good morning," she says softly, leaning over me. "How do you feel?"

My mouth is dry. "Thirsty," I croak.

As if she already anticipated it, she reaches for a prepared cup with a straw and holds it to my mouth, allowing me to sip from it with my lips. "Just a small sip for now."

Filled with a wave of gratitude, I nod. Then I take a sip from the straw. Just her presence alone makes me feel better. I swallow the liquid. "Thank you," I say, and at the same time, I realize it's not enough.

She didn't have to do this. She could have been angry with me for not showing up and gone on the excursion alone. She could have seen me lying in my van, considered me lazy, and turned back. She could have left me to my fate, and no one would have blamed her.

But she didn't.

I glance at the window. The incoming light carries a warm hue. "What time is it?"

She glances at her phone. "Just after six in the evening."

"Have you been here the whole time?" I ask cautiously.

"Of course," she answers with an obvious tone, which makes me smile. "I would never have left you in this condition."

That's… so selfless… "Thank you." I want to say more, but the words fail me.

It seems like she doesn't want to hear more either. With a caring expression, she leans over me. "How does the drink feel in your stomach?"

I listen to my body. "No more cramps." Thank God.

Her lips curl upward in delight. "Tomorrow, you'll be almost back to normal. Do you want to rest a little more?"

No. I want to be with her. I quickly shake my head. "Tell me something about yourself," I impulsively ask.

She looks at me with a furrowed brow. "What do you want to know?"

"Everything," I reply, and I mean it. I'm interested in every detail of her life. I want to know what she likes to eat, where she went to school, who her friends are, and why she speaks Italian so well.

"Everything?" She raises an eyebrow.

I nod. "From birth until today."

For a moment, she smirks to herself, then she begins to recount. It's already dark by the time she tells me about her brother.

"With Elina, he found the love of his life," she says thoughtfully. "If perhaps true love does exist, then the two have found it."

It does exist. I know it, but I don't say it out loud.

Listening to her is like listening to an enchanting melody. And the fact that she didn't mention Florian makes it even more beautiful. It's as if he doesn't exist. Not in her thoughts, and maybe not even in her heart.

Not that it would change anything. It's just… beautiful.

With each passing hour, I feel better, and eventually, I dare to sit up on the sofa. I no longer feel like a freezer, and my stomach is only slightly queasy. But that changes abruptly when my gaze falls on the bookshelf opposite.

"How did this get here?" I ask, not realizing at first that I've spoken my thoughts aloud.

Hanna gets up and walks to the shelf. "You mean this?" She carefully pulls out the album, holding it in her hands like a treasure. "I didn't want it to be lost, so I brought it to Camilla."

Just the way she says the last sentence makes me swallow hard. She didn't want it to be lost. Well, it's already too late for that. "Put it back." My voice has taken on a panicked tone, and I can hear it clearly. And so can she.

Looking directly at me, she holds the album close to her chest. "But why? I'm sure it's filled with beautiful memories."

Yes, it is.

And that's exactly the problem.

She approaches me. "Shall we look at it together?"

Oh God, no! "Why?" To feel the pain I escaped from through my new life all over again? Certainly not.

Unfazed, she sits down beside me on the sofa. "My father died young too," she says softly. "At first, it was difficult, but today I carry the good memories of him in my heart." She smiles at me wistfully. "I wouldn't want to give them up for anything in the world."

I can't imagine that. It doesn't make sense. "Why?"

Her lips curve upward. "Because I don't want to miss out on all the beautiful memories. I don't want to forget them; I want them to remain alive within me."

"But the pain…" I shouldn't have said that.

Now she knows.

She knows that nothing frightens me more than the agony that came with losing my mother. For me, for my sisters, and especially for my father. Her death shattered everything. How could I ever reminisce about the good times without despairing over the fact that they died with her?

Instead of condemning me for my cowardice, she smiles warmly at me. "Do you feel it?"

"Every day," I admit without hesitation. It's there whenever silence creeps into me. Only when adrenaline rushes through my veins am I truly free from it. I've never told anyone about it. Only Hanna is allowed to know.

"You've tried to shake it off. But it's still there," she says gently. Then she places the album on my lap with a meaningful look. "Sometimes, you have to leave old paths to grow into the new ones."

I lower my gaze to the leather cover and trace the outer edge of the album with my index finger. Even if a part of me no longer desires it, a voice in my head warns me loudly. "Everything could get worse," I say, voicing what dominates my thoughts.

"That's possible," she reaches for my forearm and squeezes it gently. "But the exact opposite could happen too."

Carefully, I slide my hand under the cover, my fingers trembling.

"I'm here," Hanna whispers.

I don't know if it's her words or the warmth that flows through me where she holds me. I don't know if it's the dim light or my still weakened body. But I no longer want to resist.

Since I returned here, it has become increasingly difficult for me to maintain the protective barrier within me. I want to try if there's a chance—even if it's minuscule—to leave the pain behind.

With bated breath, I open the cover. My parents smile at me from a scratched photo. Father wears a suit, and Mother wears a white dress.

"They got married on the fifth of August. No one does that; it's too hot, and it was a Wednesday. But that was their special day." As soon as I speak the words, I clear my throat. "My father always said that so many miracles happened on that day that no other date could have been suitable to celebrate the greatest miracle of all."

Their love.

Hanna doesn't respond; she simply continues holding my arm, giving me the time I need.

Page by page, I look through the pictures. I discover photos of the estate before the barn was built, my parents together with their grandparents during the olive harvest, and my mother at the olive press. Just a few pages later, I burst into laughter. "This is me." My goodness, how old-fashioned that baby outfit is. The onesie looks like it was hand-knitted. I tap the photo. "Would you have recognized me?"

She leans over the album. "Those eyes, I would

recognize them among thousands," she says with a grin. "Your parents look incredibly proud."

And they were. "We children were everything to them."

I keep flipping through the album, glimpsing pictures of my sisters in pretty dresses, our rare family vacations in the Dolomites, and my mother lovingly repairing cracks in the exterior wall of the estate. I see all the beauty we once had. I see the bond that carried our family through difficult times, and I see the love for our homeland in our eyes.

I see everything we lost. And it hurts even worse than I ever imagined.

On one picture, Mother holds my high school diploma from Liceo Artistico with a beaming smile for the camera. She was already sick back then. But no one knew.

She looks healthy. And happy.

"She wanted me to pursue my education even though it was always clear that…" My voice fails me. I can't say it; it's too much.

"That one day you would inherit the estate," Hanna finishes my sentence.

With tightly pressed lips, I nod. That's how it was. Until I turned twenty-three, I would have never imagined that I wouldn't become part of the family tradition. "But things turned out differently," I say bitterly and continue flipping through the album.

Hanna's breath suddenly becomes shallow, and I too feel as if I'm lacking oxygen. I feel the urge to close the album, but Hanna stops me.

Her index finger glides over the picture of my emaciated and bald mother, who, despite her illness, smiles into the camera as if it were the happiest day of her life. "What type of cancer did she have?"

I swallow hard. "A brain tumor." My words echo in the silence between us. For seconds, neither of us says anything. Hanna doesn't pressure me. I'm the one who suddenly wants to share more. "At first, she was just absentminded. Nothing more. She would forget to buy milk or call her friend and not remember why."

"It got worse, didn't it?" Hanna says as if she knows exactly how insidious such an illness can be.

"Once she bought a new car because she had forgotten she already had one." My God, the way she looked at Father when he explained to her that she didn't need it. Disbelieving. Shocked. And then, when she realized what she had done, she burst into tears. "We were only able to return it because we could convince the seller that she wasn't mentally fit to make the purchase. We even had to draft a formal document to confirm it."

"You had to declare her legally incompetent?" Hanna presses her hand to her mouth, staring at me with wide eyes.

"And that was just the beginning." In the end, she couldn't do anything on her own.

Absolutely nothing.

Images of her on her deathbed pop up inside me. And about how she smiled powerfully at me despite her weakening body. "Father fought for them. He left no stone unturned to save her. He didn't care about the incomprehension of the villagers. He ignored the urgent warnings of the doctors to prepare for the worst."

I know what Hanna is thinking right now. It's no

wonder that he hasn't been able to cope with her death until today. And she's probably right about that.

"And you? Did you ignore it too?" she asks.

How could I ever have done that? Her impending end was ever-present. We knew it was coming. We all knew.

I clear my throat to release the tightness and continue flipping through the album. Once again, I come across a photo from the fifth of August. Their twenty-fifth wedding anniversary. Despite the chemotherapy having drained all her strength, she insisted on celebrating. She wanted sparklers and balloons, a three-tiered cake, and the finest regional antipasti, even though it was clear she wouldn't be able to eat any of it. Tenderly, I trace my finger over her determined face in the picture, which suddenly blurs before my eyes.

I can't bear to see the white summer dress fluttering on her bony shoulders. And how she smiles at the family as if she wanted to give us all courage even though it should have been our duty to be strong for her. Quickly, I turn the pages, but what I see on the next ones is even worse than before.

They are empty.

Our family died with my mother.

I bury my face in my hands. Hanna scoots closer to me and wraps her arm around me. "It will get better, I promise. And one day, you'll be able to look back at the past and the future with a light heart."

I wouldn't believe that from anyone else. But I believe it from her. Not because she also lost a parent and went through something similar herself. It's more because of the way she says the words. With such certainty and hope for the future that I once again feel like I'm discovering a completely new side of her.

And she makes me feel something I've been reluctant to acknowledge for a long time. That I will never be able to fill the void inside me with adrenaline.

Chapter 25

Hanna

That I am alone in Cinque Terre today, testing a short section of the famous coastal hike, doesn't bother me. On the contrary, I enjoy being alone like never before. My breath flows calmly, and with each step I take on the rocky terrain, I feel more at ease. Now the only thing missing is that the stern breeze and the view of the endless expanse of the sea clear my mind. Perhaps this will help me focus on what has been pushed to the background over the past two weeks.

My mission. Florian. And my goals for the future.

Marriage, children, connection, security.

I have dreamed of all these things my whole life. And now, here in Tuscany, I meet a man who captivates me more and more even though he could never give me any of it.

Once again, in my thoughts, I am sitting next to him on the sofa bed in Camilla's bungalow. I see the despair in his features and feel his upper body trembling. But there's something else too. My own heart, so filled with the desire to help him that it has forgotten everything else.

Since I said goodbye to him last night with an intimate hug, I've been wondering what these feelings mean. But I can't find an answer.

Even on the way back to the estate, it doesn't reveal

itself. As I turn into the long driveway and the property appears before me in its morbid beauty, I only know one thing. In Vico's presence, I am a different person. And maybe, just maybe, it's the person I have always been deep inside.

Letting out a heavy sigh, I park in the front courtyard and get out of the car. The sun is already low on the horizon, and the evening is pleasantly mild. My gaze falls on the wrought-iron seating area with the mosaic table. There, I could enjoy life with a glass of wine. Just do nothing for a while.

"Welcome back." Vico appears out of nowhere behind my car. He looks at me hesitantly. "How was your hike?"

"The colorful villages are even more picturesque in reality than in the pictures." As soon as the words leave my lips, I realize that I forgot to take photos. Oh well, I can't change it now. I smile at him. "How's your stomach?"

"Back to normal." He pats his belly. Then his gaze turns melancholic. "Will you walk with me for a while?"

His expression tells me that he wants to talk to me. Perhaps he has been thinking about our conversation from yesterday. I nod in agreement. "I wanted to take another closer look at the estate's lands," because I really want to see the olive trees that make up the Olivettas' family tradition. Somewhere on the overgrown property they are hiding.

"Of course, boss, we'll take care of it right away." He winks at me and signals with a sweeping gesture to follow him behind the house.

Once we arrive there, he stops. "On the right side,

172

you can see open meadows," he says, completely disregarding the beautiful sight of the poppy flowers. The green is interspersed with bright red blooms, their delicate stems gently swaying in the wind.

I let the scene sink in. "It's magnificent." A picnic spot amid the floral splendor, perhaps even near a pond that invites relaxation, would be enchanting. It should be designed and built in the venerable Tuscan style of the main house to seamlessly blend in. Instantly, my imagination shows me what it could look like. The scent of freshly cut grass fills my nostrils, and the light changes its color. Guitar melodies play in my mind.

"You see something, don't you?" Vico asks. "Tell me, I want to see it too."

I shake my head. "It's nothing special." Can't I just look at something and stay reasonable for once? Instinctively, I grab my forearm.

He stops me before I can pinch myself. Suddenly, his face appears before me. He looks at me significantly. "I can't imagine that for the life of me."

I turn away, but I feel that he's still looking at me. "I…" As liberating as it would be to share my inner thoughts with him, I can't. He would just mock me. Because my daydreams are, after all, laughable. They always have been.

"What are you so afraid of?" he asks in a tone that makes it even harder for me.

"It's not fear. It's reason," I reply, putting my hands in my pockets and pressing my fingernails into my thighs.

A snort is his first reaction. "And what do you gain from being reasonable all the time?"

Though he stands at a safe distance from me, I can practically feel him cornering me. "Well, I… I mean…" People accept me. No one can stand Hanna Daydreamer, not even myself. That's the right answer, but I dare not speak it out loud.

"Sometimes you have to leave old paths to grow into new ones." He grins at me crookedly. "At least, that's what I've heard."

He's trying to beat me at my own game. Inevitably, I smile, but just a second later, I realize what his behavior means.

This man believes that what's inside me is valuable. And he thinks that withholding it wouldn't do me any good. He cares about helping me just as much as I cared about him yesterday.

I mean something to him.

Just like he means something to me.

Normally, panic should be spreading inside me right now. Because what's happening between us is wrong. But all I feel is warmth. My fingers loosen, and suddenly, there's only one delicate wish, like a streak of light on the horizon. Doesn't he deserve the same chance he gave me yesterday when he spoke so openly about his pain? Did he laugh at me when I told him about the cello music in my head at the vineyard?

No!

On the contrary. *You are the most fascinating person I've ever met*, he said.

What if I open up and show him all the things I've been hiding so steadfastly? What if he isn't repelled by my daydreams but wants to dream with me?

What if he's the one person who would accept me for who I truly am? I have to find out.

"There's a winding path," I say softly, looking at him questioningly.

He nods encouragingly.

"On both sides, there are herb beds. It smells of rosemary and lavender. Behind them, the sea of poppies opens up." Yes, that's how it could be. I point at the spot near the house. "Up here, there are old, cushioned furniture pieces, mismatched and cozy. Beside them, large terracotta pots with bougainvillea climbing up a wooden trellis. The pots have curved lines on the front, and because they've weathered a bit, they bring the right atmosphere to the area."

I step into the place where the path begins in my mind and reach out my hand to Vico. He takes it, his fingers interlocking with mine.

"Do you hear the crunch of pebbles under our shoes? Over there is a pavilion. Do you see how the cream-colored curtains dance in the wind between the dark-painted metal struts? And how the cornflowers stretch their blue heads toward the sky?"

"I see it," he whispers in awe.

It's just three small words, yet they have enough power to bring down all the walls within me. Suddenly, so much more appears before my eyes. A whole new world.

"Over here are dozens of orange trees. The wind rustles through the leaves, creating a unique melody. The sun peeks through the branches, and the blossoms exude a tempting fragrance." I take a deep breath, savoring the aroma. "We harvest them to make orange blossom water," I add with a contented smile.

He clears his throat. "There's no guesthouse?" he says, his voice hoarse.

No, there's no guesthouse.

Instead, a completely different vision appears before my eyes. So vivid that it takes my breath away.

With Vico by my side, I turn toward the estate, which now lies at some distance from us. I lean against his shoulder and point at the kitchen windows. "There's a floor-to-ceiling glass door. It's open. Can you hear the bustling from the kitchen? Pots clattering, knives tinkling. The smell of ripe tomatoes and roasted onions wafts toward us, accompanied by joyful laughter and friendly words." Yes, that's it, and I'm as certain as ever about the purpose of this place. I see it in dazzling colors before me. "Everyone is there. The whole family," I add reverently.

And there I am. Dancing in a flowy summer dress with flowers in my hair. I'm happy. Because I allow myself to be who I am. Because I've stopped constantly trying to be what others want me to be.

I live for myself.

Life is meant to be enjoyed. Never before have I felt the truth in this sentence so strongly.

This is exactly how it should feel.

And what I see before me must be the future of the estate. I feel it in every fiber of my being. And I'm just as sure I want to be a part of this future.

Chapter 26

Vico

The whole family, I repeat Hanna's words in my mind. And for the first time in so long, the idea no longer feels constricted in my chest.

"Who's there?" I ask, my voice hoarse, my gaze fixed on the estate, trying to envision the same scene Hanna sees in her boundless imagination.

She snuggles closer to me. "Camilla is at the stove. Pietro approaches her from behind and wraps his arms around her. He whispers something in her ear that makes her laugh."

Yes. Imagining that doesn't feel difficult.

"The twins are playing tag. They've grown up. They must be attending kindergarten now. Their full hair bounces with every step. They scream excitedly and almost knock over the chairs around the long dining table."

As she describes it, I vividly see the scene before me. It's like she's painting images in my mind. Images full of love.

"Over there, Alessia and Aurora set the table, and whatever they are whispering about seems to be making Alessia blush. She tries to hide the fire on her cheeks behind her curls, but Aurora has already understood what's going on." A bright giggle escapes Hanna's mouth.

My sisters. That's exactly how they were. Back when Aurora still lived here. How does Hanna know all this?

"Even your father is there," she says suddenly, sounding amazed. "He just entered the room with a dark green bottle in his hand."

Instinctively, I hold my breath. "What does he look like?"

Her mouth curls up at the corners. "Content."

For a moment, my heartbeat stops. Is it possible that what Hanna is imagining could actually happen? Could my father overcome my mother's death? And could the family one day be as happy as they used to be?

"Is there still hope?" I whisper the question that has taken shape directly in my heart. My fingers continue to caress hers.

"Where there is love, there will always be hope." Her answer is filled with such conviction that I don't even have to try to silence my doubts. They no longer exist.

I feel her warmth on my arm. On my hip. And on my leg. Her breath flows calmly. Until now, both of us have been gazing at the estate, but now I turn my head to her. "Where am I?" I dare to ask.

Still looking at the house, her lips form a charming smile. "You're at the sink, washing arugula. Your light blue T-shirt is covered in water stains, and your hair falls into your face."

I am also there. With my family.

In my homeland.

That is… beautiful.

Warmth fills my body, carrying a longing that I never wanted to feel again. But it's there. And I feel where it's pulling me. Gently, I wrap my arm around Hanna's shoulders. "And where are you?" I ask.

For a split second, she freezes, then her gaze slowly shifts to me. The sea in her eyes is stormy, her lips slightly parted. "I'm placing a vase of wildflowers in the center of the table," she whispers almost inaudibly with a tremor in her voice.

She's here. With me.

"The bouquet is beautiful," I say, for I can see it in all its colors before me. The picture she has described to me in the last few minutes is full of possibilities. And what scared me so much two weeks ago, making me want to run away at all costs, suddenly seems to be the answer to all the questions I didn't dare to ask.

Turning Hanna's vision into reality could make me happy.

I draw closer to her. "You are the most wonderful person I have ever met in my life." She alone is the reason I no longer want to run away.

She meets my gaze with a mix of desperation and longing. She tries to say something repeatedly, but no sound comes out.

I wonder if she's also imagining what it would feel like if we kissed. If she also feels the magical pull between us, which seems so much stronger than the real facts that should keep us apart.

Her hand begins to rise, and I know that she will touch my chest any moment now. She will feel how strongly my heart beats, and perhaps, she will even know she is the reason behind it.

"Vico. Hanna. Can you come over here?" Suddenly, someone calls for us.

It's Pietro.

Abruptly, we lift our heads. I remove my arm from her shoulders, and she steps back, fussily adjusting her hiking pants. I don't need to see more to know that she also feels caught.

"Are you both okay?" Pietro shields his eyes from the low sun and glances over at us.

All good, I want to reply, but my throat is so dry that I can't even hear my own croak.

Hanna hurriedly smooths her T-shirt. "We'll be right there," she says, her panicked gaze briefly meeting mine, and then she marches ahead.

I follow her, my legs feeling shaky as I struggle to clear my mind.

We almost kissed.

And I would have liked it.

Twenty yards ahead, Hanna reaches Pietro. His eyes dart between her and me.

I catch up to them and clear my throat, trying to sound as normal as possible. "What's going on?"

"Hanna has a visitor," Pietro responds with a scrutinizing expression.

A visitor? Who could be visiting Hanna here?

Hanna looks confused too as we round the corner of the house. She's walking so fast that I can hardly keep up with her. And then, just before the courtyard comes into view, I see her tense up, every muscle in her body tightening.

Seconds later, I understand why.

Standing by the entrance is a blond man with a full beard, holding an enormous bouquet of red roses.

Chapter 27

Hanna

He brought roses. Now he spreads his arms and smiles at me with excitement.

"Surprise!" he exclaims loudly and walks toward me. Seconds later, I'm in his arms, and he sways me back and forth. The scent of the flowers, which he still holds in his hand, surrounds me. "My God, I missed you so much."

Hearing his words, I have to swallow hard. But even that doesn't help against the guilt that threatens to spread all over me. "And I missed you too," I whisper in a choked voice.

He kisses my cheek and continues forward until our lips touch. Kissing Florian while knowing that Vico is watching feels awful.

I end the kiss as quickly as possible, but I still feel Vico's gaze on my back. I can't stop wondering what he might be thinking at this moment. Maybe because it's easier to think about him than to confront my own feelings.

Florian lovingly brushes my bangs away from my forehead, while scattered thoughts race through my mind. I condemn myself for not being able to enjoy his presence. For being a lousy partner to him and for not being sure anymore if buying the estate is the right decision.

Finally, Florian steps back from me and hands me the bouquet. "I just couldn't stand being without you any longer."

Words fail me, so I nod briefly and turn around. Vico's face is frozen. "Florian, this is Vico," I say, trying to say something. Then I point at Camilla's husband. "And this is Pietro."

"Pietro and I have already been introduced," Florian says as he approaches Vico and casually extends his hand. "Nice to meet you," he says in English, his smile charming, and his posture relaxed.

Vico, on the other hand, seems like an iceberg as he responds to the greeting. "I'd love to stay, but work calls."

"Of course, we have a lot to discuss too," Florian replies, putting his arm around my waist and raising his eyebrows invitingly.

For a moment, tense silence fills the air. I seize the opportunity to cast one last glance at Vico. His expression remains frozen as he shoves his hands into his pockets, turning away with Pietro. He doesn't give me a chance to signal how sorry I am that Florian appeared at this very moment. Who knows what would have transpired behind the house near the field of poppies if we hadn't been interrupted.

It was for the best. This is where it must end before something irreversible occurs.

"Alright then, let's go," Florian exclaims cheerfully, pulling me along with him.

But with each step, unease sets in. I should say something, but chaos reigns within me. "Is Natalie managing the inn on her own?" I blurt out, the first thought that crosses my mind.

His gaze turns sad. "We have no guests tonight. Again."

What? Even though things haven't been going well lately, we usually had a few bookings. "So things are still going downhill." I swallow hard, lowering my gaze. Once again, I feel like the worst person on earth. While I was here in Italy, enjoying life, he has been working for our future.

He lifts his index finger under my chin, forcing me to meet his gaze. "We have a plan. All we need to do now is put it into action."

That's right. I nod in agreement, realizing how absurd my earlier fantasies were. I belong with Florian. We've been a great team for years, and if we stick together, we'll have a wonderful life ahead.

"Show me how far you've come." He looks around eagerly. "The run-down shack looked much better in the pictures," Florian grumbles.

I immediately focus on him. "Yes, the estate is quite dilapidated," I admit, strolling alongside him on the courtyard. "But with some work and love, it will be beautiful again."

He walks over to the outer wall, tapping the stones for inspection. Then he examines the decrepit rain gutter. Although dusk has already set in, the damages are evident. "You didn't tell me about the rust."

Did I not mention it? How could I forget?

"I'm sorry." The urge to make up for my mistake overwhelms me. "The first cost estimates have come in," I quickly say, feeling uneasy about why I'm so eager to justify myself. "And I took new photos."

My backpack is in the car, and I retrieve it, taking out the camera to show him the pictures. But as soon as the display lights up, I realize what a terrible idea that was.

The first photo shows the vineyard.

It's enchantingly beautiful. But it brings a memory that now makes it hard for me to breathe. Right after this picture was taken, I sank into Vico's arms. I leaned against his chest and breathed in his scent.

It was magical.

And wrong.

At no point was that clearer to me than now. Sharing my fear of water with him at Spiaggia bianche was the first mistake. But the moment I allowed him to get so close to me at the vineyard was crucial. It was the beginning of something that currently feels like it can't even be stopped by Florian's presence.

"This is great, Hanna!" Is it astonishment or admiration that I hear in Florian's voice?

Whatever it is, it makes me glow. "I'm still learning, but soon I'll get the hang of it."

He takes the camera from my hand to look at the rest of the pictures. "Is this all?" He frowns and looks back at me. "Just the vineyard? And what's this? A nature park?"

The canyon. I only took two pictures there before I was persuaded to try the zip line, losing myself again.

Florian seems deeply disappointed. My stomach feels heavy.

"It was busy. Camilla had her babies, and Vico…" I trail off.

His puzzled look silences me. "You've been spending time with the family?"

Regretfully, I lower my gaze. Spending time with the Olivettas felt so nice. Have I been too easily swayed by them? Was that wrong? My God, I don't know anything anymore.

"Just to find out more about them," I say quickly, grateful for at least this excuse.

He hands me the camera back. "And?"

Internally, I'm torn apart. If I tell Florian they can't be trusted, he'll reconsider buying the estate. The Olivettas would have a chance to preserve their family legacy. Vico just signaled that he could imagine a life here in Collina da sogno with his family. Or did I imagine it too readily?

"Hanna? Are you daydreaming again?" Florian nudges me.

I would have reacted defensively before, but suddenly, I don't want to. Even though everything else I saw earlier was exaggerated daydreaming, this one thing wasn't. Pretending to be someone I'm not isn't right, so I look him firmly in the eyes. "And if I were?"

For a moment, a deep furrow appears on his forehead, then he waves it off. "So what about the Olivettas? Are they trying to swindle us with a bargain price?" He gestures toward the dilapidated building. "Not that we invest here and never manage to renovate this ruin."

What does his evasive reaction mean? Whatever it is, I won't lie to Florian. Not after everything I've already put him through. "I think they are okay," I say.

Now, he smiles again. "Tomorrow, I'll finally meet the seller in person. Then we can be sure." He reaches for my hand, and we stroll on. "Come on, let's continue exploring together."

Walking beside him, I don't know what to say. I still can't gather clear thoughts. A grueling silence settles between us as I keep stealing glances at him, asking myself questions that shouldn't be hard to answer.

Is Florian the right man for me?

What do I feel for him?

"Don't you even want to know about the progress with the required loans?" he asks with a disappointed look.

"Surely, you have everything under control." I caress his arm. "You always do."

"That's only possible because you have my back," affection shows in his expression. "I love you, Hanna."

I swallow. "And I love you." The words taste strangely sour on my tongue. I don't know if they're true. It could all just be a holiday fling. That's madness! "Tell me about your achievements," I ask him, trying to get rid of this terrible emotional turmoil.

As we approach the decrepit pool, he says, "You'll be impressed because I've pulled out all the stops." A broad grin makes him look mischievous.

While we pass the pool and walk toward the outdoor terrace with overgrown herb beds, he talks about things I barely understand. He speaks of short-term overdraft credits, collateral, and annuity loans. Then he mentions sums and percentages that I understand even less. He talks about repayment premiums and effective annual interest rates. My head spins. A throbbing pain spreads in my temples, and my neck stiffens.

"That sounds amazing," I still say after he finishes his explanation. "You've done a great job."

"One must give everything for their goals," he clenches his fist with a determined expression.

I nod in agreement. My throat is so tight that I can't

say anything more. Despite my migraine attack, I realize once again that I'd be lost without him. He knows the paths we need to take, lovingly takes my hand, and bravely leads the way. I may not know much, but one thing is clear: with Florian by my side, I have a future that I shouldn't risk.

My confused heart rebels.

Suddenly, Florian stops. "What's wrong, Hanna?"

Everything is wrong. But there's nothing I can talk to him about. "You're amazing," I answer, sounding as small as I feel.

Is that how it's supposed to be? Is it right to feel like this in a relationship?

With a gentle look, he strokes my cheek. "But only because I have you by my side."

I give him a timid smile as another realization forms in my thoughts.

He needs me. And I need him. We complement each other; that's the essence of our relationship. It was like that from the beginning, and it was good.

But right now, at this moment, as we stand closely embraced in one of the most beautiful spots of the estate, a sense of doubt creeps up in me. Good alone might not be enough.

Chapter 28

Vico

Throughout the entire walk to Camilla's house, despite Pietro's lively chatter, I can't shake my image of Hanna in Florian's arms. I see her smiling happily, him kissing her cheek and then her lips.

A shiver runs down my spine.

"What do you think? Can we do it this way?" Pietro suddenly asks in a deafening volume.

I turn my head to him. "Hmm?" I reply because I can't remember what he asked of me just now.

He puts his arm around my shoulders. "You seem pretty taken with her."

Taken with her? Me? As unbelievable as it is, he might be right. Nevertheless, I respond with a dismissive gesture. "Nonsense. She's taken, so…"

"Well, the way she was gazing at you behind the house… man, I'm telling you…" He winks at me and playfully punches my side.

So Pietro saw it too. It wasn't just my imagination. There was something between Hanna and me. Something so strong that I was ready to throw all principles out the window.

I wanted to kiss her. And find out if this could be the exact future for both of us that she envisioned in her fantasy.

"Quite possible there's something there," I admit,

and at the same time, I wonder why I'm saying this. "But that's not the point. You saw him. With his ridiculous roses and that silly grin." I hear bitterness in my voice. I'm probably being unfair to Florian, but I can't suppress the nagging jealousy inside me.

We head toward Camilla's bungalow. "Yes, he was there," Pietro unnecessarily confirms, as if I didn't already know what that meant. "But I could swear Hanna didn't look thrilled at all."

"Do you think?" Could that be the truth? I go back in my thoughts to replay the scene. There was something odd about the way she was in his arms. Pietro shrugs. "Sure. She was stiff as a board when he kissed her."

Absentmindedly, I nod. I remember that too. She was tense. Although I could only see her back, I'm certain she didn't feel comfortable. But that's not surprising after what almost happened between us just moments before. "So you think there's no real love involved?"

We enter the entrance area and take off our shoes. "Not a trace, if you ask me," Pietro confirms.

Even if that were the case, it wouldn't change anything. I open the door to the living-kitchen area, but before I can enter, Pietro holds me back.

"What do you have to lose?" he asks insistently.

Everything, is the immediate answer that forms inside me. Has he forgotten how my father vegetated day by day? And there's still my lifestyle, which certainly wouldn't make Hanna happy. Because despite the picturesque image of all of us at the estate for a moment, it's far from reality.

I have a dream that is not only bigger but also more

realistic than that. But I don't tell him that; instead, I shake my head and try to distance myself from him.

In the living-kitchen area, my sisters await me. Camilla, who was discharged from the hospital just yesterday, looks pale. Nonetheless, she fusses with a radiant smile, adjusting the light yellow romper of little Francesca with the dark tuft of hair.

Alessia comes from the kitchen, and suddenly, Aurora appears as well.

Since when is she here?

"Hello, stranger." With an exaggerated grin on her face, Aurora marches toward me.

She has lost weight, I would estimate at least twenty pounds, and that's despite her never being even remotely overweight before. She wears an oversized pair of glasses on her nose, her hair has grown longer, but the wavy tips are still much lighter than the rest. I hug her, feeling her bony shoulder pressing against my armpit. She smells like grappa.

"The prodigal sister has returned, how wonderful," I say affectionately. Although we are all together again for the first time since Mother's death, this meeting has surprisingly little of the bitterness I had feared for years.

"How's the cliff diving?" she wants to know as I release her from the hug. With shaky fingers, she smooths out her wide linen pants. "Are you a star already?"

"Not yet." I give her a mysterious look. "But maybe soon."

She claps her hands. "How exciting! I'm happy for you."

There's something odd about her. I don't remember

her being so hyperactive. I gaze into her eyes, searching her pupils. They're dilated. Is my sister on drugs? Perhaps she's also afraid. But afraid of what?

And that's not all. While Camilla and Alessia take every opportunity to show their sorrow over the sale of the estate, she seems carefree. Each of my sisters burst into tears upon reuniting with me, but she behaves as if she couldn't care less that we're all about to lose our home.

Wait a minute. What am I thinking? And why does it pain my heart?

"Have you seen your adorable nieces?" She turns to Alessia and Camilla, wildly gesticulating, as they each hold one of the babies in their arms. "Aren't they amazing?" Her voice threatens to break. This is not the Aurora I grew up with.

What on earth happened to her?

Again, I study her intensely, but she immediately looks away. "So what do you say?" she asks again.

As much as I hate to admit it, there is indeed something about them that I can't resist even today. I nod in agreement and hurry to the kitchen to get myself a glass of water. Not that someone might think of handing me one of the babies.

"Well, little Stella…" I hear Alessia coo behind me. "With that birthmark, you're destined to become a celebrity. One day, you'll be an actress. Or maybe a TV star."

Joyful laughter fills the room. I turn around and take a look at my family, who radiates so much warmth despite Aurora's strange behavior. Pietro looks at me expectantly.

What do you have to lose?, his eyes ask me again,

while gesturing to his own little family, filled with happiness.

I wish I knew the answer, but I don't.

Perhaps I'll lose everything.

Perhaps nothing.

And maybe, just maybe, I might even gain something.

Chapter 29

Hanna

I take a plate from the drying rack in the sink. The coffee machine gurgles. "Would you like some jam with your biscotti?" I ask Florian, who has settled comfortably on the only chair that doesn't look like it could collapse at any moment.

"Sure," he looks up from his phone. "When will the coffee be ready?"

We're running late; Florian has to leave again in an hour to make it back to Tyrol on time. "It'll be ready in a moment," I reply quickly, setting up two cups. At the same time, I wonder when this automatism between us has set in, where I serve him so naturally.

When was the last time he did something nice for me?

He brought me roses. That was very nice of him. Wasn't it?

I carefully fill the cups. "Can you help me here?" I ask afterward, feeling like a new person. I've never asked him to do anything for me, but if I want to fulfill my intention of living more for myself, that has to change too.

He furrows his brow, looking up from his phone again. I smile at him and gesture to his coffee cup and the plate of biscotti. For a moment, he seems like he doesn't understand the world, but then he gets up from the chair to help me with breakfast. "I really need to talk to Signor Olivetta. Our lawyer found some details in the contract that raised some concerns," he says, sitting back down. "Hopefully, he can speak English."

I have no idea if Vico's father speaks English. Although he supposedly lives at the estate too, I've never met him. Nobody talks about him. He's like a ghost. "Shall I translate for you?"

"I can handle it easily. After all, this Camilla will be there too." He sips the hot brew and grabs a biscotto.

"I understand." I nod convincingly because I do. There's nothing this man can't handle.

Unavoidably, I wonder who wouldn't dream of having such a partner. As I contemplate this, I lean against the rustic kitchen counter with my coffee.

"Besides, I noticed a lot of things are still left on the checklist."

I try to ignore his reproachful tone. Mostly because I'm not sure if it's justified. I have to get everything done within a week and return to help at the inn. So it's fine if he asks about the annoying checklist, right? "I'll get to work right after breakfast."

Florian takes another bite and grunts in approval. Then he jumps up from his chair, causing it to rattle loudly against the stone floor. "I really have to go now. Wish me luck."

"Good luck," I say, doing my best not to think about what his luck means for the Olivettas. "Will we see each other later?"

For a moment, he furrows his brow. "You wanted to get started too. Have you forgotten?"

Right.

I instantly feel foolish. Instinctively, I slap my

forehead with the palm of my hand. "Sorry, I guess I'm not fully awake yet."

He comes closer with a gentle expression, taking my face in his warm hands. "I trust you, Hanna."

"You can," I confirm hastily, just to make myself feel better.

He nods. "I know." His lips find mine briefly, "I'll miss you."

I should say the same in return, but instead, I wave it off. "It's just a few days."

"Still, I can't wait," he says with a soft voice and kisses me again.

"Your appointment," I mumble against his lips. I have this feeling that I should be more affectionate. I should show him how important he is to me and that I can't bear the idea of parting ways in a few seconds. But something inside me resists.

The part of me that unnecessarily keeps thinking about Vico.

"Right," he pulls away. With an inquisitive expression, he strokes my cheek one last time. Does he suspect what I was just thinking? "See you next week. I'll come back here once more. That way, we can spend a few hours together at the estate," he says with such longing that I feel even more ashamed of my uncontrollable feelings.

Florian is a great man. A caring partner and someone I can always rely on. And what am I doing? I question every word and gesture of his. I obsessively try to figure out if we truly belong together.

All because of a man I've only known for two weeks.

It's crazy. And it's completely unfair to Florian.

"Finally, we'll be together every day again," he adds with a joyful expression.

The fact that he clearly has no idea about the turmoil inside me makes my stomach clench even more. "That's great," I reply hastily, forcing a smile on my face.

***

Twenty minutes later, I stand in front of Vico's VW bus, uncertain, shifting my weight from one foot to the other. The look he gave me yesterday before walking away without a word is clearer in my mind than the beauty of the estate surrounding me.

It would be better if I didn't knock on that door. We shouldn't spend any more time together. Yet here I am, staring at the glimmering silver handle of the sliding door in the sunlight.

I couldn't resist. A part of me needs answers. I must find out what exists between us. Perhaps, it's only me who feels it. Maybe it's just an ephemeral spark, ignited by the idyllic surroundings and the vacation ambience.

With a scraping sound, the door begins to move. Vico appears before me, his shoulder-length hair pulled back at the nape. "Hanna," he says, looking at me as if I were a ghost.

I raise my hand. "Hey… uh…" Great, now I'm at a loss for words.

He continues to slide open the door, steps out of the camper, and looks around. "Is he gone?" I can't discern anything from his tone.

I nod briefly, lowering my gaze. As if I didn't

already have enough guilt toward Florian, now I also have feelings bubbling up for Vico. Because I realize that I am not an innocent in our strange situation. Again and again, I have taken a step toward him.

"Good," he responds tersely. "Let's go for a drive."

He's not angry.

If he had feelings for me, he should be, after seeing me with Florian yesterday, right? Perhaps I only imagined that there was a spark between us?

"What are we going to see?" I ask, feeling confused.

His smile makes my knees weak without reason. "I know of something that you'll surely enjoy."

I don't even consider asking what it is. I'm just relieved to be getting away from here. Strolling alone next to Vico while knowing that Florian is nearby feels strange. Even as he sits beside me in the car, and our forearms almost touch, my emotions ride a roller coaster.

Guilt. And longing.

Everything blends together, causing my heartbeat to remain unsteady throughout the entire ride. As usual, Vico doesn't reveal our destination, but unlike before, it doesn't bother me at all. I even feel excited because his surprises have never disappointed me.

Vico fiddles with the radio, and soon Umberto Tozzi's voice fills the speakers. I join in, and with each chorus, I notice the music soothing my inner unrest. It doesn't take long before I'm singing along wholeheartedly.

After an hour's drive, we arrive in a quaint village that exudes a sense of history. Vico grins at me expectantly. "Are you ready?"

I can't help but smile back because, in his presence,

everything seems effortless and uncomplicated. Enjoying life with him comes naturally. And that's what I want. This feeling is too beautiful not to savor. "Absolutely."

We leave the car behind and stroll toward the heart of the village. "This is Pietrasanta, the artistic center of Tuscany," Vico explains along the way.

Two enormous sculptures shaped like faces emerge before us, skillfully arranged beside an ancient olive tree. Their rugged surfaces carry an impressive beauty within. Instantly, a matching melody resonates within me. I sway to the rhythm, letting my gaze roam freely. "Wow, they are magnificent."

"And there are many more," he says, smiling warmly as if he delights in my delight. Then he reaches for my hand, pulling me along.

We venture into an alleyway lined with studios and art workshops. I discover elegantly curved marble sculptures, metal creations seemingly entwined with trees, and graceful stone figures. With each new find, I feel happier. I even allow my imagination to run wild, combining different artworks in my mind and listening to the music they create within me. In my mind's eye, a new world takes shape. Everything feels possible.

With my hand firmly in his, I feel like I'm breathing in this village with its medieval core and majestic architecture. Inspiration fills me in a way I've never experienced before.

"It's wonderful. Thank you for bringing me here," I say, looking up at him, seeing his gentle expression.

His thumb strokes the palm of my hand. "I'm glad you like it."

It would be better if I withdrew my hand. Because

despite everything, I know this isn't right. We shouldn't touch each other anymore until I gain clarity about my confusing feelings. So I gather my resolve and let go of his fingers.

Immediately, he steps back.

Even though I really don't want to talk about it, I feel like I owe Vico an explanation. "I didn't know he was coming."

His worn-out flip-flops snap against the concrete with each step. "It was…"

"…very surprising, you're right," I finish his sentence. "I…" My God, what should I tell Vico?

That I shouldn't have kissed him anyway? That I'm so afraid of getting entangled with him here? We've only known each other for two weeks. That's too short a time to have real feelings, if at all. Besides, I have no idea if his heart races too when we spend time together.

"Why are you with Florian?" He sighs heavily, his hands now firmly tucked into his pockets, and gazes straight ahead at the cathedral we're approaching.

I take a moment because his question isn't easy to answer. Since Florian showed up yesterday, it has already been consuming my thoughts. I haven't reached a conclusion yet.

"When we became a couple, I was eighteen," I start telling him, not only for Vico's sake but also to finally understand what's right and what's wrong.

I see his jaw clench, the muscles tense. "That wasn't my question."

True. Nervously, I fidget with my fingers. "I believe we complement each other well. He always has a plan and knows what we need to do next."

Unchanged, Vico lets me see only his profile. "So he's the boss."

"If you put it that way, it sounds like I have no say, but that…" Suddenly, I can't continue. I can't come up with a single example to prove to Vico that it's definitely not like that. "Florian is just an organized person, which can't be said about me." As I speak the words, I realize I've not only forgotten the stupid checklist in the car but also the camera. How could I let that happen again?

Abruptly, he stops and looks at me intensely. "Yet you have an incredible talent," he says, as if reproaching me for my self-critical words.

Maybe. "A talent that's good for nothing," I reply quickly nonetheless because, in the world we live in, imagination doesn't count. Numbers, facts, ambition—those are the values that truly matter. "If it wasn't for Florian, I would have ended up on the streets. That's the truth." I feel ashamed admitting it, but it's the reality. Without Florian, I would never have made it.

He raises his eyebrows in surprise. "What?"

I nibble on my lower lip and think about how best to explain it to him. Soon, I realize it doesn't matter. If I want to be myself, I don't have to choose my words carefully anymore. I can simply speak my mind.

"When my father passed away, my mother was left alone with two children and a pile of debts. We had enough to eat only because the other villagers supported us," I say, walking again to keep my inner turmoil under control. Still, I immediately feel the shame that accompanied me day by day back then.

Every time I had to leave the house wearing a faded

jacket. Each moment when the owner of the village store handed me a chocolate bar with a pitying smile.

Until then, I had no idea what poverty really felt like. It's not the hunger, nor the cold when the heating only runs on emergency mode. It's the overwhelming feeling of shame that hurts the most.

I clear my throat to push the memory away. "My brother Noah had just finished high school and started working with the mountain rescue team. But his salary wasn't enough, so I had to drop out of school and start an apprenticeship."

"That must have been tough for you," Vico says absentmindedly, hooking his arm with mine.

I shake my head. "School wasn't a pleasant place for me. I was too dreamy, constantly unfocused, forgot my homework, and mathematics felt like being trapped in a hall of mirrors." I wasn't made for that world. "I couldn't believe my luck when I found an apprenticeship at a nursery."

A smile flickers on Vico's face. "I can imagine. There, your creative flair must have been highly appreciated, and you could blossom."

If he only knew… For a fraction of a second, the furious face of my former boss appears, returning the bouquet I had arranged because it wasn't exactly as she demanded. "It was more like paint-by-numbers," I reply sadly, but that's not the point now. "I didn't complete the apprenticeship."

"Because you didn't enjoy it?"

I could never afford that luxury. "Bankruptcy," I say absentmindedly. "I was seventeen and more or less on the streets." Of course, I could have stayed with Noah, but that wouldn't have been a long-term solution. "The village where I grew up is small. I tried to find another job, but… well… people knew me. They knew that…" That I'm Hanna Daydreamer. No one wants to hire someone like that.

We pass by the imposing bronze statues in front of a museum, but not even they can distract me.

"Florian took me in," I finally blurt out, not wanting to delve into the circumstances of my job search. He was so good to me, so selfless and generous; I will never forget it. "At first, I worked as a chambermaid at the guesthouse. But over time, we grew closer, and… well, we became a couple." I hear myself, and it doesn't sound convincing at all. But that's how it happened. It came slowly, without much emotional upheaval. Does that make it any less valuable?

For a moment, Vico hesitates, as if he has to overcome something in his mind before he speaks. "Do you love him?"

By now, I know I can't answer that question with certainty. What does love feel like? What makes true love? What Florian and I have is good. And I should be grateful to have him by my side. Even if the idea of intense passion has always seemed romantic to me, it's not a necessary condition to build a life together. True love is ultimately just wishful thinking. Or is it?

My heart rebels against this rational thought.

"What is love?" I ask softly. "Feeling safe? Always being able to rely on each other? Or is it something more? Something that goes beyond that?"

Could love possibly be that overwhelming feeling that changes everything?

In search of an answer, I look at Vico. And I see a mixture of panic and longing in his eyes.

"What is love?" I repeat once more, pressing for an answer, not knowing what I really want to hear from him.

He opens his mouth, hesitates, exhales shakily, and begins again. But just as he's about to speak, my phone rings loudly, and his lips close again.

Chapter 30

Vico

"Florian," terror is written all over Hanna's face.

She looks at me, and the phone keeps ringing incessantly. I don't know whether I should be relieved or not about this interruption because I was just about to answer Hanna's question.

What is love?

It's when you can't imagine spending the rest of your life without the other person. That's what I would have said. Yet it felt like I was giving her my heart even before speaking those words. I've protected it for so long, built walls around it, and done everything to ensure it's never breached. But now there's her, with her boundless passion for colors, shapes, and music, and the way she finds beauty even in the most run-down buildings.

With her finger hovering over the phone display, Hanna looks at me as if waiting for my approval. But I can't give it to her. At the same time, I can't ask her not to take the call.

The sparkle in her eyes disappears. "I have to answer it."

Yes, she probably has to.

I watch as she brings the phone to her ear and greets Florian. She listens for a moment, then smiles gently.

Nothing has ever felt so wrong as standing here,

watching Hanna exchange affection with her partner. And there couldn't be a clearer sign that Pietro was off track. Moreover, after Hanna's story, I now know how strong the bond between the two of them is. Much stronger than I thought. And too strong for me to come between them.

Hanna alternates between listening attentively and speaking in a serious tone. She nods constantly, sometimes raising her hand reassuringly as if trying to calm Florian down.

I have no idea what they are talking about.

"Okay," she says now, followed by a few words that carry such a loving undertone that I can't bear it any longer. I turn away, take out my own phone from my pocket, and check my emails.

A message from my trainer Matteo catches my attention. *You won't believe this*, it reads.

Of course, I immediately open the message.

The talent scout has reached out. He wants to work with me. And he's even offering me a sponsorship!

I stare at my phone in disbelief, then read the message again. And again. It takes me a while to realize what this means.

My dream of a career as a cliff diver can actually come true!

I can finally do what I love the most. In a professional environment and with the help of a team from the sponsor that I can use. Physiotherapists, fitness trainers, and mental coaches would all help me take my sport to the next level. And on top of that, I'll be receiving a salary, so I no longer have to take customer assignments and can focus solely on my career.

I feel a wide grin forming on my face. It's as if the sun shines even brighter now, and the marble of the sculptures gleams even whiter.

"Yes!" I do a little jump for joy.

Automatically, I look at Hanna. I want to share my excitement with her, but she's still on the phone.

"Mm-hmm," she says now, her gaze flickering to me. She signals that she'll be done soon.

I observe her, and with every passing minute, my enthusiasm about the sponsorship fades. Because I realize that going back to the cliffs of the world also means never seeing Hanna again.

Do I want that?

As I contemplate, she turns her head to the side, and I can only see her phone. Still, I hear what she says. And this time, I understand it. "I love you too."

She loves him. I'm about to throw up. Just a moment ago, she lulled me into believing she didn't know what love was. And now, two seconds later, she's whispering love vows to her Florian?

Swallowing hard, I turn to the ceramic workshop's display window, pretending to be interested in the pieces. But they can't distract me.

"Sorry," Hanna says in Italian behind me. Her hand touches my arm.

With my heart pounding, I turn around. "No problem."

Of course, she doesn't buy into my facade. I can clearly see that in her eyes as she studies me intently. "He was surprised that mainly Camilla was handling the contract negotiation ... ah, it doesn't matter," she says then with a troubled expression. For a moment, it seems as if this topic is causing her stomachache.

I don't understand this woman. Sometimes we are so close that I feel letting her go would be the biggest mistake of my life. A moment later, she behaves so strangely that I don't know if I'm just imagining all of this.

"Where were we?" she asks now, forcing a smile.

I shrug irritably. "We wanted to see more art studios," I reply, because I can't possibly bring up the question about the essence of love from before.

Suddenly, her smile fades, replaced by a resigned expression. "Right, that's what we wanted." With those words, she turns around and heads toward the nearest alley.

Once again, I look at the message on my phone. The decision is clear; I have to accept the offer. Not everyone gets such a chance. If I don't seize it now, it won't come again.

Still, I hesitate to reply. It's madness, as there is no reason for it. Just a moment ago, I learned that Hanna will never leave Florian. Whatever spark I felt between us was only in my own heart. And there's still my father's irreparably broken heart, which stands as a monument over my life. I promised myself a long time ago that I wouldn't end up like him.

Everything goes against holding on to this fascinating woman with sea-green eyes, and there's nothing in favor of it. Nothing, except my seemingly untameable feelings.

Chapter 31

Hanna

Yawning, I enter my bedroom at the estate and head straight for the wardrobe. I feel a bit like I'm being controlled remotely, as I clumsily put on jeans and a T-shirt. My thoughts no longer come to a halt, even at night, robbing me of sleep.

Yesterday, on our way to Pietrasanta, Vico and I sang louder and laughed more as we moved farther away from the estate. But on the way back, he became unusually quiet.

And I didn't know what to say either.

A faint pounding in my temples makes itself known. It's as if my numerous thoughts just don't have enough space up there.

Sighing, I turn around and lean against the windowsill. I attempt a breathing exercise, but it doesn't help. Especially when my gaze falls on Florian's bouquet on the nightstand. The roses smell so wonderful that I can even sense it from here. The flower heads are huge; the bouquet must have cost a fortune.

I step closer to the flowers and let my fingers glide along the edge of a petal. As I do, I notice a piece of paper that wasn't there yesterday. Carefully, I pull it out.

Without you, only half of me is here. I can't wait to start our new future together. With love, Florian, it reads in Florian's scrawled handwriting.

Lost in thought, I turn Florian's message in my hands. It's a bit strange that he's suddenly so romantic. Maybe I should have gone away alone much earlier to give him the opportunity to miss me. His friendly face appears in my mind.

He is a wonderful partner.

Vico, on the other hand, is unpredictable. His love for freedom and his willingness to take risks have something exotic and alluring, but in the end, nothing he does will likely last.

Stop.

I shouldn't compare the two. It's not fair to either of them. After all, I've never spent as much time with Florian, completely free from everyday life, while with Vico, I haven't experienced a single second of everyday life.

The pounding in my head turns into a throbbing pain, accompanied by a shrill ringing in my right ear. I need to take a migraine pill quickly if I don't want to lie helplessly in bed today. I reach for the water bottle on the dresser and take out my medication from my handbag. To be safe, I take a double dose. After all, I only have five days left.

Then I have to go back.

Back to Tyrol. Back to my other life.

A pang of melancholy rises within me, but I don't want to allow it. My old life doesn't exist anymore. Even when work takes me back soon, I'll do everything to savor my time there. And who knows, doing it together with Florian could take our relationship to a new level. From good to great.

I reach for the never-ending checklist to see what's left to do. None of the open points are appealing to me. I'd much rather find out where the day takes me and do what I feel like doing.

Experience a little bit of the freedom that Vico adores so much.

A bit of *everything is possible*.

My thoughts involuntarily wander back to my zip line adventure and the liberating feeling I had. Maybe Vico isn't the reason for my confusing emotions. Perhaps it's my newfound outlook on life that makes me feel like I can soar?

The idea brings a smile to my face. If that's true, it would mean I hold my own happiness in my hands. Before I can delve deeper into this thought, someone knocks on the bedroom door.

Vico peeks in. "What's on the agenda for today?" he asks in a controlled tone, nodding toward my checklist.

I can't help but scrunch my nose. "Ugh, that annoying thing."

Suddenly, his expression changes, becoming relaxed and curious. "I don't like it either," he says with a wink, casually leaning against the dresser beside me. "But you have to tick those boxes, no way around it, right?"

Can he be serious? Ever since he saw Florian's instructions, he's been eyeing them as if they were poisoned. And now he's reminding me of their importance? "Are you drunk?" I blurt out.

His laughter brings back the lightness that I hadn't seen since my phone call with Florian yesterday. "Certo che no!" he says, playfully offended. "But it seems like you've taken something."

"Just migraine pills, nothing else." I grin, simply

because he's smiling at me. And I can feel that I can hardly resist the exuberance engulfing me right now. With enthusiasm, I toss the checklist onto the bed, and suddenly, my headache vanishes like a puff of smoke. "Let's do something exciting," I say on a whim, finding the idea splendid.

Who knows how quickly I'll have this opportunity again once I'm trapped in the routine of work. Only five days left.

"Ooookay." His expression is so delightfully bewildered that I burst into laughter. "Whatever you have in mind, count me in."

I tap my finger against my lips, gazing thoughtfully up at the ceiling. "Of course, it shouldn't be dangerous," I say.

"Of course not," he lovingly mimics me.

"But a little adrenaline would be nice," I continue, fixing my gaze on him. I'm so curious about his reaction that I can feel my own excitement building.

He looks like he's just seen a ghost. It takes a few seconds before he tilts his head to the side. "Would a bit of freedom also be welcome?"

Oh yes, absolutely. I nod decisively, pleased to note that my mother's voice inside me falls silent. "Even a little bit more."

"Come with me." He grins, taking my hand and leading me out of the room. The checklist stays where it is. And I won't need the camera either.

Not today. Today belongs solely to me.

Hand in hand, we walk across the courtyard and then farther to Camilla's house. As we did almost two weeks ago, Vico opens the garden gate, and the gleaming red Vespa beckons me with its headlights.

He steps up to the scooter, patting the creamy leather seat. "Not too dangerous, a little adrenaline, and lots of freedom. Can't get any better than that." I can tell from his expression that he doesn't believe I'll actually do it.

I take a step closer. "Me behind you?"

"Each on their own steed." There's a mischievous spark in his eyes. "We'll ride toward the sun and see where it takes us."

Admittedly, it sounds tempting. And why not? For as long as I can remember, I've denied myself any fun, afraid of taking risks. But millions of people ride scooters every day; it's probably no more dangerous than driving a car. And I drive a car too. If I'm careful, nothing can go wrong.

I glance back and forth between Vico and the Vespa. "Toward the sun?"

He nods, his legs fidgeting with excitement.

I feel my cheeks flush, and my heart already pounds. Adrenaline courses through my veins, sending tingles up my spine. "What are we waiting for, then?" I can barely contain my laughter at his incredulous stare as I approach the Vespa. "Come on. Show me how it works."

Wholly focused on me, he circles the scooter and stands beside me. "Who are you?" he asks, looking into my eyes. Searching. And so lovingly that my stomach flutters.

Instantly, my laughter subsides, making room for a different feeling I shouldn't be having.

Longing.

"How were your words at Spiaggia bianche again?" My voice sounds shaky, almost trembling. But not because I'm afraid of riding the Vespa. And I think I can see in Vico's gaze that he understands that too. "If I never allow myself to do something outside of my comfort zone, I risk missing out on so much."

He reaches out his hand as if to stroke my cheek. But when he's so close that he almost touches me, he abruptly pulls back. "That's absolutely true," he replies, then swallows hard. "Perhaps the very walls we've built to protect ourselves sometimes keep us from being happy."

Suddenly, it's as if time stands still between us. And I'm certain we're no longer talking about me riding a Vespa. Perhaps it's no longer about me at all. It's about him. About his wound.

"Maybe," I whisper breathlessly. "But what if we take the sledgehammer and tear them down? What if we do what our hearts tell us?" What if we give in and see where it leads?

"Anything could happen." His chest rises and falls rapidly. There's an almost pleading expression on his angular face. It's as if he's wrestling with himself.

I can't bear this. Being so close to him, seeing his lips twist into a pained smile, and feeling what lies deep in my heart.

"We should…" I force my eyelids down, dry my sweaty palms on my jeans, and create distance between us.

Nervously, he fiddles with his hair. "You go first."

With a strange mix of relief and melancholy, I take the helmet from the scooter and put it on. Then I push the Vespa off its stand, swing my leg over the saddle, and test what I need to do to maintain balance. Vico watches my attempts, gives me some tips, and finally shows me how to start the engine. As soon as the machine hums beneath me, the tension that had just built up so menacingly between us vanishes like smoke. Excitement wells up inside me. And also a bit of fear. Yet I'm certain that I want to do it.

I want to be reckless. Wild. And free. Just this once.

Carefully, I accelerate. My legs extend to the sides so I can steady myself at any moment, and I roll forward. I'm going so slowly that Vico can walk beside me. His presence, knowing that he's there to catch me if needed, gives me so much security that I dare to increase my speed.

Soon, the cool breeze brushes over my skin. My hair and my T-shirt flutter backward. I steer the Vespa onto the entrance road. In the rearview mirror, I see Vico following me on the other scooter. He gives me a thumbs-up.

Everything is fine, he wants to tell me with that gesture.

And he is absolutely right. It's going well. It feels good. It is good.

I turn onto the smooth country road. It lies straight before me, without potholes or bumps.

It's time. Here we go.

Confidently, I twist the throttle, the engine beneath me roars, and a few seconds later, I'm seized by a rush so powerful that I can't resist. My smile widens, and a strong sensation fills my chest. It's as if I can breathe properly for the first time.

I let out a joyous cry. I cheer, soaking in the freedom, scaling the walls of fear, and glimpsing the world that opens up beyond.

Golden rays break through the cloud cover, the

scent of deep violet lavender fields now in bloom permeates me. The wind cools my heated skin, and the motor's vibrations send tingles through my body. I savor every second.

I let go of my worries. And nothing has ever felt like this before.

The world around me spins. Shimmering dots dance before my eyes. More and more of them appear in my field of vision, each carrying the colors of the rainbow.

Suddenly, I can barely see anything else but the iridescent spots. My senses shut down one by one. I forget which way is up or down; I no longer smell or taste anything.

My jubilation turns into a shrill scream. The scooter sways like a ship on stormy seas.

In panic, I clutch the handlebars tightly.

The world turns blue-gray.

Like storm clouds.

They're everywhere.

A bright bolt of lightning flashes. It rushes toward me.

And eventually strikes me right in the head.

A scorching heat runs through my body. My hands burst into flames and can no longer hold the handlebars.

Thunder roars deafeningly.

Then a dark silence engulfs me.

Chapter 32

Vico

Huddled on the sofa in Camilla's living room, I hide my face in my hands. After fleeing directly from the hospital to here, I only found Alessia. Camilla is at a checkup appointment with the girls, and it seems that Aurora went jogging three hours ago and hasn't returned yet.

As I so often do, I let out a heavy sigh. "My God, why didn't I stop Hanna?"

Alessia sets a glass of grappa in front of me. Then she sits next to me and wraps her arm around my shoulders. "Blaming yourself won't change anything."

Distraught, I look at her. "She had to go to the hospital. Because of me!"

I still can't believe it. I don't understand how she could crash the scooter on a perfectly paved road. But she did. And I didn't protect her.

"Did you force her to go on the joyride?" My little sister's gentle tone doesn't make things any better. She shouldn't be downplaying this. It's damn serious.

Silently, I shake my head. Yet I shouldn't have handed her the scooter so carelessly.

"You see," Alessia says firmly, "she's a grown woman. It was her decision."

It's not that simple. My stupid talk about leaving the comfort zone and enjoying the adrenaline rush was

216

what even got her thinking about trying it. "I am to blame. Me, alone."

She lays her head on my shoulder, her thick curls falling over my chest down to my belly. "You said she only broke her arm. Nothing else."

I spring up from the sofa. "But that's not the point. It's about what could have happened!" And not just in terms of a serious injury. No. Hanna's accident has shown me even more clearly how quickly we can lose someone. Every breath could be our last, and we don't even need to have a brain tumor for that.

I pace back and forth in the kitchen-living room, passing by the wooden table where we've sat so many times, never fully aware of our mortality. Heading to the floor-to-ceiling window, we constantly look outside without realizing that we might be seeing the view for the last time.

"Vico, this won't help if you beat yourself up like this." Alessia's tone urges me to pull myself together, but at least she doesn't try to follow me. From the blue checkered sofa, she stares at me.

I shake my head. "How could I ever do anything else?" I ask, my voice barely audible, and I strike the wall.

This morning, I could have lost Hanna. And that, without ever truly having her for myself.

Our lips have never touched. I've never opened my eyes in the morning and looked directly into her beautiful face. Yet the thought of something happening to her makes the walls around my heart, which were already close to collapsing, grow once again.

It is better to never have loved than to lose love.

That was true then. It is true now and will always be

true. I need to be free. That alone will make me happy in the long run.

Instantly, I feel my heart rebel. It longs for Hanna, wants to hear her bright laughter and smell the flowery scent of her hair. It wants to discover how her lips taste and how her skin feels close to mine.

"This is not just about the accident." Alessia sounds surprised. "It's more than that, isn't it?" I see her rising from the sofa in my peripheral vision. She never takes her eyes off me as she approaches. "What is there between you and Hanna?"

"Nothing." Oh God, even I can hear the lack of conviction in my voice. That's enough for me to know that, despite everything, I won't be able to stay away from her.

She is taken. And now, she had an accident that could have cost her life.

There couldn't be a clearer sign. What else has to happen for me to finally realize this is going nowhere?

Alessia stands close to my side and rests her head on my shoulder. "Mm-hmm," she says absentmindedly. "Nothing. I understand."

Her words fade into the silence between us. Together, we look out the window. Where now, a flock of birds crosses the sky with so much ease, as if nothing could harm them.

Chapter 33

Hanna

My head feels muffled, yet I'm aware of the insistent throbbing. But that's not what worries me. It's the cast enveloping my forearm.

I wish I could slap myself. What the hell got into me that I threw all safety concerns out the window like that?

It was clear that something would happen, I hear my mother's worried voice in my head. *You need to take better care of yourself. Better safe than sorry. Have you forgotten that already?*

In my imagination, I see her looking at me intently. Tears well up in her eyes, and I feel ashamed for causing her such distress. To rid myself of this awful feeling, I let my gaze wander through the treatment room in the present moment.

I'm alone. The doctor who tended to my scrapes and casted my arm disappeared long ago. So has Vico, after apologizing to me countless times, even though it wasn't his fault at all.

Breathing heavily, I touch the smooth surface of the cast. I should have called Florian by now to inform him about my accident. After all, he's my partner. He deserves to know if something happens to me.

Yet I haven't even taken my phone from the backpack sitting next to my treatment chair. It could have been damaged in the fall, but it wasn't. Vico triple-checked it to ensure I could safely call him to pick me up once I'm done here.

Why am I hesitating?

I have to do it. I have to inform Florian. Instead, I keep imagining how he'll react to my call.

Worried? Upset? Maybe even both?

Even if he were disappointed, he would have every right to be. Riding the Vespa was a huge mistake. Not only did I jeopardize my health, but the cast also limits my ability to function fully. The doctor told me I have to wear it for at least four weeks.

Four weeks! How am I going to manage that?

Exactly, that's what Florian will ask. And I won't have an answer for him. What could I possibly say? That I forgot about myself and everything that should matter to me while he's busting his ass at home to secure a safe future for us?

My situation couldn't be more apparent. With each step I've taken here in Tuscany, I've dug myself deeper.

Dammit.

Dammit. Dammit. Dammit.

"Hanna Lackner?"

A gray-haired lady in a white lab coat stands before me. In her hand, she holds a medical file, and her loosely tied hair frames a pair of glasses. The golden glasses chain sways gently beside her cheeks.

I sit up. "Can I be discharged?"

"First, I have a few questions," she replies, pulling a white-covered stool closer and opening the file with my data. I notice a questionnaire. "Can you tell me how the accident happened?"

I try to think about her question, but I can only

recall a few fragments of memories. The road was completely flat. No curves. No dirt on the pavement. But there was something else. "I saw glowing dots, as if sunlight was passing through a lens."

She checks a box on her form. "Do you often experience headaches?"

How does she know that? "Migraines," I confirm. "But I've had them my whole life."

As if I gave her the exact answer she wanted, she nods knowingly. "What about perception disturbances?"

What does she mean?

Apparently noticing my puzzled expression, she starts to explain. "Do you sometimes see things blurred? Or hear high-pitched sounds?"

Restlessness begins to rise within me. I don't like this interrogation. And even less the fact that her questions are so precise. "What does that have to do with my broken arm?"

"Nothing." She shrugs. "But it could have something to do with your accident."

What does she mean by that? My accident is the result of my selfish and reckless behavior. Nothing more.

With a caring expression, she puts the medical file aside. "I'd like to run a few tests. Would that be okay?"

I'm not sure. What's the purpose of these tests?

"Don't worry, you won't experience any pain," she reassures.

"And after that, I can be discharged?" I try to muster a smile, and she nods in agreement. "Alright. Go ahead and run the tests," I confirm. The sooner I get them done, the sooner I can leave this place.

221

Minutes later, she places a cap on my head, with more cables attached to it than I can count. "This is an EEG; it measures your brain activity," she explains, plugging the loose ends of the cables into a device. "Just relax. If you'd like, you can close your eyes."

No, I don't want to. I'd rather stay awake if she's going to look into my head. I already felt uncomfortable in the MRI machine earlier, and now I feel a sense of unease again. "What's wrong with my brain?"

Her gentle smile is probably meant to reassure me, but it doesn't. "First, we'll conduct this test and a few additional ones, then we'll see from there."

She checks the fit of the cap once more and presses some buttons on the device. "I'll be back in five minutes, and then we can begin. If you need anything, press the call button." She points at the red switch on the wall.

That's very considerate, but it's not what's preoccupying me right now. My head isn't being examined for fun. She suspects an illness. Perhaps even something serious.

But I can't be sick. I don't want anyone to take care of me, and I still have a task to accomplish.

The cast on my arm is already frustrating enough, but what if there's more?

Panic rises within me, but I try not to show it. With lips pressed together, I nod, and the doctor leaves the room. As soon as the door closes behind her, all I can hear is the pounding of my heart.

Chapter 34

Vico

I hate this library. And I hate the way my father sits day after day, staring into nothingness in his worn-out leather chair. Only when Hanna visited the room, he wasn't here, and I can only guess why.

"Camilla and Alessia have gone to so much trouble," I say this sentence not for the first time in the past fifteen minutes.

As countless times before, he shakes his head. His thin hair rises and falls like feathers in the wind. "There's nothing to celebrate."

I stand directly in front of him and look at him intently. "It can't go on like this," I say seriously, lowering myself to a crouch. "Today is your birthday. Your daughters want to do something nice for you." And they specifically sent me to bring him to the celebration. They knew it would be a challenge.

"And you? What about you?" he asks stubbornly, like a child.

Even if I wanted to suppress my sigh, it would escape my lips now. I even postponed the deadline for a customer project to have time for him today. "Don't be so stubborn. Of course, we all want to celebrate with you. It's your fifty-fifth birthday after all. Camilla has invited half the village." Everyone who knows my father will come.

"Pfff," he responds weakly as if it doesn't matter to him at all that his daughter is making such an effort for him.

Another proof that he's already dead inside. "Your sweet little granddaughters will be there too." I force myself to smile at him. If his children can no longer reach his heart, maybe they can, at least the two of them.

Indeed, his eyes light up for a split second.

Finally. A first sign that I might still be able to fulfill my mission to Camilla's satisfaction.

"But they won't stay long. So we should hurry," I wink at him.

He drums his fingers on the armrest. "Is Aurora there too?"

He's asking the wrong question.

"She had to urgently return to France. An emergency at work," at least that's what she claimed when Camilla invited her to the celebration. But something about her was strange. The panic in her eyes, the nervous twitching of her bony fingers. As if she were afraid, yet I couldn't think of a single thing that could be the reason for it. "But Hanna will come. You should meet her anyway; today, you'll have the opportunity," I quickly add, trying to revive the little spark of life in my father's expression.

"Camilla and I spoke with her partner last week. I know enough. I don't need to know anything about her," he breathes out, devoid of strength.

My God, this can't be real.

I can bear his ignorance toward his own children, every heartbeat for him is sorrow, every breath is pain. But Hanna doesn't deserve such treatment. "You're missing the chance to get to know a wonderful person," I say.

"Wonderful people are dying." Doggedness spreads across his face, he clenches his fists.

Yes. That's exactly what I need right now. Thank you, dear Father, for reminding me as if my inner conflict wasn't already overwhelming enough.

Hanna's words suddenly echo in my mind. *I wouldn't want to miss the beautiful memories for anything in the world*, she said to me just before we looked through the family album. She sounded so certain, as if that were the only right way to deal with the death of a loved one.

For a moment, I thought it could actually be true. But now, seeing my father huddled, pale, and disheveled in his chair, staring into nothingness, I'm no longer sure. These beautiful memories are the ones robbing him of joy. For him, it would be better to forget what happened.

I grab his arm and pull him up. "Let's review the facts: I am not leaving this room without you. Your family and friends will never forgive you if you don't show up at your own celebration. You have two healthy arms and two healthy legs, so you are capable of dressing appropriately and coming with me." I feel a bit like a father, giving his son a stern lecture.

At least my words have an effect. Without resistance, he turns away and shuffles toward the old desk, where I've placed the freshly washed clothes that Camilla gave me for him. Once there, he lets out a heavy sigh, then looks at me. I nod, and he slowly unzips his shirt.

I should feel good about this, as I managed to break

him out of his routine. However, I already sense that the celebration could turn into a disaster. Despite everyone's efforts to make him happy.

Patiently, I wait until he changes into the clothes and combs his thinning hair, interspersed with gray streaks. Then we set off toward the village in my VW bus, which I'll use to drive him to the celebration.

The guests are eagerly awaiting us. Even before I park the car, they wave at us through the windshield from outside the restaurant.

"See? Everyone has come to spend a lovely time with you," I say to my father, who has been staring out of the window motionlessly throughout the ride.

I get no response, so I sigh and steer the car toward the parking lot. As soon as we step out, applause erupts from the guests. Joyful cheers and congratulations fill the mild evening air. Suddenly, music starts playing as well. I spot a band on a small stage just outside the restaurant, playing a fanfare.

With my arm linked with my father's, I scan the faces of the guests. There are, of course, my sisters and Pietro, Adriano with his family whom I've only seen in photos, and several of our former seasonal workers from long ago. I spot Maria, the owner of the specialty shop, and Michele, the owner of the restaurant where we're celebrating tonight. Behind him stand our neighbors and a dozen men around my father's age whom I don't know. They must be friends from the past, maybe from school. Their faces barely register in my vision. In truth, I barely see them, as I am only searching for one person: Hanna.

She had said she would call me so I could pick her up from the hospital, but my phone hasn't rung all afternoon. And I haven't dared to reach out to her; after all, I've already made enough mistakes.

Over there, next to a tall jasmine shrub, I find her. A few white blossoms have become entwined in her dark hair. She gazes into the distance, but today, I cannot discern the dreaminess that usually fills her expression.

She appears lost, as if she doesn't know why she's here.

Keeping her in my sights, I guide my father over to Camilla. "Here we are," I say, pretending to wipe sweat from my forehead, as if the effort of bringing him here has taken a toll on me.

Immediately, my sister embraces him. "It's so wonderful to have you here. We are all very happy," she says, looking at me over his shoulder. Her eyes glisten with unshed tears.

I nod at her and then turn away. Not only because of the fear brewing inside me, that this celebration could ultimately push my father deeper into his dark pit, but also because of Hanna.

And the way she's currently talking to Alessia. They're laughing together, and Hanna places her hand on Alessia's arm. They look like friends, and anyone would believe they're having a great time together.

But even from here, I can tell that's not the case. There's a heaviness in Hanna's eyes that her forced smile can't conceal. Alessia seems oblivious, chatting nonstop, laughing, and making funny faces.

Perhaps she's just sad about leaving us soon. More than once, I noticed how much she's fallen in love with the authenticity of the estate. Initially, she spoke about her renovation plans, but lately, she's been talking only about how to preserve our family traditions. The way she interacts so intimately with my sisters makes it seem as if she's already become part of this family in such a short time. Yes, that could be the reason for her sadness.

Or perhaps her smile is strained because she is deeply disappointed in me. We both know that her accident would never have happened if I hadn't encouraged her to step out of her safe shell. I need to talk to her about it, apologize again, and see if there's any way to make amends.

Swallowing hard, I march toward them. "Hello." My voice sounds hoarse.

Instantly, the two fall silent, and Alessia takes a sip of the red wine in her hand. "Oh, look, there's Laura over there. Haven't seen her in ages," she says, shooting me a meaningful look. "Be right back," she chirps and dashes off, her hair flowing behind her.

I briefly watch her go before turning my attention to Hanna. She immediately lowers her gaze.

I know it's my turn to say something, but I struggle to find the right words. Nervously, I shift from one foot to the other. "I'm so sorry."

She raises her hand with a tired smile. "We've already discussed that. There's nothing for you to apologize for. Riding the Vespa was solely my decision. And you were far away from me when I had the accident. You had nothing to do with either."

That's not true. And we both know it. But the way she defends her perspective so vehemently tells me I shouldn't press further.

She attempts another smile. Maybe she's just as unsure of what to say next as I am?

"Florian must have been completely shocked." I

228

have no idea why I bring up the man who is fortunate enough to have Hanna by his side. Maybe to punish myself. Because I couldn't care less about what her boyfriend thinks.

She presses her lips together.

"What happens now?" I don't want to ask this question, but I must.

We had four whole days left before our time together in Italy would have ended. Four days during which I wanted to find out what's between us, something that clearly cannot be controlled. And who knows, maybe we would have discovered an entirely new future for ourselves. One where we wake up next to each other every day. One where we live here together and work on the estate.

Despite the fear that overwhelms me just thinking about it, I also feel the longing for this entirely new life we could lead. One of inner contentment and love.

Suddenly, she looks at me. There's pleading in her eyes. "I don't know."

The cheerful music starts playing beside us, and some guests joyfully dance. "Will you stay?" I ask, my voice strained.

"I don't know." Her forehead seems to consist of nothing but wrinkles.

I can't help it; I have to approach her. "What's wrong, Hanna? Something's not right, I can tell. And if you're not angry with me about the accident, as you've said, something else must be troubling you. Please, tell me."

Chapter 35

Hanna

Cheerful music, boisterous conversations, and children's laughter surround us. Everyone around us seems happy, but we are not. A bittersweet melancholy lingers between us.

I should tell him, even if I can't fully grasp it myself. Since I was discharged from the hospital today, I can hardly think straight.

"No matter what it is, I'm here for you," Vico says now, even more earnestly and lovingly.

With tightly pressed lips, I turn away. I can't look into his eyes, let alone his longing face. Whatever this is between us, it's wrong. At least I've figured that out by now. I brush my bangs aside.

Suddenly, I feel his cheek against mine. His three-day beard tickles my skin, his scent enveloping me. "If you want to stay… not just until Tuesday… but for…"

His hot breath brushes against my ear, sending a whole wave of emotions flooding through my body. He doesn't need to finish the sentence; I know what he wants to say.

Swallowing hard, I take a step back. "I can't." My voice croaks.

His forehead furrows. "Because of Florian?"

He is a significant reason, that's true. Florian is good

for me and being with him feels right. But he's not the only reason. "Partly," I reply honestly.

"Because of me?" Once again, he looks as if he wants to shoulder the blame for my accident. But he doesn't have to.

Because by now, I know that my Vespa crash was nobody's fault. I haven't done anything wrong except for getting on that thing and believing that life was only meant for enjoyment.

"Don't make it so hard for me, Hanna," he pleads in a tone that gives me goose bumps.

I have to tell him. Because regardless of how he reacts, one fact remains unchanged. Whatever is hanging in the air between us, sometimes seeming like a shimmering soap bubble, so close within reach, it has nothing to do with reality. Not yesterday, not today, and certainly not tomorrow.

To feel a bit stronger, I clench my fists. "I'm sick." It's unbelievable that I've spoken those words. Just three weeks ago, I wouldn't have had the courage to tell anyone that I wasn't doing well. I would have been too worried about burdening others or risking them thinking poorly of me. But now I stand here, looking Vico firmly in the eye, and say it. "I have epilepsy."

Confused, he tilts his head to the side. It takes several seconds for him to grasp the extent of my illness. That the migraines I've been dealing with my entire life are not just headaches. That the ringing in my ears and double vision are the result of misfires in my brain.

"The doctor explained it to me today, and even though I barely understand medical terms in Italian, I got the gist of it. Not every epileptic seizure is automatically a convulsive one. So far, apparently, I've only had small ones—she called them focal seizures—that affected only a part of my brain. But it's not ruled out that one day, it might be different." And a seizure—no matter what kind—can mean my death at the wrong moment. Just like this morning during our Vespa ride. And like that time when I almost drowned in the lake while swimming.

I'm sure he understands. Nevertheless, he doesn't react. His silence drives me crazy. He tries to say something, but no words come out.

I, too, don't know what else to say. I have a thousand thoughts inside me, and I can't catch one. As I look into his eyes, the only thing I know is that it's no longer about the life I dream of but about what life is even possible for me.

I have to take care of myself and figure out what triggers my seizures so I can learn to cope with them. There are things I won't be able to do anymore. Even if the doctor couldn't tell me what those are, she made it very clear that the diagnosis will change my everyday life.

Now, sweat beads form on his forehead, and his breath quickens. I recognize the shock in his expression.

The time has come.

He understands.

Now, we're both probably relieved that we can soon return to our old lives. I will be as safe as possible, and he will experience all the adventures he longs for. We'll be fine, and we can't ask for more.

"I...," he stammers, running his hands through his hair. Then he tears his gaze away from me, turning hastily and disappearing into the celebrating crowd surrounding us.

I watch him with melancholy. I should be relieved, as all the questions that emerged in the past weeks suddenly have a clear answer. I know which path is right for me, and it always has been.

Yet it breaks my heart to see him go. I can't stop wondering why fate brought us together when there could never be a happy ending for us.

My inner turmoil sends a pounding sensation through my temples—a warning sign I should take seriously. I need to regain control. Just as the doctor explained to me today, excitement is bad for me, adrenaline especially. Stress might trigger my epilepsy, and I should avoid it whenever possible.

I take deep breaths, distracting myself by observing the celebrating crowd. Alessia and Camilla try to coax a smile from their father. They offer him cake and wine, but he touches neither. They invite him to dance, but he shakes his head. Alessia reaches for his hand, but he pulls it away. Suddenly, she looks up and locks eyes with me. Her eyes are filled with sadness, and I can't be sure of its source, but I can imagine it.

She must realize now that she has to let go of her hope for a happy ending for the Olivetta family. Until today, she might have hoped that her father would recover. But with his behavior, there's no reason left to hope for a miracle.

Maybe that's it.

Or perhaps I'm projecting my own emotions onto her expression.

I don't know.

Looking at Alessia doesn't do me any good.

Thinking about Vico, the Olivetta family, and their fate doesn't help either.

Enough, Hanna, I reprimand myself, as it's time to finally acknowledge the facts. Regardless of the daydreams that consumed me in the past weeks, none of them are real.

Least of all the one where I'm in Vico's arms, just looking at him and knowing where my heart belongs.

Chapter 36

Vico

With heavy steps, I enter the estate's library. The envelope in my hand feels weightless, yet it seems to drag my arm downward. It contains the contract that my father must sign today. Even his birthday celebration two days ago failed to bring a smile to his face, so Camilla has finally given up. She has decided that the sale should be expedited, even if it means not fighting for various clauses any longer. Once again, I am the one who must deal with Father.

The thought that soon not even the remnants of our home will exist makes me swallow hard. Hanna's dream for the future of the estate was so beautiful, so captivating that I cannot forget it. My sisters would be overjoyed. And me? No matter how much I wish it were different, no matter how hard I try to suppress it, I feel how much this place means to me and probably always has.

But without Hanna, it all loses its meaning.

And she will leave. Because of Florian. She made that clear to me.

I open the door. My father sits in his leather chair, and in a matter of seconds, I understand that the attempt to bring him back to life even just a little through his birthday celebration has failed miserably.

Nothing can reach him.

Looking at him, memories of the evening two days ago flood my mind.

I left. Just like that. Without saying a word, I ran away. Today, I am ashamed of it, yet I know deep down I would do it all over again. Because I have no other choice.

Regardless of what she may or may not feel for me, Hanna is ill. In the past forty hours, I've researched everything about her epilepsy. Though the illness itself may not cause lasting damage to her body, the consequences can be life-threatening. Even a bath in the tub can kill them.

As soon as I finish the thought, I see myself putting my arms in the water of the bathtub at lightning speed to pull Hanna out. Her body is heavy, her muscles flabby. Drops of water pour over her lifeless face and soak my T-shirt.

My heartbeat gallops, heat rises in me. With all due care, I place her on the mosaic tiles of the bathroom and feel for her carotid artery with shaky fingers.

There is no pulse. Her chest remains motionless.

I can't do this. Just the idea of it kills me.

It's time to pull the ripcord.

That I left was the right decision. However, I should have explained it to her. But how could I have done that without revealing my innermost feelings? I would have had to confess that losing someone who owns my entire heart would shatter me. And she would have known that she alone ignites this longing in me, a longing I cannot control.

A longing that will one day plunge me into the abyss, just like my father, who only now, after I've been standing beside him for minutes, looks up at me.

"Vico," he says in a frail voice. "What is it?"

I swallow hard and hand him the envelope. "The purchase contract."

Suddenly, he seems frozen. "So it's come to this."

I nod. What else should I do? We need to get it over with; there's no other way. Once the estate is sold and Hanna is no longer near me, the struggle between longing and fear in every fiber of my being will cease.

Rustling, Father opens the envelope and takes out the two printed copies of the contract. I dig the pen I brought with me out of my pocket to hand it to my father. He takes it, but I can't let go.

Our fingers, both on the pen, meet each other's gaze for a moment. In his eyes, I see his pain.

"If you could turn back time … what would you do differently?" I hear myself ask suddenly. It's that last glimmer of hope in me that compels me. That small light on the horizon that refuses to fade, no matter how much I try to acknowledge the dark reality. "Would you make different choices?"

He releases the pen. Weary, his hand falls into his lap, and I observe how he gets lost in the abyss of his thoughts.

I clear my throat. "Would you choose to live with Mother again? Now that you know how it will end?" I never thought I would ask him this question one day. For me, his answer has always been clear, as I have seen it in every movement and heard it in every word. It's better never to have loved than to lose love.

He knows that. And at least the part of me that I have under control knows that too. But the other part, the one that places this persistent longing right in the center of my chest, needs to be convinced. Hearing my father speak the truth loud and clear will achieve just that.

"Would you have ever wanted to get to know her better?" I continue with a trembling voice. "Or did you hold on to your heart with all your might?"

His lower lip quivers. At first, just a little, then more and more violently. And suddenly, I see something in his face that I have never seen in my entire life.

A tear forms in the corner of his eye. Without blinking even once, it falls, leaving a glistening trail down his sunken cheek. "My friends claimed her nose was crooked. And her eyes were too big. But to me, she was the most beautiful girl I had ever met," he says, so full of melancholy that my heart clenches. "I was blinded by love, deafened by enthusiasm, and paralyzed by longing."

That's not the answer to my question. It's a declaration of love that reminds me all too vividly of what I feel for Hanna. I'm about to repeat my question, but he raises his hand to silence me.

"Any attempt to keep me away from her would have failed." A wistful smile flits across his face. "She was the love of my life."

My God, I know that already. Not for nothing did he bury all his joy of living with her. I sink to my knees before him. "If you could undo everything, the good and the bad times, would you do it?" I plead. I have to hear it from him. I have to hear how much he regrets giving in to his feelings.

But instead of answering me, he shrugs slightly. Then he reaches for the pen. "She was the love of my life," he repeats.

Is that a yes? Is he telling me that despite his grief,

he wouldn't want to miss the time with my mother? Can that be serious, or has he lost his mind?

I need to stop interpreting his words in a way that suits me. He hasn't answered me, so I have to find my own. That's the only thing I can say for sure.

Dejectedly, I hand him the pen. "On each page, bottom right, and all the way at the end under the line where your name is." I sound a bit like a robot as I relay the instructions from the lawyer. But I have no choice if I want to keep my emotional turmoil in check.

He signs one page after another in the first contract without even looking at the clauses. It takes what feels like an eternity for him to reach the last page. He puts the pen down and traces the line of his name. Immediately after, he breaks into a piercing sob, a torrent of tears that should actually provide me with every answer I still need.

Chapter 37

Hanna

Restlessly, I pace back and forth in my room. I still haven't told Florian about my accident or my diagnosis. Both should be easy for me, yet I find myself afraid of his reaction. With each passing day, the fear grows.

What if he's just as disappointed as Vico? How will he react when he realizes that our lives may never be the same again?

My fingers tremble, but I dial his number on my phone.

It rings. I walk to the window and peer through the white side panels of the curtains. No one is here. Three days have passed since Vico fled from me. There's no reason he would suddenly show up today. Perhaps it's for the best - for both of us. I need to stop picturing his angular face, hearing his soft tone, and wondering how he's doing.

"Hanna, how nice," Florian breathes heavily. He must have rushed to answer my call. "What's up?"

"Everything's fine," I reply without thinking and immediately bite my tongue. Breaking this automatism is not easy. I make a new attempt. "It's just…"

There's a brief silence on the line. "Yes?"

"I…" *Come on, Hanna. I broke my arm. Just say it.* "When will you be here tomorrow?" Dammit. Why is it so easy for me to express what's on my mind with Vico, but not with Florian?

"I'll leave as soon as I get rid of the departing guests." I hear him typing on the computer in the background. "I'll be with you in the late afternoon."

"That sounds great." I glance at my casted arm. He'll find out about it tomorrow anyway. If I can't bring myself to tell him about the epilepsy today, at least I can mention the accident.

"Have you gone through the checklist?" Florian asks in his businesslike tone.

"Mm-hmm." Dammit, what's wrong with me? I can't lie to him. It's not a shame that I haven't completed everything.

Suddenly, it becomes so quiet that I can hear his breath. "Is something wrong?"

Now or never.

Three. Two. One. "I broke my arm," I manage to say with effort, turning away from the window and continuing to pace between the old wooden bed and the dresser.

"Oh, that's terrible!" Is it concern or astonishment in his tone?

Unconsciously, I nibble on my lower lip. "I was careless."

"But you should take good care of yourself," he replies, just as shaken as my mother used to be. He cares about me. "How did it happen?"

"An accident with the Vespa." I sigh, pausing and sinking down onto the bed. "I just wanted to go for a short ride," I say remorsefully. My *anything is possible* attitude has been shattered.

"Just a short ride?" he repeats incredulously. Of

course, he can't comprehend it all, as he doesn't know this side of me.

"It was a mistake," I say helplessly, blinking away the tears welling up in my eyes.

A loud clearing of his throat is heard. "No problem, we'll handle it. After all, it's just a matter of time until you're fully recovered," he says determinedly, and suddenly, I don't know why I was worried in the first place. "And if a hospital bill comes in, we'll manage that too."

Oh no, I hope I haven't incurred any costs; we need every cent for the estate. "I'm so sorry," I murmur.

"My dear," Florian says affectionately, "it happened, and we can't change that."

Internally, I relax. I've delivered bad news, and he responded with understanding. We are, and will remain, a good team that can talk about anything. I just need to show him more of the woman I truly am, as I've never done in the past years.

"Thank you," I whisper into the phone, and a tear of relief escapes my eye. Now, I have the courage to tell him about my illness. "I…"

"Can you still do something for me with your arm?" he interrupts before I can reveal the whole truth. He sounds so motivated for our cause that I decide not to take away his joy. Not now.

"Sure." I straighten my back. "What do you need me to do?"

The typing on the keyboard resumes. "There's a newly opened vineyard nearby. They offer dinner amid the vineyards. Can you test it and take a few photos?"

Testing, yes. Taking photos will be challenging with my cast.

"Send me the address, and I'll see what I can do," I say anyway.

"You're the best." I think I hear a smile in his voice. "There's one more thing: the bungalow on the property. I thought it could be used for the workers during the renovation."

That sounds logical, but suddenly, I feel queasy at the thought. Swallowing hard, I try to maintain my composure.

"Give me the number of rooms and bathrooms, and check if we can fit in some extra mattresses or foldable beds. You know, the essentials," he continues with fervor. His enthusiasm shows me how much this project means to him.

He's fighting for us. Always for us.

"Consider it done," I try to sound as determined as he does. "Anything else?"

The sound of rustling papers is heard. "We have the cost estimates, and the loans are ready. I've summarized the outstanding contract points. Hopefully, we can resolve them soon. But we're already moving to the next round tomorrow," he mutters to himself, as if mentally going through everything. "Also, I need to reinspect the building's condition… Oh yes, one more thing. I want to arrange with the previous owners to vacate the main house immediately after the sale."   ❮

Immediately after the sale?

"Can you keep an eye on them, see if they're slowly packing up their belongings?" he asks me with a doubtful tone. "Even though the contract will probably take a few more weeks. It would be necessary for them to prepare for their move."

No, I can't do that.

How can I watch the family, whose fate has become so close to my heart in the past weeks, as they pack up their belongings in boxes? How does he expect me to do that? To stand in the doorway and supervise them? With a tight chest, I shake the thoughts from my head. "I still have a lot to do and probably won't have time for that," I reply. It's not the whole truth, but it's a step toward being more myself with Florian.

"You'll manage, I'm sure. I know I can always rely on you. Honestly, you're amazing," his affectionate words feel like a warm embrace. That's exactly what I need after all the turmoil and emotional upheaval of the past days. Florian is my haven.

"We'll see each other tomorrow. I can't wait," Florian adds before we say goodbye to each other.

Hesitantly, I lower the phone. At least now he knows about my casted arm, and I'll tell him the rest when the moment is right.

My phone screen lights up, showing a new message. It's the promised address of the winery. *I've already reserved a table for you. Castello di Olmo, 7:00 PM. Be on time, so we can find out how well the kitchen is organized*, I read in the message. *Until then, you can keep an eye on the family's move* it also adds,

I don't respond. Instead, I let the phone fall onto the bed and head outside. I want to be in the garden, to clear my mind. There, among the wonderfully fragrant flowers and the tall grass tickling my shins, I can embrace life and the feeling of freedom in my chest.

But as soon as I close the door to my room, Camilla appears at the entrance of the house. Under her arm, she clutches a stack of folded cardboard boxes, which she leans against the damp hallway wall. She spots me before I can hide.

"Hey," she says with a tired voice, grabbing one of the boxes and unfolding it.

I raise my hand and return her greeting. A heavy silence hangs between us. And this, even though we used to understand each other so well. We were friends. Today, I'm the cause of her sadness.

"Let me help you," I say on impulse and step toward her.

She nods toward my injured arm. "You should rest."

I can barely bear her caring concern. "Please. I already feel guilty enough." I probably shouldn't admit that. I should be tougher and think more about the business. But it's the truth, and Camilla can probably see it written all over my face.

Suddenly, her features soften too. "You can't help it. I know that, and Alessia does too."

I wish it were that simple. "We're taking away your home." That's not true.

She reaches for a picture on the wall, carefully takes it off the holder, and places it in the box. "But only because we're not capable of preserving it," she says softly.

Suddenly, Tyrol and everything that's important there seems miles away. And I realize that there's still a solution that could work for all of us. Florian and I can find another property for our new inn and build our secure future there, just as we've always dreamed. It doesn't have to be this one!

I feel the fervor rising, pushing aside the guilt that has built up inside me over the past few weeks. I'm sure I can convince Florian, but as long as the Olivettas lack a plan to resume olive oil production, it won't help them.

"Is there no way to save the estate?" I ask urgently. "If Vico…" No, I won't even speak those words. Because that thought is still fuel to the fire of my quietly smoldering longing, a longing that must not flare up again.

She packs a candleholder into the box. "Vico…" she mutters absentmindedly. "He has changed." Suddenly, she looks directly at me. "Because of you."

She shouldn't say something like that. I better pretend not to understand what she means. Besides, there are more important things to discuss. "Do you think he could still take over the estate?"

She nibbles on her lower lip. "When he returned home three weeks ago, he was like Mount Vesuvius. He thought I wouldn't notice, but I always knew that beneath his unapproachable facade, a fire was burning, one he had kept small for years."

"I have no idea what she's trying to tell me. So I just gesture for her to continue and lean against the cool wall behind me.

"Mother's death hit him hard too, but he didn't let anyone see it. Instead, he ran away," she says, shaking her head, and turns to the next picture. "He keeps insisting that he wants to be free. How important his career as a cliff diver is and that he can't survive without adrenaline."

"He does," I confirm, as I've seen the sparkle in his eyes more than once when he talked about his passion.

Camilla pauses in her work and brushes the fringes of her short haircut away from her face. "There was nothing more important to Vico than his family and his homeland in the past. He wanted to be nowhere else but here."

But that's it. That could be the solution! If Florian and I buy an alternative property and Vico returns here to run the estate, everyone would win. "Do you think there's still some of the old Vico left?"

"I don't know." She lifts her shoulders with a mournful look. "He probably would have done something to stop the sale if that were the case. But when I asked him yesterday to get Father's signature on the contract, he did it without batting an eye."

The contract already has one of the two necessary signatures? My stomach feels like it's filled with rocks. No. Florian just said on the phone that there are still clauses to be negotiated. The agreement is not ready for signing. There must be a miscommunication, which is quite possible given his fragmented Italian. And who knows how well Signor Olivetta speaks English.

"Ask him what his homeland means to him," Camilla continues with a soft voice. "If he tells anyone the truth, it will be you." There's something meaningful in her expression.

"No more," I reply quickly, because I actually believe that. It might have been true once. But that's over now.

As if my response doesn't bother her, she looks at me knowingly. "Ask him," she repeats insistently.

"We won't see each other anymore. I still have a lot to do today, and in the evening, I'll be testing the vineyard dinner at Castello di Olmo." And with the way Vico has been avoiding me lately, I don't think he wants to talk to me anyway. "It would be better if you talk to him."

Her forehead furrows, and I can almost see the question on her tongue. Fortunately, she doesn't ask it but reaches for another box to unfold. "I will," she murmurs thoughtfully and walks into the kitchen.

Chapter 38

Vico

I can't believe I actually made it here. And now, as I step out of my car and look around the vineyard illuminated by spotlights, I no longer understand how Camilla managed to convince me.

Do you really want to let her go without talking to her? she asked me, looking at me as if her heart would break along with mine.

Why does it matter so much to you? I inquired.

Because I want nothing more than for you to be happy, came her reply.

As if she knew better what makes me happy than I do myself.

I shut the car door and stroll absentmindedly toward the entrance.

Being happy, what is that?

Is it knowing that Hanna probably has a better life with her Florian than with me? Or is it facing my fears and fighting for something I'm not even sure exists? And if it is indeed real, will it eventually plunge me into the same abyss as my father?

With heavy shoulders, I enter the vineyard.

"Can I help you?" An elderly server in a black shirt and apron approaches me. Her hair is elegantly tied into a knot, not a strand out of place. She looks at me attentively.

I interlace my fingers and smile silently at her, unsure of what to say. Is it better to stay or to leave?

"Do you have a reservation?" she inquires.

I have no idea. "Um...," I let my gaze wander, but the dining area is small, and I only see an elderly couple, a large family, and a group of young women. Hanna is not here. Maybe Camilla misunderstood her.

The server raises an eyebrow. "What's the name?"

"No, I..."

Suddenly, her face takes on a knowing expression. "You booked the candlelight dinner at the vineyard for the young lady from Austria, didn't you?"

Candlelight dinner?

"Oh, how shy young people are these days." She hooks her arm through mine. "Come along, you're surely being eagerly awaited."

I would doubt that. Hanna should have known about my arrival in order to announce me. Maybe someone entirely different is expected. This Florian, for example. Nevertheless, I let myself be led by her without resistance. We traverse the bustling restaurant, step out into the quiet backyard, and keep walking until we reach the rows of grapevines.

Over there, between the long rows, a space is reserved. A square table with two chairs sits amid nature. Candlelight not only bathes the surroundings in gentle hues but also illuminates Hanna's face.

With a blend of nostalgia and dreaminess, she gazes down the hill into the valley, now cloaked in twilight. She absentmindedly twirls a glass of water in her hand. Impossible as it may be, she looks more beautiful than ever before.

"I'll find the way from here," I tell the server, who

turns away with a knowing smile. Once she's out of my sight, doubts assail me once again. What would happen if I approach Hanna now and admit that I want to let her go, but simply can't? And what if I don't?

Nervously, I take a step to the side. A branch snaps loudly beneath my shoe, pulling Hanna out of the world she had retreated into. She looks over at me, and I am instantly frozen.

For seconds, we gaze at each other. I try to read her eyes, wondering if she's disappointed in me. If my panicked escape from Father's birthday party hurt her too deeply. And if her heart is also pounding too fiercely against her chest.

Slowly, the corners of her mouth turn up. I walk toward her, her smile becoming more pronounced. We repeat this dance until I reach the table.

"Buona sera," I say timidly.

She gestures to the empty chair. "Take a seat." Her voice doesn't reveal what she feels, but her expression weakens my knees.

After settling into the chair, she straightens her posture. "Why did you come?" she asks, looking deep into my eyes as though she already knows the answer to her question.

I try to steady my breath. "Would you believe me if I said I have absolutely no idea?"

"No," she replies gently, taking a sip of water. "So why did you come?" she asks again.

To ask you to stay with me.

"To apologize," I blurt out even though this conversation's start might lead to a point I never want to reach. I rest my elbows on the table and lean forward. "Again."

251

"Why?" She struggles to keep herself composed, as if there are so many words inside her that she deliberately holds back.

Not wanting to endure her gaze any longer, I lower my eyes. "I shouldn't have run away. I'm sorry, that was—"

"Does it even matter anymore?" She interrupts me.

Surprised, I look up at her. Her face appears closed off, but her breath is rapid. "Isn't it?" My heart tightens.

Her index finger glides over her fork. "The estate is being sold. Your sisters are losing their home."

Ah, that's what it's about. Not me or us. But Camilla, Alessia, and Aurora. I don't know if I should feel relieved or cry. I manage no more than a nod.

"*You* are losing your home," she adds with a pleading expression.

What does she want from me, anyway? She and her stupid boyfriend are the ones buying the estate. She shouldn't be concerned about the sellers' feelings. "Why does it even matter to you?" I blurt out.

With trembling fingers, she reaches for her napkin. "Because you can still prevent it," she says, her voice breaking, and suddenly, I realize how much it must have cost her to utter those words. How long has she been wrestling with herself? "This estate means everything to your sisters."

"I know that." My God, why does she think I'm not aware of that? "The three of them are incredibly important to me. Only when they are happy can I be happy," I add. Yet I feel that trying to uphold the family tradition will suffocate me. The half-decayed walls will remind me every day of what happened. And my father will hold up a mirror to me in every

252

second, one I don't want to look into. There is only one way I can see that becoming possible.

If Hanna stays with me. Forever.

"Then do something about it," she pleads, reaching her hand out toward mine. "What colors do your wishes have?" she asks meaningfully.

The delicate pink of her cheeks. The velvety brown of her hair.

And the deep sea green of her eyes.

I want to tell her. She must know that my wishes bear only her colors. So we can find out if they are the same as hers.

"Stay here. Save your home," she says earnestly. "Florian and I can build our future somewhere else."

Florian and I. The future.

Like spirits, the words flutter through my mind, seeping into my thoughts and building a wall around my heart. No matter if I were ready for the most significant leap of my life, she won't stay. That much is certain. "I can't," I hear myself say.

Her lips press together in disappointment, and she withdraws her hand. "A sponsor wants to support my career. It's a once-in-a-lifetime opportunity." Not that it's a good excuse for leaving my sisters behind, but it's the only one I have. "I've been working toward this moment for years. It's my dream, you see."

Her facial muscles soften. "Since when have you known?" She feels betrayed. I see it in her eyes.

"Just a few days ago," I reply, crossing my arms over my chest. Out of pure self-defense. Nevertheless, I feel as lost as I've ever been.

She swallows hard. "And when will you leave Collina da sogno?" Her voice is controlled.

"Tomorrow. It's better this way. For all of us." Even though it was beautiful to momentarily immerse myself in her dream world and see a future filled with life and love. Ultimately, it was nothing more than a dream.

A silent tear escapes from the corner of her eye. The candlelight refracts in the drop as it runs down her cheek. I want to kiss it off her velvety skin, to take away her sadness and mine as well. However, I just watch idly until the tear reaches her jaw and falls into the darkness from there.

"Time to wake up, isn't it?" she asks me, her voice hoarse.

I nod, my throat tightening more and more. I wish I could ask her to help me conquer my fears so that I can return home. But she has made it clear that her concern is only for the future of the estate. Not for ours.

"Time to wake up," I confirm in a toneless voice, and I lower my eyelids.

Chapter 39

Hanna

I maneuver through the tall grass, securing my broken arm in the sling, until I reach the decaying wooden door with the old-fashioned slide latch. The metal fittings look as if they could lose their grip at any moment, but still, I step closer and open the door.

Better safe than sorry no longer applies. At least not like it used to. Because now I know that I'm not clumsy, and I never was. Thanks to my conversation with the doctor, I know the potential signs of an impending seizure. Even if there may not always be any, a heavy head seems to be part of the package for me. Today, however, it feels fine.

Unlike my heart, which Vico shattered yesterday, even though it shouldn't have been possible. But I won't allow myself to dwell on that. Whatever I thought I saw in his eyes, it wasn't real.

There's no future for us.

At least now I know what's right. Turning this estate into a guesthouse isn't my dream. But what comes after can become my dream again if I put in enough effort for that future.

With a heavy sense of guilt toward Florian, I step into the twilight of the shed and look around. I spot barrels and antique equipment that the Olivettas must have used for their olive oil production. I gently let my fingers glide over the grain of the wood. Dust swirls and tickles my nose. Sneezing, I circle around the barrel, where I notice a sign on the front. I free it from cobwebs and dirt to read the text.

In elegantly curved writing, I discover the family name of the estate. It looks just like the label on the bottle of olive oil from the village store. Absently, I lift my gaze and let myself be consumed by the emotions the surroundings evoke in me.

The room transforms rapidly in my mind's eye. Sunbeams stream through the windows, illuminating everything. I see Vico's father in the best of health, operating the olive press, sweat on his forehead, yet he smiles as he gazes at the woman labeling the barrels.

His wife.

Children's laughter fills the barn. Ten-year-old Vico plays with his sisters amid the equipment and shelves in a game of hide-and-seek.

With the taste of olive oil on my tongue, I wander through the space. As beautiful as the images are that my imagination paints, my heart grows heavier with each step.

This can't be the end.

Even if Vico gets to live his freedom, and even if I continue with Florian, the Olivettas need a home. But what good would it do them if I were to convince Florian not to buy the estate? It's for sale for a reason, and they can't keep it themselves. Perhaps I'd plunge them even deeper into unhappiness if I were to ruin the deal.

Lost in thought, I lean against the long table that was once surely used for filling and labeling the olive oil.

If I can't save the family, at least I can ensure their legacy lives on. We could restore all the beautiful objects in this barn and integrate them into the guesthouse, so they remain a part of this estate. The main house must stay as true to its original state as possible, and we'll adorn the walls with pictures from the past. Yes, we will create a tribute to this wonderful family. Preserving the soul of this place and paying the respect the Olivettas deserve. Who knows, maybe they'll come to visit from time to time and take joy in what we've made of their home.

Vico, too, would have a small piece of home, in case he ever decides to return.

It's not the ideal solution, but it's the best I have.

I wipe my forehead with the back of my hand and exhale shakily. Then I push away from the table, walk to the door, and step out into the bright afternoon sun. I carefully close the shed and make my way to the main house, immediately searching for places where we could position the Olivetta family's treasures.

Before I reach the main house, I spot Florian's black station wagon in the courtyard. I glance at my wristwatch.

Indeed, it's already half past three; once again, I lost track of time. But these daydreams were not futile, that much is certain. My imagination is nothing to be ashamed of; that's what I've learned here in Italy.

Smiling to myself, I set out to find Florian.

I find him by the pool, lifting a floor tile with a look of disdain as it crumbles under his touch. Seeing him should fill me with joy, yet all I feel is melancholy when I look at him. Melancholy and guilt.

It's certainly not his fault, but rather what has

happened here in the past weeks. Even though Vico and I never kissed, on a deeper level, I betrayed Florian.

I force an unconcerned smile and step beside him. "Hey."

His eyes light up as he pushes himself up from the ground. "Hey," he responds with a gentle voice, and he cautiously touches my shoulder. His gaze wanders to my cast. "Does it hurt a lot?"

How caring he suddenly is. For all these years, I never wanted to burden him or let him see when I felt bad. I wanted to be what I thought he wanted me to be. That was a mistake. "Just a little," I reply truthfully.

He reaches out his hand to caress my cheek. "That's good. After all, we have big plans." There's something promising in his look, something I've rarely seen before.

"You're up to something, aren't you?" I ask skeptically.

A broad grin appears on his face, and then he takes my healthy hand and pulls me with him. "Come on, I need to show you something."

Whatever it is, it seems to make him nervous. His palm becomes clammy on the way, and he keeps glancing between me and the estate.

I'm not sure if I like that, but my curiosity outweighs the nagging guilt, and that's a good thing. I stumble along beside him, allowing him to lead into the house. When we reach the door to my room, he stops. Then he looks deeply into my eyes, cradles my face in his hands, and kisses me passionately.

"You're scaring me a little," I say cautiously as he pulls away from me. That, too, is the truth. And it feels good to speak it out loud, even though I'm starting to feel uneasy now. "What's going on?"

A whole range of emotions is reflected in his expression. Love. Joy. Nervousness. There's even a hint of concern. He exhales heavily and places his hand on the doorknob. "Are you ready?"

I don't know.

He opens the door and gently nudges me to enter the room before him.

"Wow." That's all I can say in front of the sight that greets me. "This is…" Words fail me. I don't know how to describe it.

Beautiful. Unique. A dream.

The entire room is adorned with roses. Even on the white sheet, Florian has arranged a heart of petals. The fragrance is exquisite. I step inside and let the moment wash over me.

Suddenly, I hear Florian clearing his throat behind me.

I turn around and just manage to see him dropping to his knees.

Oh. My. God.

"Hanna," he says with a husky voice and a hesitant smile. "The past few weeks have been hell. They've shown me how meaningless my life is without you."

I can hardly sort out my thoughts. Is this really happening, what I've been dreaming of for years? Just now, when meeting Vico has stirred my feelings for Florian?

He looks up at me with longing. "You're the best thing that ever happened to me, and I love you with all my heart."

I put my hands over my mouth in disbelief. He has

never said anything so beautiful to me before. But the turmoil his words evoke is not where it should be. My heart should be pounding hard, screaming yes with joy. Instead, a storm brews in my stomach. Guilt over my closeness with Vico collides with my affection for Florian, who has always been there for me. On top of that, there's the familiar comfort of our long-standing partnership and the fluttering sensation in my stomach when I'm near Vico. All of it blends into a tempest that I can barely withstand.

Breathing heavily, I watch as Florian reaches into his pocket. He takes out a small box and turns it to face me.

It's going to happen now. He's going to ask me. And I don't know what this certainty is doing to me.

"Hanna," he begins, but he immediately has to clear his throat. "We're stronger together." He nods at me, as if seeking my confirmation.

I inevitably nod back. That seems to be enough for him to fumble awkwardly with the box until he finds the opening mechanism.

The world suddenly moves in slow motion. Infinitely slowly, the lid of the box lifts. A slim silver ring, nestled in blue velvet, appears before my eyes.

"Will you be my wife, Hanna?" Florian's words stretch out unnaturally. His tone is filled with emotions. "I can't imagine anything more beautiful than sharing my life with you."

He can't imagine anything more beautiful than marrying me. Wow. This is…

Slowly, the information sinks into my consciousness and collides with a truth that shouldn't even exist. The truth that I'm not sure if I feel the same way.

I swallow hard, feeling immensely ashamed of this thought.

In front of me is a man to whom I've done so much in the past few weeks. He loves me, and he's asking to take care of me. In good times and bad. We've had a comfortable life so far. And we will continue to have a comfortable life in the future. Especially because here in Italy, I've found a part of myself that will make it possible.

What more can I ask for?

"What do you say?" Florian asks now, his gaze filled with longing.

He needs an answer. It should damn well be easy for me to give him one.

Timidly, I lower my head, only to lift it again a moment later.

The sun rises in Florian's face. Filled with tenderness, he reaches for my hand and slips the ring onto my finger.

Chapter 40

Vico

Florian looks up from the two contract versions with a puzzled expression. "Your father signed this?" he asks me in English.

That's obvious. I nod.

"But when we last spoke, there were still some unclear points. Here, for example…" He taps his finger resolutely on one of the contract clauses. "It states that he must vacate the estate immediately after signing the contract. Just a week ago, Camilla insisted vehemently that the same two weeks agreed for the annex building should apply here as well."

Does it even matter? "Well, it seems her opinion has changed." All I wish for is to get through this moment quickly. Once again, I'm the one who has to be strong for the family and take the final step alone. Being in Camilla's kitchen with this Florian and his smug grin is bad enough. My mind can't stop showing me images of him and Hanna.

How he gently brushes her hair from her forehead.

How she lovingly kisses him.

How they laugh together.

Bitter jealousy rises within me, though I have no right to feel it. My last conversation with Hanna was clear.

"Where is Camilla anyway? Why isn't she here

262

herself?" Florian's complaining snaps me out of my thoughts.

"She couldn't make it," I reply curtly. He doesn't need to know that she wouldn't be able to bear watching him seal the end of the estate.

He scrutinizes me with his bright eyes. "And your father?"

"Busy too." I shrug.

For a moment, he squints his eyes. "I'd like to go through the contract again."

I can't suppress a sigh, nor do I want to. "Go ahead. Let me know when you're finished." With a headshake, I gesture toward the dining table, where he takes a seat and begins reviewing the documents.

Feverishly, he compares the texts in the contract he brought and the one my father has already signed. I watch as he ticks off the clauses like an eager student aiming for a top grade. The longer it takes, the greater the conflict inside me becomes.

Hanna wants nothing more than to keep the estate in the family. And for a moment, I even thought it could be possible. If she could be a part of this family. As the woman by my side. And together, we could work to carry on the Olivetta tradition.

But that future doesn't exist. The hurdles are too great, and the burden of the past weighs heavily on my soul. We are who we are. No matter how much I wish I could be someone else. I'm not.

I walk to the window and gaze out at the green hills. Once again, memories of my time together with Hanna flood my thoughts. I see her wonderfully dreamy face, hear her carefree laughter while zip-lining, and experience her boundless imagination that she initially wanted to keep hidden from me. I feel her back against my chest, her hair on my neck, and her breath on my cheek. I smell her floral scent. And I see her vision for the estate before me.

What if it could still come true?

What if I face my fears? Would she be willing to let go of her old life? Do her feelings match mine? We've only spent three weeks together. Can love truly develop in such a short time?

I have only a few seconds to change the course of things. If I turn around now, take the contract from Florian, and tear it into a thousand pieces, there will still be a chance.

I tear my gaze away from the window. Florian flips to the last page. Only one clause remains without a tick.

My heart pounds so forcefully that I'm afraid it might explode. Yet I approach him because this irrational longing inside me is so overpowering that it overshadows all fear.

He draws the last hook and then leans back heavily on his chair, looking up at me with a satisfied nod. "Everything looks good," he confirms before his expression twists into an arrogant smirk. "Has my fiancée told you about our plans for the estate?"

His fiancée? Did he just call Hanna his fiancée? When did that happen?

I gasp for breath, but it feels like I can't get any.

Everything around me seems to darken. It suddenly dawns on me that it doesn't matter if my longing can overcome my fear.

Hanna has made her choice. She said yes. That's all I need to know.

Arrogantly grinning, he raises an eyebrow. "Well, it seems I beat you to it."

I stare at him in disbelief. What does he mean?

Now he springs up, the chair rattling loudly on the tiled floor. "Do you think I'm stupid?" he asks, agitated. "Do you think I didn't notice you trying to put ideas in her head? Her daydreaming is even worse than it already is." He glares at me with malice. "And the way you looked at her during my visit the other day. Do you think I didn't notice that either?"

I haven't done anything. I never wanted Hanna to get hurt or for feelings to develop between us. That was never the plan!

"I have no idea what you're talking about," I reply in a tone so neutral that even I am surprised. Emptiness spreads inside me. "Are you going to sign now?"

He takes a step toward me, puffing out his chest. "With pleasure."

Then he should just do it. Swallowing hard, I walk around him and go to the table to retrieve the two contracts. "What are you waiting for?"

He can spare me the smug look. We both know he's won. He takes the papers from me and dates and signs the dotted line on the last page of each.

"This will be a wonderful surprise for Hanna," he mutters absentmindedly. Then he fixes a smirk on me. "I'll tell her at our engagement party in two weeks that I made our shared dream come true for her. That's my gift to my bride."

I clench my fists. He's only saying that to torment me.

What an asshole.

"We'll start the work tomorrow. Make sure your

father is out of the main house by then," he adds as I struggle to maintain my composure.

"Understood," I force out, then take one of the contracts from his hand and gesture toward the hallway. "I'm sure you can find your way out on your own."

With an amused smirk, he starts making his way out. "It was a pleasure doing business with you," he calls out from a distance before finally disappearing from my sight.

I'm left with the painful ache in my chest. And there's only one thought I'm allowed to entertain now.

Life must go on.

Matteo is still waiting for my confirmation for the sponsorship. He'll get it now. I've neglected my training for far too long. That ends today.

I have a life, and I have a goal. Both will help me forget what happened in the past few weeks and finally feel free again.

Because it simply has to be that way.

Chapter 41

Hanna

We've long left behind the gentle hills of Tuscany. When we departed from the estate, Vico's VW van was nowhere in sight. Perhaps it's for the best.

What else would we have said to each other?

It is what it is, and there's no point in dwelling on it any longer. We are both on our way back to our good old lives.

The mountains rise beside the highway as Florian and I drive toward Tyrol together. Leaning my head against the window, I gaze up at the sky, where the moon is already visible, even though the sun hasn't fully set yet.

Florian reaches for my hand and squeezes it tightly. "Are you tired?"

"Yes," I reply, feeling at least a little bit free. Finally, I manage to openly express how I feel and what's going on inside me. I turn to him. "When will we return to Collina da sogno to get my car?"

Focused on the road, he shrugs. "With your broken arm, you can't drive anyway. So there's no rush."

I hum in agreement, as he is right. Nonetheless, it feels strange to know that my car is in Italy, and I'll now be dependent on someone else to take me where I need to go for weeks. "But you'll have to go back to Tuscany soon for the contract signing, right?"

He takes his hand off the steering wheel, giving me a gentle pat on the thigh. "Mm-hmm."

Something in his expression puzzles me, but I can't put my finger on it. It's probably just my own tiredness, making me see things that aren't there. "Look." He nods toward the road sign right in front of us.

Semmtal.

"Welcome home," Florian says affectionately, but all I can do is stare at the letters on the sign, unable to grasp that I'm actually back. I should be happy, but that feeling eludes me.

"Thank you," I whisper absentmindedly, stroking Florian's hand. I don't need to look to feel the ring on my finger. We haven't discussed a date yet, but it'll probably happen next year, at the latest.

Does Vico know about our engagement?

Is that why he fled without saying goodbye?

Stop. I shouldn't even be asking myself these questions.

We pass through the entrance of the village, and I focus on the world outside our car. Since my departure, a lot has changed. Spring has transformed the village into a blooming oasis.

The flower decorations on the quaint houses add wonderful accents to the dark-painted wooden windows with their red, pink, and yellow spots. The meadows are so lush green that they glow even in the twilight. I crack open the car window, and the spicy scent of the alpine meadows fills my nose.

"Are you happy to be back?" Florian signals and turns the car into a side street.

"It feels strange. Foreign and familiar at the same

268

time." Once again, I speak exactly what's on my mind. "And that's even though I've only been away for a few weeks. Crazy, right?"

His mouth curls upward. "Soon you'll have two places where you feel at home. Semmtal and Collina da sogno."

And two places where I'll have trouble keeping up with work. One of them now comes into my view. "We'll need staff. Maybe we can hire Natalie permanently after she finishes the school year. She's proven herself, hasn't she?" I ask, as I can't possibly manage to run both inns alone. And that's independent of my illness, which Florian still knows nothing about.

He needs to know. Best now, right away.

"No worries, I've already calculated everything. We'll manage without Natalie," he replies in his businesslike tone, slows down the car, and parks under the carport next to the woodpile.

The way he talks about her is odd. "Has something happened?" I unfasten my seat belt and extricate myself from the seat. The long drive has made my legs stiff, and he seems sluggish as he exits the car.

For a split second, he looks at me over the car roof with an expressionless face, but then he shakes his head.

"She quit the internship. But I'll tell you about it later. Right now, something else is much more important." ❮

When did this happen? Why did she leave? And why hasn't he told me anything about it until now?

Several instances in the past few weeks when he sounded odd on the phone immediately come to my mind. Could Natalie's departure be the reason for that?

I scrutinize him intently, but his expression gives nothing away. "I'm curious," I say pensively, deferring not only this conversation but also the talk about my epilepsy for later. I follow him into the house, where he leads me directly to his study and grabs a large roll of paper.

"Are you ready?" His expectant gaze makes me smile. "I present to you…" He almost ceremoniously unrolls the paper, revealing the content.

It's a drawing. A plan of the estate.

"… our future." He raises his eyebrows, his eyes shining.

I step closer to study the plan. But Florian seems so excited that he can't give me a second to process it.

"Okay, let me explain. Up here in the front, we're putting in a completely new pool. We'll build one of those super chic stainless-steel pools. Surround it with black granite. The sun loungers will be white. Everything will be luxurious. And modern," he gushes.

Luxurious? Modern? That doesn't fit the estate at all.

"This way, we can charge even more for nightly stays than if we just had standard accommodations like everyone else in the area," he says, his cheeks glowing with enthusiasm. "I've already spoken to the pool company and placed the order. They have long lead times, so I didn't want to wait." His index finger moves on the plan. "See this? It will be a bar. We'll pave this area, and in the center, we'll have a fan palm. And we'll get cool orange lounge furniture. You know, the ones without cushions."

Cool lounge furniture? "You mean the plastic ones?" I ask, dismayed. He can't be serious.

He nods eagerly. "Exactly. The guests will love it. And that ugly patch of grass in the back will be gone too. We're building a golf course there; that'll attract wealthy customers as well."

The area he refers to as an *ugly patch of grass* is my poppy field. The place where I envisioned a winding gravel path and a romantic pavilion in my mind. But that's not all. Frowning, I look up from the drawing to him. "It was supposed to be an inn, not a luxury hotel for the rich and famous."

"The plans have changed," he dismisses my objection as if he didn't want to hear it. "This is better, I promise. It will help us reach our goal much faster." He spreads his arms wide. "This old inn here isn't prestigious enough. We'll sell it off once the estate starts running."

"What?" I'm so taken aback that I can barely sort my thoughts. We're going to emigrate? He can't decide that without me.

As if he expected a completely different reaction from me, he lowers the plan with a disappointed expression. "What's wrong? Don't you like it?" He sounds offended.

"I don't like it at all!" I reply in horror.

A mixture of disbelief and anger spreads across his face. "I thought you'd be happy." He sounds hurt.

Immediately, I bite my tongue. Have I hurt him with my words? Should I have been more careful? Pondering, I step closer to him and place my hand on his forearm. "I'm sorry," I say conciliatory. "It's just…"

He backs away as if he doesn't want my proximity. "What?" he asks.

Automatically, I lower my gaze. I feel small. It's the

exact feeling I've carried within me all my life and had long accepted as a part of me. Until Vico showed me that I don't have to. That what I have to say is valuable. That my opinion matters. And so do my desires—in all their colors.

I won't let this feeling take hold of me again. Not after I now know how life can feel.

Taking a deep breath, I lift my head and gaze firmly into Florian's eyes. "I, too, have been thinking about how the estate could look after the renovation," I say resolutely.

A steep furrow forms between his eyebrows. "Why on earth would you do that?" His words carry bewilderment.

Of course, he doesn't understand. How could he, when he doesn't know the new Hanna yet? The one who is aware of her worth. The one who knows what she wants. "I let my imagination roam," I can barely believe I just said that. At the same time, I'm filled with pride that thanks to everything I experienced in Tuscany, I can finally embrace my artistic soul and no longer be ashamed of it.

"Pfff," he scoffs and rolls his eyes. "You and your daydreams."

Now, it's me who takes a disappointed step back. "Just listen to it before you judge." My voice is firm, just like my gaze.

"Come on, Hanna Daydreamer," he spits out the words like spoiled milk. Did he really call me that? Even though I've always tried not to show him this side of me?

Since when has he been like this?

"Weren't you listening to me earlier? I've already set

272

everything in motion. I had drawings made, made down payments, and placed orders. The look of the estate has already been decided," he snaps at me.

I can hardly organize my thoughts.

Why did he do this? Just because he's the sole borrower, he thinks he can decide everything without me? Who does he think he is? And who does he think I am? His obedient servant?

The estate hasn't even been sold yet! Who knows, maybe Vico…

"Don't look at me like that. Of course, I've taken care of everything," he rants, waving his hands in the air. "I've always made the decisions. Why should that change now?" There's a hint of *because you're not capable of doing it anyway* in his words.

"What other decisions have you made without me?" I ask with growing unease. He's hiding something from me, I'm sure of it. Stoically crossing my arms over my chest, as much as I can with the cast, I observe how his movements become more and more agitated. "Out with it."

He swallows hard, then turns away. "It's for our own good," he says. Upset, he paces back and forth. "You have to understand, I've done everything to ensure we have a secure future. For you, Hanna. Only for you!" He stops by the window, turns around, and presses his fingertips together, forming a triangle with his hands. "That's what you always wanted. Nothing was more important to you than that."

Perhaps he expects me to approach him now. To thank him for taking such good care of me and to be happy that he's willing to shoulder this burden for me.

But it can't go on like this. I've let him have his way

for years, forgetting about myself in the process. That has to stop now.

"That's true. However, you can't decide over my head about the path we're going to take together," I reply.

With a frosty expression, he approaches me. "Now suddenly you have a problem with that?" His voice almost breaks. "What's wrong with you, Hanna? Did that gigolo put these ideas into your head?"

Gigolo?

No. This won't work. I know exactly what he's trying to do here, but it won't work. Not today.

"Don't try to deflect from the topic. I asked you something, and I want to hear the answer. Right now," I say firmly, not allowing myself to look away. "What other decision have you made?"

He snorts disdainfully. "I used the bed-and-breakfast as collateral for the loan. I had to do it. Otherwise, I would never have gotten so much money from the bank."

Wait a minute. He mortgaged our bed-and-breakfast to take out a loan in his name? The place he only refers to as *the* bed-and-breakfast instead of *our* bed-and-breakfast even though I've invested thousands of unpaid working hours and the little money I had from selling the family jewelry into its renovation?

If all this is dissolved, he will ultimately have enriched himself through me!

"You can't do that!" I gasp, but words fail me.

He shakes his head in incomprehension. "Of course, I can do that. The bed-and-breakfast is mine. Have you forgotten?"

"On paper, maybe. But when I sold my father's ring to invest in the roof repairs, you promised me that…" I can't continue. Because I hear how naive I sound. Tears well up in my eyes.

Now of all times, his expression softens. He comes closer and gently takes hold of my upper arms. "Why are you making a big deal out of nothing? We're getting married, Hanna. Then everything will be ours together," he says in a soft voice. "Can't you see that you're being unfair to me right now?"

Is that the truth? Am I being unfair to him? Or is it the other way around?

I sob, not knowing what to think anymore. I've never once stood in the way of Florian's plans.

He was the focused doer. I was the useless daydreamer.

Who are we today?

Are we still the same?

And if we are, is that right?

In his eyes, I search for answers to my questions.

"Wasn't I always there for you?" he asks, so full of disappointment that my heart tightens painfully. "Didn't I always give you what you needed? First a job, then a home. And now even the prospect of a financially secure future."

"You did," I acknowledge, and everything he says is true. Yet deep inside me, I feel that beneath this logical surface, another truth is simmering. "But every coin has two sides, and you've always made sure I only see the one that benefits you," I say, surprising myself with my words. My tears suddenly cease. I lock eyes with him. "Did you ever truly care about me?"

He tilts his head. "Of course."

"Then why did you never ask for my opinion?" I clench my fists, sweat forming in my palms. "Why did you dictate the course of our lives as if mine belonged exclusively to you?"

Actually, I can answer the question myself. Because I allowed it. It was just as much my fault as his. He was the absolutist doer. I was the silent order follower.

I press my lips together, so he won't see how much they tremble. We are closer to the core of our relationship than ever before. And I know it's time to reveal the essence.

I lock eyes with him. "Do you love me?" I ask intently.

Without a moment's hesitation, he nods vigorously. Before he can reply any further, I raise my hand.

"Me, Florian. Not the diligent Hanna who bakes you bread, cleans the huts without complaining, and always strives to please you," I pause for a moment to emphasize my words. "But the person I am in here." I place my hand over my heart. "With all my dreams, strengths, and weaknesses."

At first, I see confusion in his eyes, but then his facial muscles slowly soften. His mouth opens, but he says nothing.

"You can't answer the question, can you? Because you don't really know who I am," I realize. He has never been interested in my thoughts. And a few moments ago, I understood why.

To him, too, I was always just Hanna Daydreamer.

"I…" He begins.

Shaking my head, I look down at my engagement ring. I gaze at it for a few seconds, then I exhale deeply and lift my gaze to meet Florian's. "Sometimes you have to leave old paths to grow on new ones," I say in a choked voice. Slowly, I remove the ring from my finger, feeling as if I'm freeing myself from a shackle.

Chapter 42

Vico

Gliding seagulls screech overhead, and below us, the waves crash loudly against the coast. Here in Bari, even in early April, the temperatures are pleasant in the evenings, though the water remains cool. The gentle sea breeze tugs at my hair. I pull it back with a single gesture to study the display of the video camera in Matteo's hand.

My coach plays the recording in slow motion. In the video, I step to the front edge of the cliff in my swim shorts, checking my position. Then with a powerful push, I execute a somersault with a twist.

"Here," Matteo stops the footage, pointing with his finger at my legs. "See how crooked they are."

I nod absentmindedly. "I'll tighten up more, got it."

For a moment, his gaze flickers to me. It's better if I pretend not to notice the questioning expression on his face.

"What else?" I try to sound at least somewhat engaged.

He lets the video play again. "The entire somersault is rubbish. Your lack of body tension continues into the twist." Shaking his head, he stops the video once more. "Look at your calves and toes. What is that? Jello?"

"Mm-hmm," I mumble, annoyed at myself. If I show up at the competition in two weeks with such a performance, I might lose my sponsorship. The criteria in the contract are strict. If you don't deliver, you're out. "I'll try again now." I quickly turn to head back to the take-off point.

"But this time, please concentrate," Matteo calls after me.

He noticed. As much as I try to be fully present in what I love—cliff diving—I can't stop thinking about Hanna. We didn't say goodbye to each other. The news of her engagement hit me so hard that I couldn't bear to see her one last time. It's over. I should be indifferent to Hanna, yet my heart rebels.

She will marry Florian. And with him, she'll turn my home into a bed & breakfast.

I clench my fists and shake my head to free myself from the tightness in my chest. These thoughts have no place here. What surrounds me now—the cliff, the tempestuous sea, my sport—that's what matters. So I take a deep breath of salty air and march all the way to the front edge of the rock.

"Show me your best somersault with a twist," Matteo shouts from below. "You can do it."

I know he wants to help me, but he's only adding more pressure this way. In moments before the jump, where there used to be calmness within me, chaos reigns today. Nevertheless, I nod energetically.

My thoughts dictate my life, and I control my thoughts. As long as I remind myself that I can do it, I can.

I can do this.

Focus. Tighten my muscles. Eyes on. Takeoff.

Arch into the somersault. I embrace my legs—and I wish I were embracing Hanna.

Glimpse at the water for orientation. The sea green—just like her eyes.

What now?

What comes next?

Suddenly, I hit the sea surface hard. My muscles give way, and a dull pain shoots through my entire body. Split seconds later, my legs touch the sandy seabed.

Fuck.

I messed up again. This was the twentieth attempt in this training session, and with each try, my performance got worse.

I stay underwater for as long as I can hold my breath. Eventually, I know how Matteo will react to this jump. But what am I supposed to do? I'm already trying everything, but not even thinking about Hanna's life-threatening illness helps me get her out of my mind. Let alone my heart.

With strong strokes, I swim toward the rocks and pull myself out of the water.

Matteo sighs, exhausted. "What's going on with you?"

Instead of answering, I shrug and grab the towel.

"Is it the pressure from the competition?" He sets the camera aside and nods toward the folding chairs we brought. "Come on. Talk to me."

Weary, I sink into one of the chairs and gaze out over the vastness of the sea as I dry my shoulders. "I don't know what's happening either."

"You haven't trained for several weeks. Of course, you might be a bit rusty. But what I saw today…" He hesitates to speak the truth, but his perplexity is evident. "And it's not just about your diving."

So he noticed that too. And here I thought I was hiding it pretty well from him. I rest my head in my hands and take a deep breath.

"Wherever your thoughts are, they're certainly not here," he says earnestly, and suddenly, I feel his hand on my shoulder. "We're friends, man. Maybe I can help, but only if you spill the beans."

"Thanks for the offer, but there's nothing you could help with anymore," I reply. During dinner at the vineyard, I had the chance to change the course of events. I could have gone all in to find out what Hanna truly feels and whether there's a future for us.

But I didn't.

Instead, I let her go. Maybe I even pushed her right into Florian's arms. On top of that, the estate is now sold. "It's too late."

He pats my shoulder. "I understand," he says, even though he has no idea what's going on with me. How could he know that suddenly I'm filled with longing for a woman, when I've always told him how much I cherish my freedom? "What now? How do we get this under control?"

If I only knew. I look at him, seeking help. "They say time heals all wounds, right?" I immediately see my father before me. With all his grief and despair. And the realization dawns on me, how naive it is to hope that one day I'll forget Hanna.

"It does, I suppose," Matteo sounds more optimistic than I feel. "But the competition is in two weeks. If you don't—"

"I know." Despite the turmoil of my feelings, I'm fully aware of what's at stake.

The only future I have left could go down the drain

if I don't manage to let go of this other dream, which will forever remain out of reach.

With clenched fists, I quickly get up from the folding chair. "Time for another try."

Chapter 43

Hanna

With the suitcase I packed in Italy in my hand, I stand before Noah's white-plastered house nestled in the middle of the forest. It's already dark around me, and the frogs croak by the nearby mountain lake.

Inside, there's a warm glow of light. Through the floor-to-ceiling windows, I see my brother and Elina cooking together. He's slicing carrots, dressed in his usual plaid shirt with a white T-shirt peeking out. His three-day beard gives his rugged face a daring charm. Elina stirs a steaming pot and can't seem to take her eyes off him. Now he sets the knife aside, takes a carrot slice, and takes a step toward her. With a mischievous grin, Elina shakes her blond hair back and lets him feed her.

The way they look at each other, as if there's nothing more important in the world than their love, makes me smile involuntarily. I notice that the sight no longer hurts me. On the contrary, I'm genuinely happy for them with all my heart. It becomes clear to me that true love exists, and Florian and I have never felt it.

As for Vico and me…

Tears fill my eyes, and I'm unsure of their origin. Are they from the sadness of realizing I've allowed myself to be suppressed in my relationship for years? Or are they from the anger at myself for accepting the marriage proposal when I knew something was wrong?

Don't think for a moment that Vico is waiting for you. I told him about our engagement. He'll never forgive you, Florian had yelled at me after I left the inn. At that moment, I realized he had suspected something all along. That's why he surprised me with a visit to Collina da sogno, even bringing roses. He was afraid of losing me—as his workforce.

How could I have been so blind? And to hurt the man who helped me find myself again, of all people?

Feeling heavy-hearted, I climb the stairs to the wooden veranda and knock on the door.

Elina opens it with a joyful giggle. "Hanna." Her smile fades instantly as her eyes fall on my suitcase. "Oh my God, what happened?"

My throat feels tight. I bite down on my lower lip and blink rapidly.

She comes closer, lovingly putting her arm around my shoulder and guiding me inside. "Could you take Hanna's luggage, please?" she calls out to Noah, who is still in the kitchen at the stove.

He turns around now, immediately grasping the situation. "Um… sure." He hastily wipes his hands on a dish towel and walks to the door. It's clear that seeing me in such a state makes him uncomfortable, and I understand why. For many years, I hid my true feelings, even from him.

"Sit down," Elina directs me to the sofa. "What would you like to drink? Tea, coffee, juice? Or perhaps a shot of Schnapps?"

I wave her off and sink into the orange cushions. "Can I stay with you for a few days?"

With a sympathetic expression, Elina joins me on the sofa and hugs me tightly. "As long as you want."

Grateful, I nod, and now I can feel the tears welling up, impossible to hold back any longer. I cry on Elina's shoulder, and she hands me tissues and gently strokes my back until I calm down at least a little.

"Do you want to talk about it?" she asks afterward, without putting any pressure on me.

I want to talk because I no longer want to hide myself and my feelings. But where should I start? Probably at the end of the story. "I broke up with Florian."

For a moment, Elina looks as if she's seen a ghost.

"Actually, the only unbelievable thing about it is that I didn't do it much earlier," I confess, and then I proceed to tell her about the dynamics that kept me tethered to Florian all those years. I grab a pillow and knead it as I share every thought swirling in my head with her for minutes on end.

"That's why I was certain I couldn't survive without him. I knew he would take care of me as long as he was by my side. In my mind, I was dependent on him," I conclude, feeling ashamed even as the words leave my lips.

Was I myself possibly being with him only because of that? Did not only he take advantage of me, but also I of him?

"That's what he wanted you to believe," Elina looks at me intensely.

I pluck a loose thread from the pillow on my lap. There might be some truth to that. He was always trying to keep me small. "Do you think so?"

"I'm afraid so," she shrugs. "Noah and I talked about

it often. He was always skeptical of Florian but didn't realize how bad it really was."

So this man not only deceived me, but he locked me in a gilded cage, and no one truly saw it. I nod absentmindedly.

"What happened that made you realize it now?" my future sister-in-law asks next.

A wistful smile spreads across my face, because there's only one person responsible for this realization. "Vico." My heart feels heavy.

"Ooooh, that sounds intriguing," Elina fidgets on the sofa. "Tell me everything."

Noah, who has been quiet in the background, steps closer and nods encouragingly. There's no reason to hide something that's been affecting me, so I share with them the story of our encounter.

I tell them about the moment I first looked into his magical eyes. About the closed-off sadness that surrounded him at first. And about his longing for freedom, which I could feel in every moment with him.

Our deep conversations. And the way he looked at me when I talked about my dreams.

"We showed each other the colors of our desires. And it was… so liberating." The memory rises bittersweetly within me.

Elina clasps her hands to her chest. "Oh, how wonderful," she exclaims with delight. "It sounds amazing."

"That was the thing. However, with each passing day, it became clearer that there can be no future for us," I continue sadly.

I share in detail about the estate, the broken family, and Vico's big dream of cliff diving.

286

"He wants to be free. Lead an unattached life. Adrenaline is his happiness engine," I shrug.

Elina tilts her head thoughtfully. "And do you think he wouldn't be willing to give up his freedom for you?"

Not in my wildest dreams would I think of asking that of him. But that's not the point. By getting engaged to Florian, I deeply hurt him. Even if he might have honestly hoped at some point that we could have a future together, I surely destroyed that possibility.

Instead of answering Elina, I just wearily shake my head.

"What about you? Would you be willing to give up your security for him?" She looks at me expectantly.

"You mean, travel with him in his camper and live hand-to-mouth?" I had never thought about that. All I had in mind was the vision of both of us on the estate. Although breaking up with Florian meant giving up more security than I ever thought possible, it doesn't mean that I can just do whatever I want now, right?

Could I really give up any form of stability? And even if I could, would it be enough to let Vico know how much he means to me? Could it heal the hurt I caused him?

Elina's eyes sparkle conspiratorially. "Why not?" she says, as if it were the easiest thing ever. "That's how it is with true love, as you told me just a few weeks ago."

"But I don't even know what he really feels," I counter.

Maybe I was the only one feeling the sparks whenever we were close. Besides, he acted so strangely distant after finding out about my epilepsy. Perhaps my engagement was just the final blow, but there was already a wall between us before.

She seems completely unfazed by my objections. "Then find out."

It's not that simple. "Even if I could leave everything that ever mattered to me behind, that wouldn't be…" I pause as a thought emerges from nowhere. "Vico will never be truly free as long as his family is unhappy," I say. His sisters mean everything to him.

Elina might say something in response, but I don't hear it. I'm too busy continuing my train of thought.

"…and his family will be unhappy if they're homeless," I murmur, touching my forehead as if that would help me think better. "So if I manage to take away his worries about his family…and thus give him the freedom he longs for…"

Yes. If I make that possible for him, maybe he could forgive me.

Breathlessly, I grab Elina's hands. "I will save the estate from being sold." Who knows if Florian even wants to buy it now that he has lost his only employee?

She blinks in confusion. She must think I'm crazy. And maybe it is a bit crazy. Because if it were that easy, I would have already come up with an idea of how to do it.

"There must be a way," I say because I want to believe in nothing else. "I will find it." And once his family is safe, I'll give up my own security for Vico.

Chapter 44

Vico

I pour myself an espresso, open the sliding door of the van, and sit on the floor to breathe in the cool morning air. Camping is not allowed here in this parking lot, but I couldn't stand the company at the campsite for another second.

Everywhere, there were only happy couples. I was surrounded by loving glances and romantic gestures. Candlelight. Music. Affectionate touches.

Here, on this plain parking lot, it's better. Only a lone seagull wanders back and forth in front of my van, searching for food. The sea murmurs peacefully in the background, and the sun climbs over the horizon. It's the perfect moment to focus on what lies ahead.

Tomorrow is the day. Tomorrow is the big competition that will decide my future as a cliff diver.

I take a sip of my coffee and try to keep my thoughts solely on the dives I've perfected over the past twelve days. It was hard work, but now I'm ready.

For safety's sake, I go through the movements again and again. Every time the dive ends in the water, Hanna's sea-green eyes appear in my mind.

Perhaps the very barriers we've built ourselves sometimes hinder us from being happy. That's what I told her shortly before her accident. At a moment when I first suspected that it could actually be the truth.

But what if we take the sledgehammer and tear them down? What if we do what our hearts tell us? she responds again in my thoughts, and then, as well as now, I know that it's no longer about whether she climbs onto the Vespa or not.

Desperately, I shake my head. How am I supposed to compete in this competition that suddenly seems so insignificant because I can't forget this woman?

Since my mother's death, I was certain that it would be better never to have loved than to lose love. But now, I can't help but feel that I may have been mistaken. I've done everything to hold my heart, to avoid getting hurt. Yet I feel as if I may never be truly happy again.

Does it even make sense? Shouldn't one savor what they have while it's still possible? Enjoy every moment? Every touch? And every kiss?

The ringing of the phone interrupts my thoughts. Hope rises within me.

What if it's Hanna calling? What if she can't forget the picture she painted for both of us?

She doesn't want the inn, I'm certain of that. And I know she doesn't truly love Florian either.

What if she's calling to give us both a chance?

I find my phone under the pillow, but as soon as I see the display, disappointment washes over me. How foolish of me to hope that Hanna would reach out. What reason would she have to do so? She has her precious Florian. And her oh-so-secure future, which means everything to her.

Camilla, on the other hand, has every reason to call me. Since my departure, I haven't had the heart to contact her. My fear of experiencing her grief over the sale of the estate is too great. Thoughtfully, I hold the phone in my hand as it continues to ring. I must answer the call. At the very least, I owe her that.

"Hey." I try to sound casual as if my world is light and carefree. "How's it going?"

"It's been incredibly busy. You know, the move and… renovations at the main house are already underway…" Her voice breaks. She clears her throat with effort. "We're managing."

Immediately, my shoulders turn as hard as concrete. "I'm sorry I couldn't stay."

"Your competition is important, we understand," she says in a tone that makes it clear she knows my departure isn't solely about cliff diving. "Pietro's friends have been a great help to us. And Alessia comes whenever she can. We're almost there." The last words come out strained.

I want to apologize to my sister urgently, to take away some of her sadness, but I can't find the right words.

What can I even say? A lame *I'm sorry* won't be nearly enough.

At the other end of the line, there is silence. Then I hear her trembling exhale.

"How are the twins?" I ask quickly, hoping that changing the subject will lighten both of our moods.

But the opposite happens. A heavy sob reaches my ears. I set the espresso aside, feeling my throat tighten so much that I'm certain I won't be able to swallow it now. "What's wrong, Camilla?"

It takes her a long time to compose herself enough to respond. "The little ones are doing well," she says with a hoarse voice.

"But?" I can tell there's something more.

"Father…" She breathes heavily. "Since he left the estate, everything has gotten much worse. Yesterday, he was so out of it that he didn't even recognize my two girls."

My God. I was sure a change of scenery would help him leave the past behind. But it seems to have had the opposite effect. "How could that happen?"

"You've seen him. He hasn't been himself for a long time. And the sale of the estate dealt him the final blow." Suddenly, she sounds distant. As if she needs to switch off her emotions to be able to talk about it at all. "I'm afraid he'll…"

She doesn't have to say it, and I don't want to hear it. "Fuck."

Unconsciously, I clench my fist so tightly that my fingernails dig into my palms. My fear of my own emotions has destroyed everything. The estate, my family, and - worst of all - my chance for an entirely new life with Hanna. It's all connected, and only now am I able to see it.

"If there were a way to undo it…" My God, if only that were possible. I would do it. Because Hanna's dream is my dream too. I've never seen it as clearly as I do right now.

"There isn't," Camilla interrupts. "We have to look forward." An infinite sadness echoes in her words. "You too, Vico."

Every fiber of my being resists. Because if I do that, I see days filled with emptiness that not even the adrenaline rush of cliff diving can fill. Since I've been back, I've tried my best to pick up where I left off, but now I realize that I don't even want that life back.

I want Hanna. Despite all the obstacles standing between us, just one day with her would be worth more than a lifetime without her.

There must be a way to show her how serious my feelings are for her. And that I would be willing to face my greatest fear for her. But how can I prove to her that my heart beats only for her?

"Vico? Are you still there?" Camilla asks.

I mumble absentmindedly because my mind is somewhere else.

An idea is forming inside me. With each passing second, it becomes clearer. A picture builds up in my mind's eye and eventually turns into a solid plan. An exciting tingle floods my body. Suddenly, I know exactly what I have to do next. And it certainly isn't jumping off a cliff to win some meaningless competition.

Chapter 45

Hanna

Nearly two weeks have passed since my breakup with Florian. Twelve days and nights in which I've done nothing but rack my brain over how to save the estate.

Today, I find myself once again sitting at Noah's handcrafted kitchen table, surfing the internet in search of ideas.

Taking out a loan is out of the question. No bank would give me the money for that. And I don't know anyone I could ask for financial support. The crowdfunding campaign I started last week in my desperation is progressing slowly, despite my efforts to attract attention.

I rest my head on my healthy hand and gaze out the window at the mountain lake at the end of the clearing. What else could I try?

Playing the lottery and hoping for a miracle?

Asking for donations?

I blow the bangs from my forehead with a sigh of frustration. Then, in my desperation, I type *saving buildings* into the browser's search function.

An article about activists barricading themselves in a house to prevent demolition appears on my screen. There's also an advertisement for a book on building renovation and real estate listings.

"That was a dead end, once again," I say to myself.

Despite my unsuccessful search so far, I can't give up. On the contrary, I need to step up my efforts, as the sale of the estate could be imminent. Semmtal is a small village where everyone knows everyone and everything. I'm aware that Florian hasn't returned to Tuscany yet, which means the sales contract hasn't been signed. But that doesn't mean it couldn't happen tomorrow.

"How do you get money?" I voice the question, hoping that saying it out loud might help.

How do you get money?, I repeat in my mind. *How did Florian get money for the inn whenever we needed it?*

Funding.

Yes. That's it. I need to search for funding opportunities!

My joy is short-lived, though. Because I have no idea how these subsidies work. Florian never let me help when we applied for funding. No, I correct myself with a touch of bitterness in my heart—he applied for funding. But in the next moment, I refocus on my goal.

Where did he learn about possible funding opportunities? Where did the money come from? I rummage through my memory and find some helpful information.

Florian used to boast that there are funding opportunities everywhere. Regions, countries, states—even the European Union has multimillion-dollar funds just waiting to be tapped into.

That sounds fantastic. And it's the first real glimmer of hope.

Feverishly, I type the corresponding terms into the browser's search box using my index finger. I start by scouring the websites of the State of Tyrol and the federal government, and then move on to the European Union's website.

There, I find a list of subsidies, which I translate one after the other into German with the help of a website.

I click on *Restoration of Cultural Heritage* and painstakingly work my way through the sections that describe the funding, relying on my limited knowledge of English. With each passing second, my excitement grows.

This could be the right fit.

If I manage to declare the country estate as culturally significant, I can apply for the subsidies. I search for the button to submit the application, but I can't find it. Instead, I notice a bolded piece of information at the bottom of the page.

Application deadline: 31st of March, it says.

It's already April. And there are no other suitable fundings listed on this page either.

Dammit. My hope dissipates, and I lean back in disappointment, staring at the screen.

Could this really be the end? Do I have to give up?

Frustrated, I continue to explore various subpages of the website, and I'm eventually redirected to a page of the Italian government.

Of course! Subsidies are also granted within Italy. But can I, as a foreigner, even apply for them? Especially when I don't even own the country estate?

Never mind. I'll deal with that later. I search the website, but nothing seems to fit. So next, I look for regional subsidies for Tuscany, and surprisingly, I find something.

"Fund for the Revitalization of Original

Agriculture," I translate and delve into the application details. The Italian language used is so complex that I can barely understand it. I have to look up words multiple times until I have a somewhat clear understanding of the requirements.

I need a revitalization plan—whatever that is. Moreover, not only the plan but also a cost estimate must be presented to an allocation committee.

The application deadline is… today!

I have neither a plan nor anything else, but I click on the button labeled *Electronics Preregistration*. As soon as the new page opens, I encounter my first problem.

In the top fields of the online form, I have to enter the name and address of the property owner, who also seems to be the applicant. With my heart pounding, I type in the information—I don't have any other choice anyway. The rest of the details come easily to me, as I have already gathered most of them for Florian's checklist. I provide the construction year, area measurements, condition, and the size of the agricultural land.

The next field is a free-text box. Here, I have to describe the purpose for which the money is needed. Without hesitation, I write about a new oil press, renovation work on the house, setting up a farm shop, and funds for acquiring additional plants. Then I scroll down, filling in the missing information as best as I can, until I finally reach the button labeled "Submit Now."

I exhale with effort. My finger hovers over the Enter key.

I shouldn't doubt myself, but it happens automatically.

Pressing this button means I will have to face a committee and convince them of a project that doesn't even exist yet.

I, Hanna Daydreamer, have to deliver an impassioned speech and risk being ridiculed.

Am I really ready to do this?

"You can do this," I tell myself, clenching my fist.

My heart gallops, my hands are sweaty. But I do it.

I press the Enter key.

Seconds later, a new page appears.

Thank you for your application. Please have a signed copy ready for your hearing.

Your presentation appointment: April 15th, 2:00 PM, Palazzo Vecchio, Florence, Room 12.a.

My heart comes to an abrupt halt. My breath stops.

Oh my God, that's tomorrow already!

With my casted arm, I can't draw up a plan, nor can I drive a car. How on earth am I going to manage this?

Chapter 46

Vico

I breathe a sigh of relief and press my mobile phone closer to my ear. "Thank you so much. This is amazing," I say to the lawyer on the other end of the line before ending the call.

For the past fifteen minutes, I've paced back and forth in front of the van because my legs just wouldn't stay still. Ever since my phone call with Camilla yesterday morning, a fire has been lit inside me. At first, it was just a small flame, but now it has grown into a raging wildfire.

I can't be stopped now, especially after receiving the confirmation that changes everything. With my heart pounding, I open the internet browser to search for Florian's guesthouse website. Contacting him is the next step of my plan. Without much thought, I write him an email, telling him that we urgently need to discuss the contract. I attach contact details for a video call because I want to look him in the eyes when he hears the news.

After sending the message, I look around. Waiting for his response here would be a waste of time. I have a lot to do, including informing Matteo that I won't be participating in the competition. Not this one or any other.

There's only one jump left for me, and that's into a

new future that I'm determined to fight for with all that I have.

Before I can talk to my coach, my phone announces an incoming call from Florian. That he's calling back so quickly is strange. Did my message scare him? I straighten my back and answer the call.

His grim face appears on the screen. "What's up?" he asks curtly in English.

I smile openly at him. "Good morning to you too," I reply in English.

"Um… yeah. Sure," he says with a disdainful snort, furrowing his eyebrows. "So what do we still need to discuss? Is there a problem with clearing out the estate? If that's it, I can't grant any extensions. The contractors…"

"We don't need an extension," I say firmly, cutting him off.

He rolls his eyes impatiently. "Then what else? I don't have all day, so…"

I'm more than happy to get straight to the point. "Like I said, we don't need an extension because we won't be moving out." Boom. The bomb has been dropped. I can't help but grin.

Florian responds with a mocking laugh, but then falls silent and looks at me sternly. "How dare you waste my precious time with such nonsense?" he asks imperiously.

Should I tell him now? Doesn't he deserve to stew a little longer? Maybe. But that's not the kind of person I am. That's who he is.

"I'm sorry to inform you that it's not nonsense. The contract is void, and the estate remains in the possession of the Olivetta family," I say calmly.

"The contract is valid," he retorts brusquely, reaching for something off-camera. "I have a neatly drawn-up agreement here, reviewed by lawyers. Signed by your father." The contract appears in his hands, and he flips to the last page. "Here you go, everything is here."

"Of course, there's a signature. I'm not denying that," I reply, remaining completely composed.

His cheeks under the full beard flush red. "That's your father's signature, right? Or did you try to pass off a forgery on me?" His facial expression becomes more aggressive with each word. "I'll sue you until you're left with nothing, pal."

It's hard to keep my composure, but I won't stoop to his level. "Save yourself the legal fees; the signature is undoubtedly genuine," I reply.

He audibly exhales. "Then there's nothing more to discuss. The outbuilding of the estate must be vacated by tomorrow evening." There it is again, that sinister grin. "It was nice talking to you." I can tell there's a curse word on the tip of his tongue, and I wonder immediately why he doesn't say it. Is Hanna nearby? Can she hear our conversation? And if so, does she suspect what I'm planning?

If that's the case, Florian will experience something he'll never forget and regret it for the rest of his life.

"Not so fast." I raise my index finger. "My father did sign, that's true. However, it has come to light that he is not authorized to sign on behalf of the estate."

That's the truth, and nothing but the truth. Camilla's information about my father's final decline gave me the idea, and the lawyer earlier confirmed it. Father is not legally competent in his current state, just like my mother wasn't when she forgot that she already had a car and bought another one. It won't be difficult to prove this fact with a medical assessment and then proceed with the annulment of the contract.

"How stupid do you think I am? Of course, he is authorized to sign," Florian snaps. "I had my lawyer investigate the ownership beforehand." His face glows with pride.

"That's also true. The estate belongs to him," I explain calmly. "The catch is that he is not authorized to sell it."

Suddenly, all the restlessness leaves my body. I don't need to keep moving to release energy anymore. Filled with inner tranquility, I lean against the driver's door of my van and let the sun warm my face.

Although the bright light makes it difficult to see the display, I can clearly tell that Florian is searching for words but can't find any.

Perhaps it's better if I continue speaking. Despite the remaining risk that the medical assessment might not turn out as expected, I don't let it show. "My lawyer will gladly send all the necessary documents to your lawyer," I say with a self-assured grin, sounding like a businessman. "For now, I would still recommend you withdraw the construction workers from the estate. Just to avoid further costs for you."

I strain my ears, hoping to catch any sounds in the background. A muffled exclamation. Or heavy breathing. But there's nothing. Hanna doesn't seem to be here. It's just Florian, and the pure fury etched on his face.

"The estate is mine," he says forcefully, as if he believes he can impress me with that statement. His

302

eyes narrow to slits. "Just like Hanna," he adds. "Got it?"

No, I don't get it at all. "Hanna belongs to one person only: herself," I hold his gaze firmly. So he knows what an idiot he is to think he could ever possess her like an object.

"What do you know…" He lets out a forced snort, but it doesn't impress me.

"Enough," I reply succinctly.

He rubs his forehead.

It's time to end this call. I have far more important things to do than explain to Florian that he doesn't deserve the woman by his side. "You'll receive the documents next week. Whether you withdraw the construction workers today or then, I'll leave that to you. After all, it's your money."

In an instant, he appears weary, as if he has realized he's lost. And maybe he even senses that more is about to happen. "I guess I need to make some urgent phone calls."

"I'm sorry it had to come to this," I say, and I mean it. I never wanted to hurt anyone. Not Hanna, not my family, and not even him.

He sighs wistfully. "You have no idea…" he says, then abruptly ends the call.

Puzzled by his last words, I lower the phone. What did he mean by that?

Whatever it is, it doesn't matter anymore. Because my focus is now solely on my goal.

Time for the next step. I climb into the driver's seat of the van and start the engine.

Chapter 47

Hanna

Elina's cheeks are burning red. Focused, she navigates Noah's car onto the highway, heading south. "Oh my God, I can't believe I'm doing this."

Gratefully, I smile at her. "You're the best, you know that?"

She accelerates to merge into the heavy traffic. "And you're not the first to tell me that on a fiery road trip to Italy."

"How do you mean?" I lean forward in the passenger seat, curious.

"Love trips to Bella Italia are my specialty," she replies, flipping down the sun visor. "My friend Maya once had an urgent need to go to Rome because of love. She didn't have a broken arm, but she had no driver's license. So I stepped in." She grins mischievously.

"I hope it had a happy ending?" I inwardly pray that it was the case. It would be a good sign, and I desperately need that. Because apart from the printed application, which Vico's father still needs to sign before we continue to Florence, I have nothing else.

No project plan, no cost estimate, no drawings.

In such a short time and with this cursed cast, it was impossible to put something together. All I have is the vision in my mind, which I've been refining all night.

"No. It wasn't a happy ending," I hear Elina say. "It

was even a spectacular ending! With fireworks, sparklers, and thunderous applause." Her dreamy expression says it all. "Every time someone finds the love of their life, I could cry with joy. And that's how it was with Maya and her Josh. Absolutely magical."

Her romantic mood takes hold of me. "And it was the same with you and Noah," I say, hopeful that Vico and I will have such an ending too. If it's true love, it just has to be, right?

She nods dreamily. Then she reaches out her hand to me. "Today, you'll get your happy ending. I can feel it."

I wish I were as certain as she is. But the closer we get to Tuscany, the more nervous I become. Without even speaking to the Olivettas, I've submitted the funding application.

What if Vico's father doesn't sign it?

And how will Vico react? Especially when he finds out I'm doing this so he can pursue his dream of cliff diving. And that even with me, if he wants.

These and many more questions haunt me throughout the entire journey. They make me grow quieter with every passing minute as the lush green landscape flashes by. Elina notices too. She keeps smiling over at me and playing cheerful music to lift my spirits.

By the time we arrive, I'm sweating profusely. As we pass through the entrance to the estate, my head starts pounding.

No, not now. This is the most inconvenient moment for a seizure. Thankfully, a doctor is sitting next to me. She knows about my condition, and if it were to happen, no one could help me better than her.

"This is absolutely beautiful!" Elina exclaims with excitement. "Do we need to go to the main house or there in front?" She points at the single-story, red-brick building.

Lost in thought, I nod, looking at the stately estate. Someone has trimmed the wild vines, and the rickety chairs have disappeared. "To the bungalow, please. Camilla probably knows where her father is," I mutter, noticing a white plastic tarp fluttering over the half-ruined wall.

What's going on here? Are they renovating? No, that can't be, as I don't see any workers around.

As soon as Elina stops the car, I leap out and hurry to the door. Only in passing do I notice how empty everything looks. The house seems almost abandoned. The doormat with its dark ornaments is missing, and the plant pots are gone.

Anxiously, I look at the doorbell.

The name is gone.

My God, has Camilla already moved out? And this even though the estate hasn't been sold yet?

Under the doorbell, I spot a sticky note.

We have moved, it says in Italian, followed by an address. I tear off the note, dash back to the car, and enter Camilla's new address into the navigation system.

It spits out a route with a fifteen-minute drive time.

That's good. We can't afford any more delays, as ninety miles still exists between us and our final destination in Florence. It's eleven o'clock, and I have to be at Palazzo Vecchio in three hours.

On the way to Camilla's place, we hardly talk. My excitement has a firm grip on me. I try to breathe evenly, hoping to prevent any potential epileptic episode. But when Elina stops the car in front of a Tuscan house with a flat roof and stone facade, I can barely contain my inner turmoil.

"Wait here, I'll be right back," I say breathlessly, grabbing the funding application and rushing to the front door.

Luckily, Camilla opens the door immediately. Her surprise is evident. "Ciao, Hanna."

"Is your father here?" I plead, feeling my hand damp with sweat holding the paper.

She nods, but her expression remains skeptical. "But he's not in a state to receive visitors. What do you want to discuss with him?"

With lips pressed together, I step closer. "I need to see him. It can't wait," I say urgently. "Please."

Still wary, she backs away, then turns and signals me to follow her. "We need to be quiet. The little ones are sleeping," she whispers as she leads me down a hallway filled with half-packed moving boxes. She stops in front of a white-painted door, raising a warning finger. "You have three minutes, no more."

That'll have to do. Hopefully. Despite my excitement, I gently knock on the door. There's no response from inside, so I open it. "Signor Olivetta?"

As soon as I enter the room, I see Vico's father sitting on a worn leather chair. He looks pale, his hands tremble, and he appears even thinner than at his birthday party. With lifeless eyes, he gazes into nothingness.

Swallowing hard, I step closer to him and crouch down. "It's me, Hanna."

He doesn't react.

"I'm here to help," I say, hoping to shake him out of his lethargy. "We have a chance to save the estate before it's sold." Instinctively, I reach for his hand. It's ice cold. "Signor Olivetta, can you hear me? You don't have to sell. There's another way." Quickly, I show him the application form. "I have a funding application here. You just need to sign it, and I'll take care of the rest. But it has to be done right away."

In the corner of my eye, I see Camilla turning away and disappearing down the hallway. My focus returns to Vico's father. I keep pressing his hand, hoping for any response.

A feeble whimper escapes his mouth. It's the first sign he gives me, telling me that his heart still clings to the traditional family estate.

With an encouraging nod, I show him the application. "It's not too late, but we need to act quickly."

His head moves jerkily from side to side. "The estate has already been sold," he murmurs so softly that I can barely hear it.

"You're mistaken," I reply with conviction. Florian made it clear on the drive back almost two weeks ago that there were still open points to be discussed before finalizing the deal. And since he hasn't left Semmtal since then, he wouldn't have had the opportunity to sign the contract.

No, Signor Olivetta is too confused to grasp reality.

However, he shakes his head again. This time, more forcefully. "It's over. See for yourself." With a barely noticeable gesture, he points at the half-height cabinet next to his chair.

A wave of unease washes over me. Full of concern, I

rise from my crouched position and open the top drawer.

There lies a contract.

I take it and hastily flip through the pages until I reach the last one.

It's signed.

Both by Florian and Signor Olivetta.

No, this can't be true.

The pounding in my temples intensifies, and the room around me suddenly feels distorted.

I sink to my knees, feeling drained of energy, as I slowly begin to grasp the significance of the document in my hands.

Chapter 48

Vico

As fast as my old crate carries me toward home, I race along the highway. I've already passed Rome, but I still have about four hours of driving ahead, and I know how to use them.

I turn off the radio, connect my headset to my phone, and dial Adriano's number.

"Well, look who's back," he says moments later, the sound of rushing waves in the background. He's probably at Spiaggia bianche.

I didn't even say goodbye to him in my desperation surrounding Hanna's engagement. A simple apology isn't enough at this point. I clear my throat, feeling ashamed. "I didn't know what to do with myself," I admit openly.

He laughs forgivingly. "Mm-hmm, so it's true then, what Alessia hinted at last week."

"Seems that way." The thought that so many people in my life already knew what was going on with me while I still thought I could fight it makes me smile. I step on the gas to overtake a truck whose exhaust fumes are creeping into my car through the ventilation.

"I'm happy for you, Vico." He sounds unexpectedly sentimental. "I hope you'll be happy with her."

And now he hits a sore spot. "She's still engaged to someone else," I say through gritted teeth. "And she has no idea that I…" For a moment, it's hard for me to continue speaking. Just the thought of saying it out loud overwhelms me. "…that I'm going back to my hometown to make her dream come true." And do everything in my power to show her how much she means to me.

My God. I'm actually in the process of turning my whole life upside down even though I can't be sure that Hanna carries the same longing deep inside her.

Nevertheless, I won't give up. Because where there's love, there will always be hope.

Those were Hanna's words just before she gave me one of the greatest gifts I've ever received. She showed me a future that I had forbidden myself from dreaming about. I haven't forgotten her, and that's good because she gives me the strength I need. I have nothing to lose and only everything to gain.

"How can I help?" Adriano asks on the other end of the line.

"You're the best." My seat creaks as I sit up straight and signal again to change lanes. "Here's the plan."

I quickly explain to him how I intend to save the estate. Adriano promises to activate his contacts, and I immediately get to work after ending the call.

During the rest of the drive, I make calls to restaurants and specialty shops in Tuscany and beyond. Through my work as a graphic designer, I have met many people over the years, and they are the ones I'll be reaching out to soon.

It's necessary because if I want to save the estate, I need to secure the funding. And what could be more fitting than doing that with what has always been the family's pride and joy: the best olive oil in the region.

Many of my contacts remember the Olivetta family's oil and place orders immediately. Maria, the owner of the local store, cheers with joy on the phone, and with each successful call and every mile I get closer to my hometown, I become happier.

Now that I know my plan will actually work, I can't wait to see Camilla and Alessia laughing from the bottom of their hearts again. And even though Aurora acted strangely during her last visit, I'm sure she'll be thrilled as well.

Who knows, maybe even Father will find some joy in the fact that soon we can relive the good memories. He'll reach the point that Hanna described to me about herself and her father's death.

She said she didn't want to miss out on all the beauty. She didn't want to forget but keep it alive within her.

That's what I wish for Father. And that's exactly what I'll do if I'm ever overcome by my own grief someday.

With this thought in mind, I write Camilla a short message. Even if I don't have time for lengthy explanations, she should at least know that there is hope again.

Chapter 49

Hanna

"The estate is sold?" Holding the signed contract in my hands, I scrutinize Vico's father. "How can that be?" Everything within me refuses to believe that it could really be over.

There is no response, only a pair of sad eyes staring right through me. I let the paper fall to the ground, massage my throbbing temples, and concentrate on breathing in and out. "We have to undo it."

"We don't have to," Camilla whispers in disbelief, standing in the doorway with the phone in her hand, her shoulders trembling. Alessia is here too.

"But our roots are what define us," I argue. It's what I said to Vico at Spiaggia bianche, and I still believe it. Those who still have roots should hold them, and the Olivettas have them.

"We don't have to undo it," Camilla repeats hesitantly as if she can't believe what she's saying. Then she steps toward me and pulls me into her arms. "Because it's already done."

I don't understand anything now. "How…? What…?" I stutter clumsily, looking past Camilla's shoulder to Alessia, who takes a handkerchief from her pocket.

Camilla strokes my back. "I just found out. The contract is void."

My God. I push away from her to look at her. "How can that be?"

She shrugs. "We'll find out more details soon. But right now, all that matters is that it's true, isn't it?"

You're right. "So that means…"

Tears well up in the corners of her eyes, her lower lip trembles. Unable to say anything, she nods.

For a moment, I'm paralyzed. I can hardly gather a clear thought and look around, searching for what's next.

The funding application.

Vico's father needs to sign it.

Almost in a trance, I pick up the paper from the floor and hand it to Signor Olivetta. "Can I have your permission?"

A glimmer of hope flashes across his face. With eyes glistening, he takes the application from me and puts his signature on it.

"Grazie mille," I say, touched, as he hands the application back to me. To bid farewell, I plant a kiss on his unshaven cheek.

Out of nowhere, he wraps his arms around me and pulls me close. He says nothing, just breathes out in bursts. But his gesture alone is enough for me to understand how much my help means to him.

"I won't give up, I promise," I whisper in his ear, then gently disentangle myself from him and turn to Vico's sisters. "I have to be in Florence in about two hours for the presentation with the application. Are you coming?"

Alessia nods so vigorously that her long curls fall into her face.

Camilla smiles at me. "I wouldn't miss it for the

world. Just give me five minutes. I need to arrange for someone to look after my little ones," she says, rushing into the adjacent room while I bid farewell to her father.

A short while later, she stands before me with her handbag. "Should I drive?" she asks, glancing at my cast.

I quickly shake my head. "Everything is arranged."

"Perfetto. Then I can inform Pietro on the way." She heads to the front door with an exhilarated expression, where Alessia impatiently taps her foot.

I follow her on unsteady legs.

It's really happening. The chance for a happy ending is alive.

Now, it all depends on me to make it come true.

Chapter 50

Vico

Yawning, I slow down the pace of my van. The engine stutters dangerously loud. "Don't fail me now," I warn it, tapping on the steering wheel as if that would positively affect the motor.

Surprisingly, the noise subsides. Thank goodness. I've invested so much in the past few hours, and breaking down now, so close to Collina da sogno, would be an unnecessary delay that I can't afford. After all, I still have a long way to go.

Only a few yards more, and I'll arrive at the estate. I can already see it on the horizon. I drive toward the main house with its majestic beauty, wild meadows, and cypress alley. With a warm feeling in my chest, I roll down the window and breathe in the aromatic air.

Yes, I feel it clearly.

This is where I belong.

This is my home.

However, for now, it's just a stopover to see if Florian has indeed given up and halted the construction work. Then I'll head farther north. Across the border to Austria, to Semmtal.

To where Hanna is.

I don't yet know exactly what I'll say to her. I can only hope that by the time I arrive, I'll find the right words.

Excitedly, I turn into the driveway and rattle toward the estate. There, I spot a small truck parked next to Camilla's bungalow. I park my van beside it and despite my weariness, jump out of the vehicle. At that moment, I see Pietro carrying a large box labeled cucina, with the tip of a cooking spoon sticking out between the flaps.

"Vico?" He abruptly stops and looks at me as if he can't believe I'm really here. "What…"

My sister replied to my message ten minutes ago, saying she'd immediately return here to meet me. But I don't see her anywhere. "Where is Camilla? And is Alessia here too?"

Before he can answer, Pietro's phone rings. He takes it out of his shirt pocket and sighs heavily when he recognizes the caller. "I love this woman, but sometimes she drives me crazy."

Despite my inner turmoil, I can't help but grin as he answers the call. "Moving service. How may I assist you?" he asks with an affectionate smile.

I can't hear Camilla, but I can see the effect of her words on Pietro's face. Slowly, his forehead furrows. First, I see skepticism, then surprise, and finally, haste.

"My God," he says finally, covering his mouth with his hand.

"What is it?" My pulse quickens, and I step closer, searching his face.

Pietro nods. "Got it." Bewildered, he looks at me and takes the phone away from his ear. "You won't believe this."

The way he says it makes me suspicious. It's not something bad that happened. It's something… significant. "What is it?"

He hurries back to the house and locks the door. Then he points at my camper. "Get in the driver's seat; we have to leave immediately."

Automatically, I move. "Why?"

Arriving at the van, he grins at me with promise. "You'll see soon enough."

Chapter 51

Hanna

Elina screeches to a halt, and two massive stone pots with tall oleander bushes block our path. "We can't go any farther; the rest of the way you'll have to walk," she says.

"There's a no-entry zone in front of the Palazzo," Alessia confirms, nodding vigorously.

Camilla reaches for the door handle. "What time is it?"

"You have ten minutes left," Elina replies, her blond mane swirling around. Her hand is on mine, and I look into her concerned eyes. "Are you okay?"

I'm not sure. "It feels a bit strange," I nervously reply. "But the colors are real. No bright lights, just a slight headache."

"Tinnitus? Distorted taste? Dizziness?" She squints, as if trying to better assess my condition.

I shake my head in response.

"Okay. I'll catch up once I find a parking spot." She quickly turns to Camilla and Alessia. "Take good care of her, alright?" she asks the sisters, then nods encouragingly at me. "You've got this, Hanna."

The door next to me is flung open from the outside. Alessia's curly head appears in my field of vision. "Ready?" she asks breathlessly.

"Ready," I confirm, though the excitement already

gives me a queasy stomach. I leave the car and weave through the crowds of tourists in the pedestrian zone, with one of Vico's amazing sisters on each side, until we reach the vast paved square.

Alessia points toward a square building with stone facade that reminds me of a castle. "It's over there, ahead."

We head toward the entrance with the stone steps, guarded by life-sized figures. Only a few minutes later, we rush into the building. A courtyard with arched arcades and a cheerfully splashing fountain appears before us. The columns on the sides are adorned with ornaments and exude a dignified calmness despite the many tourists.

"Room 12.a, right?" Alessia hurries to the information board and frantically looks for the way. Then she waves us over. "This way."

I don't dare to ask for the time, but my intuition tells me my ten minutes are nearly up.

And that's exactly the case. When we reach the first floor, the door to room 12.a is already open. I stop as I arrive at the doorway.

Breathing heavily, I peek into the room. It only takes a split second for my excitement to turn into fear.

This is not just a simple project presentation in front of two or three officials, as I thought. No.

In this venerable room, there are more rows of spectators than I can count, and they are filled to the brim. At the front, on a small stage, tables are set up where the panel sits. Four men and five women look at me expectantly. Next to them is a podium with a laptop.

A young man with round glasses fixes his gaze on

me, stands up from his chair, and buttons his jacket. "Signora Olivetta?"

My throat tightens.

"Si," Camilla suddenly appears behind me, nudging me into the room and giving me a gentle push toward the stage.

That's all it takes to make me realize: Until now, I had many helpers. But for the last stretch of the journey, I must walk alone.

Despite the unease crawling incessantly within me, I straighten my shoulders and take a deep breath. Then on shaky legs, I stumble forward to the podium. Once there, I place the funding application in front of me and grip the table firmly, seeking at least a bit of support.

Showing Vico what's in my mind was one thing. Explaining to Florian that it's no longer just about pleasing him but also myself was another.

But this, this is bigger.

Much bigger.

I let my gaze sweep over the rows of spectators and then on to the panel. The lady with the short blond haircut looks kindly at me, but she impatiently taps her pen on the table at the same time. The man with bushy eyebrows beside her appears skeptical. With growing panic, I scrutinize the other jurors.

Suddenly, I feel like that time in school when I stood on stage, and the presentation of my visions turned into a disaster. I feel the shame like a heavy weight on my chest.

What if the man with glasses asks me afterward how I even came up with the idea to show up here with nothing but ridiculous utopias? Will the lady in the black-and-white-checkered suit laugh at me? In my panic, I can already see her parting her bright red lips to release her mocking laughter.

"Prego," the man with glasses signals with a hand gesture and a quick nod, urging me to start.

I swallow.

Restlessness spreads among the audience, and the murmuring reaches me even at the front.

"What's wrong with her?" someone whispers in amusement in Italian. Soft chuckles follow.

My mind goes blank all of a sudden. Even if I wanted to show the people in this room the images in my mind, I couldn't. There are none!

"Signora, begin your presentation, please," the spokesperson of the jurors repeats, tapping his watch warningly.

Shivering all over, I turn to face him. "There is no presentation," I say in a voice so soft that I can barely hear it myself.

He raises an eyebrow.

Oh God. This is going to be a complete disaster. What was I thinking, showing up here without everything prepared?

I look at the exit, where Alessia and Camilla stand with pressed lips, showing their support with crossed fingers. All their hope rests on me. It's their future I'm fighting for, Vico's happiness.

Even if I embarrass myself in front of the audience, laying out my dreams for the estate. Even if the jury deems me crazy, and Hanna Daydreamer haunts me forever.

I have to try.

For the Olivettas.

For Vico.

Because he always believed in me and never saw my dreams as futile. On the contrary, he considers them a talent I should be proud of. What do I care about the opinions of others, when thanks to him, I've learned to appreciate the value of my unique imagination?

Until now, I've clung to the podium, but now I let go and spread my arms. "There is no presentation," I say again, this time with a resolute voice.

The jury members wear shocked expressions. "But Signora, we were expecting…" The head juror begins.

I raise my hands reassuringly. "At least not the kind you might have anticipated." With a hesitant smile, I address the audience. The elegant lady with the bright red lips gives a small smirk. "Because I am convinced that nothing I could show you on a projector would be as impressive as the images in your own imagination."

I gather the courage to step out from behind the podium and face the audience. Amid the questioning and skeptical looks, I notice some curiosity and openness. I steal a glance at Vico's sisters. They nod emphatically.

"Ladies and gentlemen, dear jurors, please close your eyes with me." The queasy feeling in my stomach persists, unsure if anyone in this room would indulge my request. Nevertheless, I lower my eyelids.

Now, all I can do is listen to what unfolds around me.

Silence spreads. A chair creaks. Someone sighs.

I direct my thoughts to the estate, imagining myself there, right at the spot behind the house where I showed Vico all the colors of my dreams. Within moments, I am transported there. I inhale the scent that the warmth of the sun coaxes from the grass and feel the gentle breeze caressing my hair. All tension melts away.

"Think of the best olive oil you have ever tasted. Remember the intense aroma on your tongue and the silky sensation in your mouth," I say to my audience, guiding their thoughts along with mine.

"Picture yourself drizzling a little oil onto a plate. Do you see the golden shimmer on the surface? How would it feel to dip white bread into the oil and savor each bite?"

The thought makes my mouth water. I taste the oil on my tongue and feel a smile forming on my lips. The image in my mind widens. It's not just the olive oil; no, I also see everything around it.

"Where are you now?" I ask, taking my audience along. "Perhaps in your garden? Under a pergola or in a pavilion? Is the sun still shining, or has the twilight settled over the land?" For me, I remain unchanged, standing behind the estate. "Crickets chirp. The wind caresses your legs. You sit at a wrought-iron table with the people who mean the world to you."

Vico appears in my thoughts. Smiling, he leans over the table, reaching for my hand.

"Life is meant to be enjoyed," I whisper longingly.

Vico nods, bringing my hand to his lips, kissing each of my fingertips. I am so lost in this vision that I tune out the last remaining bits of reality around me.

"If we forget to enjoy life, we forget ourselves," my heart weighs heavily. "And so it happened to the Olivettas," I say with a choked voice. "Death took Signor Olivetta's love of his life. Four unique children lost their mother. And from this once-strong family that produced the best olive oil in the region for centuries, they became uprooted souls, desperately searching for stability."

I see them before me. Signor Olivetta and his four children. They have all forgotten how to be happy, each in their own way.

"Today, the estate has fallen into disrepair. The olive press stands idle, and the olive trees are overgrown with weeds." I clench my fists. "But it doesn't have to stay that way. We can't bring back the old times, but we can create something worthwhile from what we have. A home for a remarkable family. A tradition that must not be lost. A business whose product enriches people's lives."

My heart warms at the beautiful vision I paint.

"Life is meant to be enjoyed, just like the olive oil of the Olivetta family," I continue passionately.

By now, I've lost track of who I'm saying all this for. Of course, it's for the jury, the audience, Vico's sisters, or even his absent father. But even more so, it's for Vico, whose face is constantly before my mind's eye. In my imagination, he nods with emotion at my words.

In my thoughts, I gaze deep into his eyes.

"No matter where we are, and no matter what we do, as long as we are with those we love with all our hearts and savor the beautiful moments to the fullest, we will be happy," I say.

A sense of tranquility spreads within me. I listen inward, but no more words come to me. I stay with myself and my daydream for a few more seconds before slowly raising my eyelids.

The people in the front rows of the audience still

have their eyes closed, as do the members of the jury. A gentle smile graces their faces, as warm as the colors of the setting sun. I let my gaze wander farther back, to where Alessia, Camilla, and now Elina stand.

They are completely lost in my words, still daydreaming.

No one in this room has their eyes open.

Except for me.

And Vico, who suddenly steps out from behind his sisters and looks at me with longing.

Chapter 52

Vico

No matter where we are. And no matter what we do. As long as we are with the ones we love with all our hearts and savor the beautiful moments to the fullest, we will be happy.

Hanna's last words resonate within me as I lose myself in her glowing sea-green eyes. I feel no fear. Only love—for this incredible woman.

She places her hand on her heart, and I immediately notice the absence of the engagement ring on her finger. Although I don't know what happened, I understand its significance.

"All the freedom you love, I want to live with you. Yet we will never be without a home," she speaks loudly, ensuring everyone in the room can hear.

Gradually, the audience awakens from their trance, blinking to find themselves again. But neither Hanna nor I pay attention to them. It's as if only the two of us are here.

Without taking my eyes off her, I approach. We draw closer to each other. "My greatest love is not freedom," I smile at her, and she radiates back. Then with my heart pounding, I step onto the stage beside her. "It's you."

Confused, she tilts her head. "You mean…"

I nod. "Let's restore the estate to its former glory together."

She takes a step forward, our upper bodies touching. A tingling sensation spreads through me, just like that first time we met. I reach out my hands and do what I've dreamed of for so long. I gently cup her head and pull her closer.

Our noses touch, her warm breath brushes against my lips. She lowers her eyelids, and I do the same.

Seconds later, we lose ourselves in a kiss like I've never experienced before. It carries everything my heart desires.

I surrender to her closeness, unable to get enough of her soft lips and the scent of her skin. My hands roam from her shoulders down, I wrap my arms around her, holding her tight, so she knows I will never let her go.

Around us, applause breaks out, along with some whistles.

"Ladies and gentlemen, please," someone says soothingly. "Shall we continue?"

Reluctantly, I break away from Hanna. I've waited so long for this kiss, and even though I know countless more will follow, I don't want to let her go. I trail my mouth to her ear. "That was incredible," I breathe, and I don't just mean the kiss, but also what she has accomplished here in the last few minutes.

I can imagine how much courage it took for her to display her talent. But she did it. And the enthusiastic reactions of the people around us are not just due to our performance on stage.

Tenderly, I stroke her cheek. "You're not a dreamer," I say earnestly. "You're a visionary."

As if she's only just realizing where she is and what she has accomplished, Hanna covers her mouth with her hands. With tears in her eyes, she looks at the audience, who rise from their seats, applauding even more vigorously. I step back and gesture a bow.

This woman is as unique as each of the worlds in her mind, and everyone here can see that.

"I request for silence," the young man with the nickel glasses tries to calm the audience again. "Prego, Signore e Signori."

Hanna reaches for my hand and pulls me along to the standing table where she held her presentation earlier. There, we wait until the audience settles down, and the head of the allocation committee speaks up.

"Signora Olivetta," he says, looking over his glasses at us. I like that he addresses Hanna this way. "Thank you for your—let's call it extraordinary—project presentation. If you submit it in writing, we will review it."

So he can't approve the funding yet. Not now. I quickly glance at my sisters and nod encouragingly. Even if the review turns out negative, they must not think this is a lost cause. Because it can't be, after all, I have plans for how we can revitalize the estate even without funding.

"With pleasure," Hanna says firmly beside me, reaching for the funding application to hand it over.

At the bottom, I notice my father's signature. I quickly take the application from her. "Just a moment, there's a small mistake here."

With an apologetic smile, I dash to the committee and ask the lady with the red-painted lips for her pen. The confusion is evident on her face, but she hands me the ballpoint pen, with which I then write my own name next to my father's on the application.

Out of the corner of my eye, I see Hanna tilting her

head in question. She can't see what I'm writing, but once this is done, I'll tell her everything. Smirking, I hand the completed form to the juror. A smile flashes across the man's face. He lowers his gaze and studies it for a moment.

I can feel the tension in the air. Not just my own, but also Hanna's and the people in the audience.

With a prolonged clearing of his throat, the head of the jury captures everyone's attention. "Well, I'm sure there will be no reason to exclude you from the funding," he says with an approving nod.

Immediately, thunderous applause erupts again. The people in this room don't know us, yet they cheer us on as if their hearts are just as invested in the future of the estate as ours.

"My God, I think we did it," Hanna says, looking stunned.

I wrap my arms around her, lift her up, and spin her around. A liberated cheer escapes her lips, and I feel that from now on, things will only get better.

"This calls for a celebration," Camilla announces joyfully. Suddenly, they—Pietro, Alessia, and a blond woman I've never seen before—are right beside us.

Carefully, I put Hanna back down and stroke her forehead. Now that we can finally be together, I never want to let her go again. "What do you think?"

Hanna's eyes shine. "Definitely."

With Hanna in my arms and the unending jubilation of the audience, I leave the hall. I don't leave her side all the way back to Collina da sogno, and when we arrive there, I don't waste time asking for my father's permission. I simply take him with us to the Ristorante to celebrate.

The next hours are spent exactly where I belong—among the people who mean the most to me.

At the side of the woman who saved me from myself.

Late in the evening, I call for silence and raise my wineglass. "To Hanna."

Hanna's friend Elina lets out an enthusiastic whistle. Camilla and Alessia applaud while Pietro smirks knowingly, and I can already guess what he's thinking.

He was right. About everything.

"To both of you," he calls out loudly, and the others immediately join in. Even my father nods imperceptibly.

"And may all your wishes come true," Camilla adds, her eyes glistening with tears.

They will. I've never been more certain of anything in my life.

Confidently, I turn to Hanna and pull her into my arms. "What colors do our wishes have?" I ask her even though I already know the answer.

Her lips curve into a relieved smile. "All the colors of this world."

Epilogue

Hanna

Two months later

With a contented sigh, I brush my hands on my short jeans and adjust my sun hat. A pleasantly mild breeze dries the beads of sweat on my neck. Taking a deep breath, I feel the sheer essence of life flowing through me. Despite my exhaustion after a hard day's work on the olive grove, I am filled with bliss.

All of this. The estate, the olive trees, the Tuscan way of life. It's so beautiful that even after two months, I still wonder every day if I'm not just dreaming.

My gaze falls on Vico, who is a few yards away, carefully inspecting the growth of the plants. With a devoted expression, he runs his hands over the leaves, checks the fruit's skin, and examines the condition of the bark. Since we began clearing the olive grove of weeds and pruning the trees a few weeks ago, he has become increasingly serene. As if he has reclaimed a piece of himself with each passing day.

Tears of joy well up in my eyes. And as I watch the gentle smile forming on his lips, everything around me suddenly seems bathed in golden light. It warmly touches my skin, causing a pleasant tingling sensation. Birds happily chirp their songs, accompanied in my mind by the sound of a solitary violin. Its melody is melancholic yet filled with happiness. The breeze strengthens, tugging at my T-shirt and carrying the scent of summer to my nose.

As if Vico senses that I'm watching him, he turns to me. Our gazes meet, and suddenly, an entire orchestra plays in my mind. The music carries me away as he approaches to embrace me.

"Are you dreaming?" he lovingly whispers into my ear.

I breathe in his scent. Feel the beat of his heart. "No need for dreaming," I reply with a smile. For no dream could ever be as beautiful as the reality I get to live with Vico.

He detaches himself from me, stands beside me, and puts his arm around my shoulder. I take off the sun hat, resting my head against his chest, and together, we watch the setting sun behind the olive trees.

"Sometimes, I can't believe it's really true." Vico's chest trembles. "But we did it."

The olive grove will soon be completely revitalized. The barn patiently awaits our attention to bring it back to life. But until we need it after the harvest, we have a few months left.

And the estate?

I gently turn, so that both of us can see the venerable building. We've renewed the shutters and repaired the damages in the stone facade. I've trimmed back the ivy all around, and the new rain gutter gleams in a warm red hue.

"The orange trees at the back entrance were a wonderful idea," Vico says.

"Next February, they will bloom." I can already smell their fragrance. I have their aroma on my palate, and I am filled with anticipation for the day when we will harvest them and turn them into orange blossom water.

"It will be just as you dreamed it." His tone filled with love and reverence.

"It will be." Even though we've only implemented a part of everything that I can already see so clearly in my imagination, the estate already feels different.

Warmer. Cozier. More alive.

It's a home again. Not just for Vico and me but also for Camilla, who emerges from the door at this moment with a stack of plates. Alessia's curly head appears behind her. With radiant faces, the two of them set the table for dinner. They don't notice us observing how lovingly they arrange the plates, fold the red-and-white-checkered napkins, and set the cutlery. A little later, they disappear into the house, laughing and full of joy.

"They are happy." With these words, I snuggle even closer to Vico's chest. I know how much the happiness of his sisters means to him. And I also know how much it pains him that Aurora has not visited even once. "Aurora will come. I'm sure of it."

A melancholic sigh escapes his lips. "I'm not so sure," he says absentmindedly. I feel his muscles tense up. We both fall silent for a moment. Then Vico clears his throat. "There's something wrong with her. It was evident when she was here for the twins' birth."

I gently sway him back and forth to ease the tension.

Vico plants a soft kiss on the top of my head. "Her nervousness and overexcitement, that's not her. That wasn't my little sister, but... a stranger."

"Camilla mentioned that she has also lost a lot of weight." As much as I want to help, I've only seen Aurora in photos so far. To me, she is the most beautiful woman I've ever seen. With a radiant smile and a presence that captivates me every time I see her.

Shaking his head, he strokes my arm. "Something must have happened. Something terrible. Something that changed her whole life."

I gaze into Vico's angular face. "We should visit her in France."

He nods with a grateful smile. At the same moment, I catch in the corner of my eye that the entrance door of the estate swings open again. But it's neither Alessia nor Camilla who steps out.

It's Vico's father.

Vico has spotted him too.

I sense him holding his breath.

"What…?" he whispers tonelessly.

I know the question dominating his thoughts, but I don't know the answer. I've never witnessed Vico's father leave his worn-out leather armchair on his own initiative. And now, he steps into the garden, albeit with unsteady steps, but clearly under his own power, and surveys the scene.

Nostalgia and sadness dominate his expression. Slowly, he makes his way toward us and finally stands quietly beside us. I link my arm with his and squeeze his hand.

Together, we gaze at the olive grove. Together, we breathe in the scent of the new era we are embarking on.

Suddenly, he turns his head and looks directly at both of us. I don't know what to do, and I think Vico feels the same. So it remains as it is. We look at each other, trying to decipher the unspoken words in our faces.

Not yet, perhaps.

His lips tremble, as does his thinning hair. Then he slightly lifts the corners of his mouth.

He nods at us. Just once, and so faintly that I can barely discern it. Yet I'm sure he did it. And I believe I know what it means.

Moved, I reach for Vico's hand, our fingers entwining.

I feel our affection.

Our hope.

And that one truth that nobody can take away from us.

Our path may still be long, but we'll navigate it with certainty.

None of us will ever forget that life is meant to be enjoyed. Because deep inside, we know that loving with all our hearts is the best thing we can do. We will never stop seeing our wishes in the most beautiful colors of this world.

How it continues …

Two broken hearts. One reunion. A love story without an end.

Every storm comes to an end someday. That's what I always wanted to believe. But for almost five years, I've been unsuccessfully trying to leave my past behind. I want to erase every kiss, every touch, and every one of my terrible mistakes from my memory.

But above all, I need to forget Maxime.

My heart belongs to him alone, yet we can never see each other again. Until today, I was sure he wouldn't find me here on the French Atlantic coast. However, after all these years, we face each other again, and I realize he won't give me a choice.

He'll force me to tell him exactly what he must never know: that one truth that will destroy his life.

Find out about the story of Vico's sister Aurora.

<u>Available as an e-book or paperback.</u>

What has happened so far …

Two hearts. One mistake. A single truth that changes everything.

I long to escape back to Vienna. I should be saving lives in a prestigious hospital, immersed in the bustling city. However, due to a fatal mistake, I am forced to complete my medical training in a rural practice deep within the mountains.

Here, there is nothing but silence. And Noah. From the outside, he is like the mountains—unapproachable and rugged. But deep inside, I am certain he is vulnerable and gentle. Even though he keeps his distance, I feel fate may have brought us together in the middle of nowhere.

But what if I fall for the wrong man again? I cannot

bear another disappointment, so I guard my heart closely. Especially since he is my patient, making him off-limits if I want to hold on to this job...

Find out about the story of Hanna's friend, Elina.

<u>Available as an e-book or paperback.</u>

Dear Reader

I'm glad you enjoyed the story of Hanna and Vico, and I hope it touched your heart.

Throughout the creation of this novel, I have been accompanied by many wonderful people. First and foremost, my family and the love of my life. Additionally, the tireless book professionals, beta readers and release helpers, who have become so numerous that I can no longer mention all their names. Without you, this book would not exist. I am at a loss for words to express how grateful I am.

But most of all, I want to thank *you* for purchasing and reading this book.

You would greatly support me by leaving a short review on Amazon or any other platform. Thank you in advance!

Do you want to stay up to date on new releases? Sign up for my newsletter today! (www. belindabenna.com)

This way you won't miss any new releases and get insights into my life as an author.

Lots of love,

Belinda

Printed in Great Britain
by Amazon